Ursula K. Le Guin

Twayne's United States Authors Series

Warren French, Editor

Indiana University, Indianapolis

TUSAS 453

URSULA K. LE GUIN

(1929–   )

Photograph courtesy of Lisa Kroeber

Ursula K. Le Guin

By Charlotte Spivack

University of Massachusetts—Amherst

Twayne Publishers • Boston

Ursula K. Le Guin

Charlotte Spivack

Copyright © 1984 by G. K. Hall & Company
All Rights Reserved
Published by Twayne Publishers
A Division of G. K. Hall & Company
70 Lincoln Street
Boston, Massachusetts 02111

Book Production by John Amburg

Book Design by Barbara Anderson

Printed on permanent/durable acid-free
paper and bound in the United States of
America

Library of Congress Cataloging in Publication Data

Spivack, Charlotte.
   Ursula K. Le Guin.

   (Twayne's United States authors series; TUSAS 453)
   Bibliography: p.
   Includes index.
   1. Le Guin, Ursula K., 1929–   —Criticism
and interpretation.   I. Title.   II. Series.
PS3562.E42Z92   1984   813'.54   81-18560
ISBN 0-8057-7393-2 (Hardcover)
ISBN 0-8057-7430-0 (Paperback)

To my son Loren
"Bright the hawk's flight"

Contents

About the Author

Charlotte Spivack received her B.A. from the State University of New York at Albany, her M.A. from Cornell University, and her Ph.D. from the University of Missouri at Columbia, where she specialized in the drama of Shakespeare and his contemporaries. She is now professor of English at the University of Massachusetts at Amherst, where she teaches courses both in her original area of specialization, the Renaissance drama, and in her new interests, contemporary fantasy literature and science fiction. She has published three books: *Early English Drama* (coauthor, 1966), *George Chapman* (1967), and *The Comedy of Evil on Shakespeare's Stage* (1978). In addition she has published several articles in scholarly journals on a variety of subjects including Shakespeare, Goethe, Dante, Webster, Dekker, Strindberg, the book of Job, the figure of Merlin in modern fiction, and the nature of mythic fantasy. Professor Spivack first became interested in Le Guin when she discovered the Earthsea trilogy, which she now includes in her course in fantasy fiction. She also teaches a course devoted entirely to the works of Le Guin, and she has presented scholarly papers about Le Guin at several conferences. At present Professor Spivack is preparing a study of contemporary women writers of fantasy.

Preface

This study, both analytical and critical, of Ursula K. Le Guin's work is intended to help the general reader understand and appreciate the range and quality of this writer's literary achievement. Le Guin is probably best known for her fantasy and science fiction, for which she has won several awards during the last two decades. But she transcends her acknowledged eminence in these two fields, being in fact a literary artist whose imaginative brilliance and stylistic excellence spread far beyond her usually acclaimed achievements in fantasy and science fiction. The sheer literary and inventive merit of her novels, short stories, poetry, and essays serves to establish her as a major voice in contemporary American literature.

My organization is primarily chronological. The first chapter focuses on those aspects of Le Guin's early life which were influential on her subsequent career. Her parents, Alfred and Theodora Kroeber, both anthropologists and both writers, stimulated her early interest in mythology and literature, thereby preparing the way for her vocation of imaginative writing. Subsequent chapters trace the development of her fiction from her earliest novel *(Rocannon's World)* through her most recent *(The Beginning Place)*. Within this chronological framework, separate chapters are also devoted to her short stories, poetry, and essays, dimensions of Le Guin's work generally neglected by critics. In the next to last chapter I discuss several short works which have not been included in anthologies and which are, therefore, difficult to find. There are a few inevitable omissions in this category, but these omitted items are virtually unavailable to the reading public. The final chapter offers an overview of critical writing about Le Guin to date.

In this endeavor I am grateful to more individuals than I can possibly acknowledge. My debt to other scholars and critics will be clear from the notes and references, but I wish in particular to thank James Bittner for his useful suggestions when I first began this project. I also owe much gratitude to the friendly and conscientious staff of the Interlibrary Loan Office of the University of Massachusetts, especially fellow Le Guin reader, Ute Borgmann. In addition I gratefully recall the inspiring enthusiasm of my Le Guin class in the spring semester of 1980. Finally I wish to thank my daughter Carla, who proofread the manuscript and made valuable editorial suggestions, and my son Loren, who carefully prepared the index. To him this book is dedicated.

Charlotte Spivack

University of Massachusetts—Amherst

Chronology

1929   Ursula born 21 October in Berkeley, California, daughter of Theodora and Alfred Kroeber.

1947   Enters Radcliffe College.

1951   Is graduated from Radcliffe College, member of Phi Beta Kappa.

1952   Receives Master of Arts degree in French from Columbia University.

1953   Begins work on doctorate in French at Columbia University. Receives Fulbright award for research in France. Meets Charles Le Guin en route to Europe on *Queen Mary*, marries him in Paris on 22 December.

1957   Daughter Elizabeth born in Moscow, Idaho.

1959   Moves to Portland, Oregon, where daughter Caroline is born.

1960   Alfred Kroeber dies.

1961   Publishes first story, "An Die Musik," in *Western Humanities Review*.

1962   Sells first story, "April in Paris," to *Fantastic*.

1963   Publishes first science-fiction story, "The Masters," in *Fantastic*.

1964   Son Theodore born in Portland, Oregon; publishes "The Rule of Names" and "The Word of Unbinding" in *Fantastic*, initiating the world of Earthsea; attends the Oakland Science Fiction World Conference.

1966   *Rocannon's World; Planet of Exile*.

1967   *City of Illusions*.

1968   *A Wizard of Earthsea*, winner of the Boston Globe-Horn Book award.

1969   *The Left Hand of Darkness*, winner of Hugo and Nebula awards.

1971   *The Lathe of Heaven; The Tombs of Atuan;* teaches science fiction writers' workshop at Pacific University.

1972   *The Farthest Shore,* National Book Award winner; *The Word for World Is Forest,* Hugo award; delivers guest of honor speech at Vancouver Science Fiction Conference.

1973   "The Ones Who Walk Away from Omelas," Hugo award.

1974   *The Dispossessed,* winner of Hugo and Nebula awards; "The Day Before the Revolution," Nebula award.

1975   "The New Atlantis," Hugo and Nebula nominee; *Wild Angels; The Wind's Twelve Quarters;* special issue of *Science Fiction Studies* devoted to her work; honored at the science fiction "Aussiecon" in Melbourne, Australia.

1976   "Diary of the Rose," Nebula nominee; *Very Far Away from Anywhere Else; Orsinian Tales,* National Book Award nominee.

1977   Withdraws "Diary of the Rose" from the Nebula competition to protest the expulsion of Stanislas Lem from the Science Fiction Writers of America.

1978   "The Eye of the Heron" in *Millennial Women.*

1979   *Malafrena; The Language of the Night.*

1980   *The Beginning Place.*

1981   *Hard Words.*

Chapter One
Life and Intellectual Background

Life

Ursula K. Le Guin has always valued her privacy. She neither seeks publicity in the media nor bares her soul in her own writings. On the other hand, she has made no attempt to be unduly secretive, and her basic biography can be easily gleaned from interviews and other published records. What is she like as a person? Her appearance was recently described as "slender, slightly tall, with uncluttered lines and soft, dark hair beginning to gray."[1] In personality she has been characterized as "witty, strong, emphatic and empathic, wise, knowledgeable, easy going, and electric, seraphic, gracious, sanguine, and sane."[2] It is her own conviction, however, that only her fiction, not her biography, is of interest to the general public. Her personal life in Portland, Oregon, with her husband of thirty years and their three children, is consequently a private matter.

Born in Berkeley, California, on 21 October 1929, Ursula was named for her patron saint. She was the youngest child and only daughter of Theodora and Alfred Kroeber. Her illustrious parents, both scholars and writers, were major influences on her development. Her mother had a graduate degree in psychology but did not begin her own successful writing career until she was almost sixty. She is best known for her *Ishi in Two Worlds* (1961), a biography of a "wild" North American Indian who was a friend of her family. The "two worlds" of the book are later reflected in the repeated theme of cultural contrast in her daughter's fiction. Ursula dedicated one of her novels—*The Tombs of Atuan*—to her mother, the "redhead from Telluride." Alfred Kroeber was an anthropologist of international repute. A learned and multilingual man, he developed an outstanding department of anthropology at Berkeley, along with his other major contributions to the discipline. Ursula dedicated her poetry collection *Wild Angels* to him.

The Kroeber household was filled with books and people. The flow of interesting visitors to the home included faculty and graduate students, along with American Indians and such distinguished individuals as Robert Oppenheimer who was later to become in part a model for her hero in *The Dispossessed.* Ursula found this generation of anthropologists who visited her father to be an exciting group of people with an "intense interest in individuals and individual cultures." Equally exciting were the family's books, and Ursula, along with her three older brothers (Karl, Theodore, and Clifford), developed an early zest for reading.

The Kroeber family lived in Berkeley during the academic year but spent summers in their forty-acre country estate in the Napa valley. Theodora described this summer place, called Kishamish, as "a world for exploration, for reading, for one's own work, for swimming and playing games, for sitting by the outdoor fire until late in the night talking, telling stories, singing: for sleeping under the stars."[3] As well as being an intellectually stimulating household both in Berkeley and Kishamish, the Kroeber home was also a happy one. Ursula was fortunate in her upbringing and in the relaxed, satisfying relationship with her parents and her brothers. She notes in retrospect that she suffered no adolescent hang-ups.[4]

The reading available to the young generation in this exciting home was both extensive and varied. Even before learning to read, however, Ursula had heard her father tell Indian legends, so that the oral tradition of folk tales was part of her earliest memory. She was also introduced to mythology very early. She found that she preferred Norse myths to the Greek, and these distinctive tales from the northern peoples have had a direct influence on her own works. Probably her favorite childhood book was Lady Frazer's *Leaves from the Golden Bough,* a children's version of the classical study in anthropology.

As she moved from her childhood into her teens, Ursula's reading turned from myth and legend to science fiction. Like her brothers she read widely in *Thrilling Wonder Stories* and *Astounding.* One of her favorite authors from this period, the early 1940s, was Lewis Padgett. Her greatest literary discovery at this time was a work of fantasy on the family bookshelf: Lord Dunsany's *A Dreamer of Tales,* a favorite of her father's. The "inner lands" in Dunsany's book she recognized as her own imaginative world.

This early period of extensive reading was accompanied by writing.

Ursula wrote her first fantasy story at age nine, and submitted for publication her first science-fiction story at age eleven. It was rejected, and she was to wait another ten years before trying another submission.

By the late 1940s, she abandoned science fiction, which by then seemed to her to be "all about hardware," and turned to mainstream literature, where her favorites were Tolstoy and Dickens. It was not until the 1960s that she rediscovered science fiction when a friend lent her some SF magazines which introduced her to the work of Cordwainer Smith. In his stories she found a new direction for her own writing.

Meanwhile her personal life moved in new directions as well. After being graduated with a B.A. from Radcliffe College in 1951, Ursula went on to graduate study in French at Columbia University. She earned her M.A. in 1952, began work on a Ph.D., and soon won a Fulbright grant to undertake further study and research in France. While crossing the Atlantic on the *Queen Mary* in 1953, she met Charles Le Guin, whom she married in Paris later the same year. The marriage meant "the end of the doctorate,"[5] but it was the beginning of a long happy relationship which still continues. Her dedication of *The Dispossessed* to "the partner" is a tribute to that marriage bond.

In 1959 the Le Guins moved to Portland, Oregon, where Charles began teaching history at Portland State University. Two daughters, Elizabeth and Caroline, had been born to them by this time, and Ursula had also lost her father, who died in Paris in his mid-eighties. In 1964 the Le Guins' youngest child and only son, Theodore, was born. Although she had young children to care for in the late 1950s and early 1960s, Ursula continued writing but on a limited schedule, mostly in the evenings after the children were in bed.

By 1962 Le Guin's extensive writings had produced only two minor publications: her first acceptance, "An Die Musik," appeared in the *Western Humanities Review* in 1961, and "April in Paris," her first sale, appeared in the September 1962 issue of *Fantastic*. After this relatively late start (she was thirty-two when she published her first paid story), the publications came rapidly: the Hainish novel trilogy and several major works in both science fiction and fantasy as well as mainstream fiction, poetry, and essays. In the two decades since that first acceptance, Le Guin's publications have been many, various, and of consistently high quality.

Intellectual Background

Le Guin is an entertaining writer, and all of her fiction can be read with enjoyment and adequate understanding without reference to anything else. She is also a novelist with a genuinely mythopoeic imagination. The highly original cosmos that she has created through her fiction is not only rich in populated planets but also peopled with morally and psychologically complex characters and thronging with images, ideas, and archetypes. The mythopoeic achievement of all her works transcends the literary achievement of any single work. For the reader who wishes to read several of Le Guin's books, therefore, some awareness of her key ideas and motifs will enhance the pleasure and increase the understanding, serving to intensify a rewarding reading experience.

Because of her intellectual and imaginative background, Le Guin has much to bring to her career as writer. Just as her own knowledge of psychology and anthropology, of Norse myths and Indian legends, of Oriental philosophy and foreign languages uniquely equipped her to fulfill her writing talents, so at least a basic knowledge of these ingredients can equip her readers with a perception of nuances and levels of meaning that might otherwise be overlooked in favor of the larger sweep of the narrative.

Although many of these details of background influence will be discussed in the pages ahead, three subjects central to an appreciation of Le Guin's fiction are worthy of a prior introduction: cultural anthropology, Jungian psychology, and Taoist philosophy.

Cultural anthropology, although a relatively new discipline, has become a standard part of the basic college curriculum. Alfred Kroeber as a pioneering twentieth-century anthropologist helped to establish this study of other cultures as a basic item in higher education. In his personal field work he devoted himself largely to the study of North American Indians, in effect turning his own household into a classroom of living anthropology. His daughter thus not only read the fascinating material in the *Golden Bough* but also lived in the middle of an ongoing exploration of an alien culture.

Closely allied with the study of cultural diversity as the subject matter of anthropology is the equally important factor of an anthropological attitude toward other cultures. The anthropologist must be a close and impartial observer, with an objective eye toward the culture he is investigating. At the same time he must also participate in what may seem to him the most alien features of that culture in order to see them fully and clearly. The role of anthropologist thus involves a tension between observation and participation. To the extent that he is able to participate sympathetically in the culture that he can never become a part of, he also becomes an outsider to his own culture. Contemporary anthropologist Claude Levi-Strauss remarks that the anthropologist is destined never to feel "at home" anywhere.[6]

Most of Le Guin's protagonists assume the role of anthropologist, if not by profession then by circumstance.[7] Rocannon *(Rocannon's World)* and Genly Ai *(The Left Hand of Darkness)* are both ethnographers sent to other planets to record their observations, and both Shevek *(The Dispossessed)* and Lyubov *(The Word for World Is Forest)* take on themselves the role of cultural observer in other worlds. Furthermore in almost all of her books the central conflict involves a confrontation between alien cultures, often mediated by the protagonist. For most of these anthropologist-heroes, the journey outward to an alien society is at the same time a journey inward toward self-discovery. Alienation and isolation are their lot, but for these very reasons they are unusually perceptive and sensitive observers. The perspective of anthropology thus affects characterization as well as content.

Equally important to Le Guin's fiction is the perspective of Jungian psychology. She has acknowledged and elaborated on this influence in several of her own essays.[8] An awareness of the Jungian theory of archetypes is, therefore, quite helpful to the reader of her science fiction and fantasy.

Although C. G. Jung was essentially a follower of Sigmund Freud, who first discovered the major role of the unconscious in determining human behavior, he developed his own theories about the nature of that unconscious. Jung perceived two levels in the unconscious stratum of the psyche. One is the personal unconscious, a repository of forgotten or repressed individual experiences. The other is the collective unconscious, a repository of universal human experience shared by all members of the human race. Through the long evolution of the human psyche, these common experiences have produced certain inborn predispositions called archetypes. Since all human beings have mothers, for example, this collective experience yields the archetypal Mother, which is in turn realized in the actual mother as well as in such cultural extensions as Mother Nature and the Blessed Virgin. Since the archetypes in themselves are only predispositions, they emerge on the conscious level as symbols.

Jung called these symbolic constituents of our collective unconscious "the little people" because they appear to the conscious mind
as personifications. Along with the Mother, archetypes include the
Wise Old Man, the divine child, the trickster, the animus (the masculine experience of the female) and the anima (the feminine experience of the male). One of the most important archetypes is the
Shadow, a personification of the dark side of human nature. In an
essay devoted to this archetype as it occurs in literature, Le Guin
comments:

It is Cain, Caliban, it is Frankenstein's monster, Mr. Hyde. It is Vergil who
guided Dante through hell, Gilgamesh's friend Enkidu, Frodo's enemy Gol-
lum. It is the Doppelgänger. It is Mowgli's Grey Brother; the werewolf; . . .
it is the serpent, Lucifer.[9]

These archetypes as the psychic heritage of the human species figure prominently in mythology and religion as well as in some works
of art and literature. As a mythopoeic writer, Le Guin is especially
rich in archetypal characters and situations. The Earthsea trilogy includes the Wise Old Man, the Mother Goddess, and the Shadow; the
Beginning Place has Anima and Animus figures; and all of her fiction
focuses on archetypal situations, such as the Coming of Age and Rebirth. Recognition of the archetypal dimension of Le Guin's work
thus adds a resonance to the reader's experience.

Along with cultural anthropology and archetypal psychology, a
third pervasive feature in Le Guin's fiction is the philosophy of
Taoism. An ancient Chinese school of thought going back at least to
the third or fourth century B.C., this doctrine was introduced by Lao
Tse in a profound but cryptic work, the *Tao Te Ching*, later inter-
preted and supplemented by his disciple Chuang Tse.[10] Le Guin discovered Taoism early in her career, for the *Tao Te Ching* was one of
her father's favorite books. She was immediately attracted by its precepts which appealed to her own cast of mind as a "congenital non-
Christian."[11]

The word "Tao" refers to the Way, which cannot be precisely defined but which refers to the basic moral law which underlies all
human behavior. Rooted in nature, it is the fundamental precept underlying all religions.[12] One of the principles of Taoism is the
doctrine of inaction, or what is called the Theory of Letting Alone.
This asserts the superior virtue of not-taking-action over action, of

passivity over aggression, of patience over initiative. The imagery of the highly metaphorical *Tao Te Ching* draws on nature for examples demonstrating the strength of passivity and receptivity. Water is an often repeated example.

> The softest substance of the world
> Goes through the hardest;
> That-which-is without-form penetrates that-which-has-no
> -crevice.

This Theory of Letting Alone in the world of nature applies directly to moral and social behavior:

> Stretch (a bow) to the very full,
> And you will wish you had stopped in time,
> Temper a (sword edge) to its very sharpest,
> And the edge will not last long.[13]

Many of Le Guin's protagonists embody the virtue of inaction. The primary lesson of magic learned by Ged in the Earthsea trilogy is never to use it unless it is absolutely necessary; the protagonist of *The Lathe of Heaven* is depicted as the Taoist ideal of letting things alone; and most of her anthropologist-heroes try not to tamper with the cultures they investigate.

A second principle of Taoism is the relativity of opposites, which directly refutes the dualistic philosophy of historical Christianity. Whereas the Christian tradition postulates a continuing struggle between good and evil, Taoism asserts the mutual interdependence of light and darkness. The Earthsea trilogy, the Hainish trilogy, and *The Left Hand of Darkness* are all centrally concerned with this theme of reconciling dark and light. Taoism asserts, furthermore, the mutual interdependence of male and female, visually depicted in the yin-yang symbol of interlocking dark and light semicircles. This particular manifestation of the Taoist doctrine also figures prominently in the Le Guin books, along with other facets such as anarchy, which will be dealt with in the pages that follow.

All three of these thought patterns—cultural anthropology, archetypal psychology, and philosophical Taoism—merge into and help to shape the overall conceptual framework of Le Guin's fiction. The result is a rich intellectual substructure which gives body to the equally rich mythopoeic texture of her imaginary worlds.

Both an entertaining story teller and a serious novelist of ideas, Ursula K. Le Guin is now in the prime of her writing career. The chapters ahead will examine, in roughly chronological order, her literary achievements so far. The years ahead will undoubtedly extend that chronology.

Chapter Two
The Hainish Trilogy

The appearance of Ursula K. Le Guin's first three novels (1966–67) was scarcely noted by reviewers and not even acknowledged by critics.[1] These three slim volumes—published by an obscure paperback house—later to be called the Hainish trilogy, exhibit, however, both the significant themes and the refined style which distinguish this writer's mature work. As novels they may be faulted primarily for their abbreviated structure which tends to make the plots seem somewhat contrived and which also introduces more ideas and situations than can be adequately disposed of in such a short compass. On the other hand, for the casual reader of science fiction looking for exciting adventures, they offer a plenitude of imaginative episodes. Even the serious-minded reader of the admittedly greater later works will readily confess to a sheer delight in the early trilogy that the more massive and mature work does not quite afford for all its fine literary quality. In short, the Hainish trilogy is first-rate escape reading enhanced with definite intimations of greatness.

The major themes which become the focus of Le Guin's writing first appear in the interplanetary adventures of this trilogy. These themes include the archetypal journey, the search for identity and the concomitant problems of alienation and isolation, the problems of human communication and acculturation, the reconciliation of opposites, and the moral tenets of Taoism. These themes are repeatedly worked out through a plot structure which, although it will become more sophisticated in later books, remains fundamentally the same in all of her work. In this plot structure an isolated and alienated hero journeys to a strange far-away place where, through a series of contacts with creatures alien to him, he discovers himself. The strange new land thus becomes a symbol for the newly discovered personal identity. The saying "To go is to return" occurs in some form in almost every novel. It serves as an epigram to virtually all of Le Guin's stories.

Although all of Le Guin's work is influenced by her extensive readings in myth and legend, the Hainish trilogy in particular reveals the inspiration of Norse myth. The author acknowledges this influence. "I had heard Norse myths before I could read, and read *The Children of Odin* and later the Eddas many, many times, so that that mythos was a shaping influence on both my conscious and unconscious mind."[2]

Rocannon's World

Rocannon's World, the first novel in the trilogy, offers a blend of fantasy and SF, indicating the polarized tendencies of Le Guin's future work. Some readers may find the blend objectionable, while others find rather that it enhances the overall imaginative effectiveness of the story. In retrospect the author found the mixture more of a weakness than a strength: "Fantasy and science fiction *are* different, just as red and blue are different; they have different frequencies; if you mix them (on paper—I work on paper) you get purple, something else again. *Rocannon's World* is definitely purple. . . . There is a lot of promiscuous mixing going on in *Rocannon's World*. . . . This sort of thing is beginner's rashness, the glorious freedom of ignorance. It's my world, I can do anything! Only of course, you can't."[3]

The core of the novel is clearly mythic fantasy, based on the story of the Breisingamen necklace in Norse mythology. The seminal short story which introduces this episode first appeared separately as "The Dowry of the Angyar" in a 1964 issue of *Amazing* magazine. This same story, with minor changes, appears in the novel as "Prologue." The original episode in Norse mythology concerns the goddess Freya's overpowering desire to possess the precious and artfully wrought necklace of Breisingamen, held by three evil giant women.[4] She leaves her husband Odur and her child Hnossa in Asgard as she travels to earth to seek out these giant women who possess this golden treasure. She enlists the aid of both the benevolent elves and the ugly dwarves, even submitting to the unwelcome caresses of the latter in her mad lust to obtain the necklace. When she finally acquires it and returns home to Asgard proudly displaying it, she learns to her dismay that Odur has left, and no one knows where he is. Once more, Freya leaves her child behind, mounting her car, drawn by two cats, to begin a long and fruitless search for Odur. Eventually she returns alone to her palace in Asgard.

Although Le Guin essentially retells this story in the prologue, the rest of the novel develops around a new protagonist and involves many new elements of cultural complexity and of SF inventiveness. Semley, as protagonist in the prologue, is a proud and beautiful woman, goddesslike in her manner and bearing. Her motive in acquiring the necklace, however, is not mere greed or vanity but rather her determination to recover her rightful dowry. Like Freya she must abandon her husband and child and journey to another world; also like the Norse goddess, she drives a car drawn by cats, in this case huge flying cats called windsteeds. She also finds that when the airy and benevolent elves cannot help her, she must turn to the skillful but sullen dwarves in their underground abode. Her journey to another world, however, enters the realm of science fiction, for Semley travels while unconscious through "a long night" that lasts several years, so that when she returns home, her husband is long since dead and her daughter a grown woman. Whereas Freya is left weeping piteously over her lost husband, yet still wearing the necklace, Semley throws the precious blue sapphire before her daughter and flees to the forest to wander in madness until her death.

In the revised story serving as prologue, the new protagonist of the novel enters the narrative. Rocannon, a somewhat less than objective ethnologist, is captivated by the strange beauty of Semley to whom he released the necklace which has been kept in a museum on his planet. He becomes intensely interested in investigating what his handbook calls the "High Intelligence Life Forms" (Hilfs) on her planet. His fleeting experience with Semley and the blue necklace stirs within him an awareness of a new dimension of life. He admits that "I have as it were blundered through the corner of a legend, of a tragic myth, maybe, which I do not understand" (24).

Rocannon assumes direction of the first ethnographic survey of Semley's planet, identified in his handbook as Fomalhaut II but known by its own inhabitants simply as "the World." Shortly after the arrival of the members of his mission on that planet, however, Rocannon finds himself alone, the sole survivor of his crew, all the others victims of a vicious attack by invaders from distant Faraday. Marooned on this unfamiliar world, Rocannon undertakes a quest to avenge his fourteen dead companions. In the course of his adventures he not only comes to make the new world his home, conferring his name on it as well, but also develops inwardly into a more sensitive and perceptive human being.

The three-part structure of the book reflects this gradual change in the hero. In the prologue he is an outsider; a mere spectator who has blundered into a myth. In part 1, called "The Starlord," Rocannon as hero plays the active role of avenger for his slain comrades. The emphasis in this part is on action and event rather than on character. In part 2, called "The Wanderer," the emphasis shifts to the inner development of Rocannon, who takes on a new name, Olhur, which means the Wanderer. He is at the same time stepping into the role of the Norse God Odin, also known as the Wanderer.[5]

Rocannon's adventures constitute a picaresque plot rich with inventive episodes. He is burned at the stake by the barbarous Zgama and his clan, but escapes injury and death because of his impermasuit. "The Wanderer wears a second skin" (64). Captured by wild hunters, he must surrender the blue sapphire necklace (now in his possession, a gift from Haldre, Semley's daughter). Later Haldre's son, Lord Mogien, seizes it back from the same ruffians and returns it to Rocannon. The Wanderer barely escapes being bled to death by the eerie Winged Ones, whose larvae suck their paralyzed victims dry. Ultimately he adopts the planet, which he has ritualistically joined by shedding blood there, and marries the Lady Ganye who wears the blue jewel at her throat long after his death.

In his role as the Wanderer, Rocannon comes to be regarded by some of the world's inhabitants as a god. Like his mythic prototype, Odin, he gains godly knowledge but at a high price. Just as Odin had to sacrifice an eye in order to gain wisdom from the magic well of Mimir, so Rocannon must be willing to sacrifice what he loves most in order to gain the gift of mindspeech from the guardian of the well, who lives in a cave deep in the unnamed mountains. This Ancient One asks that Rocannon give what he holds dearest and would least willingly give, be it "A thing, a life, a chance; an eye, a hope, a return: the name need not be known" (118). Rocannon agrees to give it freely, without suspecting that what he is about to sacrifice is the life of his dear friend Mogien.

The gift of mindspeech enables Rocannon to locate and destroy his enemy. The gift is "a skill of the senses that his race and the men of Earth had witnessed and studied in other races. . . . Mindhearing . . . not speech but intentions, desires, emotions, the physical locations and sensual-mental directions of many different men jumbling and overlapping through his own nervous system" (120–21). What he seeks from the gift of mindspeech is only a limited endowment, since he wishes only to destroy enemies; on a larger scale, a more extensive command of mindspeech will become for his descendants an important ability, a symbol of human communication on the highest level.

In spite of his rejection of total mindspeech and his obvious difficulty in communicating in depth with his fellows, Rocannon achieves a close relationship with the several companions on his quest. The characterization of these companions is deftly handled. These friends include the young Lord Mogien, Semley's grandson, "arrogant and loyal, ruthless and kind, in his very disharmony Mogien was lordly" (65); Kyo, of the delicate race of Fiia, "childlike and uncanny" (69) with "strange, large, light eyes" (43); and the loyal servant Yahan, who sings of legendary heroic deeds to the accompaniment of his silver-stringed bronze lyre.

Most effective are Le Guin's characterizations of races, of species. Indeed one of the ironies of the book is the sharp contrast between the flat statistical handbook listing of the "hilfs" of the unexplored planet and Rocannon's complex and developing experience of relationship with them. There are two races of little people (both about 130 cm. tall), the Gdemiar who are "nocturnal troglodytes" (5) with light skin and dark head-hair and the Fiia, who are "diurnal" and generally light in skin and hair. Originally the Gdemiar and Fiia were of one race, but at some historical point the former chose the way of technology and of underground life and darkness, whereas the latter chose the way of sunlight and forests and eschewed technology. The split was also profoundly psychological, for the Fiia have repressed the dark side of their nature and have no memory of anything evil. "The Fiia have no memory for fear, Olhor. How should we? We chose. Night and caves and swords of metal we left to the Clayfolk, when our way parted from theirs, and we chose the green valleys, the sunlight, the bowl of wood. And therefore we are the Half-People. And we have forgotten, we have forgotten much!" (108).

As the little people are divided into two groups with opposite traits, so the most human species, the Luiar, are split into two classes, the passive Olgyar, who are light-skinned and dark-haired, and the aggressive Angyar, who are dark-skinned and yellow-haired. Two unconfirmed species cited in the Handbook are also confirmed by Rocannon, for better and for worse respectively, as he encounters both the lovable Kiemhrir, animal in form but elevated in spirit, and the nightmarish Winged Ones, angelic in appearance but subhuman in nature. The Kiemhrir, or Name-eaters, are small furry brown animals with limited speech but unlimited good will whereas the

Winged Ones are ethereal in their delicate stature and gracefulness but have "brains degenerated or specialized to the level of insects" (102). In each case, of course, the subspecies are precise opposites: light and dark, diurnal and nocturnal, airborne and earthbound.

Le Guin thus deepens the meaning of the contrast between the airy elves and subterranean dwarves of Norse mythology by adding the psychological implications of opposites. The need for reconciliation of opposites, an important concept in both Taoism and Jungian psychology, is manifested on many levels in her several novels. The idea is personified both externally, as in the polarized races of Rocannon's world, and internally, as in the case of the hero of *City of Illusions,* who has a divided mind.

When Rocannon ultimately achieves his mission, destroying the enemy who killed his crew, the reader feels satisfied with the strictly narrative outcome of the plot in spite of its rather abrupt ending. Somewhat less satisfying is the character of the hero, not for any lack of skill on the author's part but simply because the novel ends just when the reader has come to know and care about Rocannon. His growing awareness of the new planet and his deepening relationships with its inhabitants endear him to us. As he establishes new intimacies with members of alien species, he becomes a more interesting person. After his successful battle with the Lord-Errant of Plenot, during which he loses blood from an arrow wound (he is too proud to wear his invisible impermasuit for protection), he relaxes and drinks with his new friends who also tend his wound: "Rocannon sat drunk and contented, riding the river of song, feeling himself now wholly committed, sealed by his shed blood to this world to which he had come a stranger across the gulfs of night. Only beside him now and then he sensed the presence of the little Fian, smiling, alien, serene" (60).

His ability to communicate remains severely limited, however, and in response to the sensitive Kyo's probing questions, he closes his mind, "retreating from the touch of a strange sense into his own humanity, his own identity" (93). Even when he finally learns the telepathic gift of mindspeech from the guardian of the well, his natural reticence prompts him to request a self-imposed limit to the skill: "Clinging to his humanity, he had drawn back from the totality of the power that the guardian of the well possessed and offered" (120). He wants to hear one voice only, that of his enemy; with that limited power, he can complete his revenge.

Although the new world acquires Rocannon's name—and the Lady Ganye of the Angyar, whom he weds, acquires the blue sapphire— Rocannon himself remains a partially realized figure. But the reader identifies with him in his very limitations. The enemy remains totally unknown to us because the Faradayans are unknown to Rocannon. And though the Fiia and the Kiemhrir are appealing, they are also elusive and shadowy, because they are so to Rocannon who has come to love them but not to know them. The technique is that of the evolving point of view: the reader's moral angle of vision widens along with that of the narrator.

It is gratifying to the reader to know that Rocannon, though only a partially realized character in his own book, not only had a world named after him but also contributed his own descendant as hero of the next book of the trilogy, *Planet of Exile*.

Planet of Exile

Even shorter than its predecessor, the 124-page *Planet of Exile* is really a novella rather than a full-fledged novel. As such it is more unified in theme and more tightly woven in its narrative structure. It is also stronger in characterization, although the devoted SF reader may find it somewhat lacking in the sheer imaginative variety of the earlier book. On one level, *Planet of Exile* is a Romeo and Juliet love story with a happy ending; on another, it is an anthropological account of the relationship in crisis of two very different cultures living in close proximity. Both levels illustrate the reconciliation of opposites.

The young, star-crossed lovers are Jakob Agat Alterra, a descendant of Rocannon (twenty-three generations later), and Rolery, a member of a primitive nomadic society. They are opposites in more than the usual ways. He is dark-skinned, a member of a "far-born" race of peoples who still feel alien to their home planet after six centuries. The new planet continues to reject them, or so it seems, for they cannot bear children by cross-breeding with the natives. Nor are they able to breed prolifically among themselves, and their numbers are drastically dwindling. Rolery is light-skinned, native to her planet but like an alien in her own tribe, for she was born "out of season" and will as a result probably never bear children. Whereas Jakob's people are technologically advanced and also have a command of mindspeech, Rolery's kind are a primitive people, nomads who have not even achieved the wheel, and who regard mindspeech as witch-craft. Because of the law of cultural embargo effective in the League of planets, the new settlers (Jakob's ancestors) were not supposed to use technology advanced beyond that of the native peoples. As a re-sult, the knowledge long ago acquired by this more technically so-phisticated group has been gradually lost and is in imminent danger of extinction.

On this planet, with its long years (each season is fifteen earth years long) preparations are in progress for the coming winter, of 5000 days duration. While Rolery's kin, the Tevar, are busy with food storage underground, Jakob, a leader among his own people, the Alterrans, comes to warn them of a new impending danger, an in-vasion of a barbarian race called the Gaal. Communication between the two major species has been severely constrained all these centuries not only because of the obvious cultural differences between them but also because each is convinced that the other is not human. "Are the farborns men or not—who knows? Maybe they fell out of the sky as in the tale" (36) muses Wold, the Eldest of Rolery's kinfolk, and "this is a hilf, not a human!" (71) cries out an old woman of Jakob's people in respect to Rolery.[6]

Jakob enlists the aid of Wold, the Eldest, in fighting off the Gaal, and almost succeeds, but his newly conceived love for Rolery stirs up the old enmities, and the alliance fails. While the Tevar consult the shaman and engage in their Stone-Pounding ceremony, the thin ranks of the Alterrans are unable to hold back the advancing hordes of the savage Gaal, white-faced barbarians who wear red plumes in their hair. Soon the city is under siege, and both races must, against their wills, join forces to fend off the invader.

The central chapters relate the invasion, the siege of the city, and the concurrent beginning of the severe winter, with its overwhelming blizzards and its seasonal monsters, the Snowghouls. The graphically related actions are matched in depth by the inward development of the major characters, not merely the lovers but also Wold, the old man who is in some ways the best drawn character yet in Le Guin's fiction. Wold's characterization is in many ways of a piece with the portrayal of his clan and their way of life, but it rises above the an-thropological detail as a moving and universal picture of old age. Not a stereotype, Wold's character gains depth through tension of oppo-sites. In relation to his society, he experiences both antagonism and participation; he is at once a leader and an outcast. Within himself, he balances detachment and involvement, vitality and surrender, memory and anticipation. Cantankerous and courageous, heroic and pathetic, he is unforgettable.

The ending of the novel is by no means a simple resolution of the action. The city does survive the siege, the Gaal are defeated, and the lovers are united, but the outcome involves much more than these mere events. On the social level, the old enmity is at last overcome. Jakob addresses the mixed crowd at the wall of the city: "The Men of Tevar kept our walls side by side with the Men of Landin. They are welcome to stay with us or to go, to live with us or leave us, as they please. The gates of my city are open to you, all Winter long" (123).

Even more significantly, after the long evolution over six centuries of time, there is evidence that the planet has at last accepted the far-borns. Their isolation and alienation had one great advantage for them all this time: they were immune to local infection. The bacteria have refused to attack the alien species. But the battle reveals cases of infection, which means that the favorable adaptation has at last occurred, along with its very positive implication, that cross-fertilization might take place. As Rocannon learned at the well, there is a price to pay for every gain. The people of Alterra will be able to breed with those of Tevar, but their ability to bear children is at the cost of their new susceptibility to bacterial infection. Rolery learns all of this as she is busy tending the wounded. "She sat there among the sleep of wounded men, under the ruined city full of death, and brooded speechlessly on the chance of life" (117).

Both Jakob and Rolery develop as individuals, particularly Rolery, who quietly and receptively learns Alterran ways, including mindspeech for which she has a natural gift. She even learns to look into Jakob's eyes, outgrowing the taboo her people had placed on the direct look. Even the Eldest, Wold, grows in his ability to be at one with the real changes taking place in his world. When the invasion begins, he searches somewhat pathetically for his heavy spear, the one with which he single-handedly killed a Snowghoul long ago. But the sense of pathos turns to heroism as he uses the spear to kill one of the invading Gaal. Through the combined onslaught of army and winter, he touchingly but realistically identifies himself with the Winter sun, "old, weak in its old age" (64). He also recognizes winter as his ally, the one force that is strong enough to defeat the enemy. The realization tickles his fancy. "Wold suddenly cackled out loud, and turned from the darkening window. He had out-lived his chiefdom, his sons, his use, and had to die here on a rock in the sea; but he had great allies, and great warriors served him—greater than Agat, or any man. Storm and Winter fought for him, and he would outlive his enemies" (88). Wold dies at the moment of victory: his death and Agat's triumph coincide. At that moment also Agat is at last accepted by the clan, as his race has been by the planet. No longer an exile, he goes home with Rolery. The epigram in this case might be "To go home is to be home."

As in *Rocannon's World,* in this book the portrayal of whole cultures is as effective as individual characterization. Le Guin's background in anthropology provided her with the material for a highly convincing—and sympathetic—account of the Tevaran way of life. They are nomads and as such their attitudes toward time and space are fundamentally different from those of the city-dwelling Alterrans. As Jakob perceives the difference: "Hilfs did not consider either time or space in the linear, imperialistic fashion of his own species. Time to them was a lantern lighting a step before, a step behind—the rest was indistinguishable dark. Time was this day, this one day of the immense Year. They had no historical vocabulary; there was merely today and 'timepast.' They looked ahead only to the next season at most. They did not look down over time but were in it as the lamp in the night, as the heart in the body. And so also with space: space to them was not a surface on which to draw boundaries but a range, a heartland, centered on the self and clan and tribe. Around the Range were areas that brightened as one approached them and dimmed as one departed; the farther, the fainter. But there were no lines, no limits" (74).

Also distinctive is the role of ritual in their lives. The formal meeting of the clan involves a ceremony of Stone-Pounding, organized by its shaman-herald. A hundred men sitting in a circle pound rhythmically in a "hypnotic toneless trance of percussion" (34). The contrapuntal rhythms have meaning on the group level: "*Ak, ak, ak, ak,* the sound went on for a long time, until suddenly a second pounding joined it in counterpoint, *kadak ak ak kadak.* Another came in on a higher note, giving a tripping rhythm, then another, another, more, until any measure was lost in the clatter of constant sound, an avalanche of the high dry whack of rock hitting rock in which each individual pounding rhythm was submerged, indistinguishable" (34).

The intriguing role of the shaman-herald who summons this ceremony is not, however, developed in the society of the Tevarans.

Because of these features, *Planet of Exile* is of special relevance for those readers interested in anthropology. With its central romantic theme of star-crossed lovers and its tightly suspenseful heroic plot, this second volume of the Hainish trilogy will appeal to general readers, not just those in search of hard-core SF. Perhaps its one flaw is the inclusion of the Snowghouls, an extraneous Gothic element which has little relation to character or theme, does not further the plot, and evokes a somewhat ludicrous vision of an Abominable Snowman.

Of particular interest to women readers is the character of Rolery, coprotagonist of the novel. An adolescent rebel and loner, with plenty of courage and integrity as well as devotion, she is a very appealing figure. By no means a passive heroine, she is, in fact, the moral center of the book. As Le Guin pointed out, "the central mover of the events of the book, the *one who chooses,* is, in fact, Rolery."[7] Admittedly hers is not an aggressive role, but in Le Guin's Taoist scheme, aggression is futile whereas "wu wei" or "action through stillness," accomplishes much. Rolery's physical courage and resourcefulness save Jakob's life when he is attacked and left for dead by her irate kinsmen, and her quiet but firm receptivity to the ways of the farborns helps to bring the hostile groups together. Bright, curious, and tough, she becomes a symbol of the planet's final acceptance of the alien race as well as of the merger of two totally different cultures.

City of Illusions

It is ironic but fitting that Rolery's descendant should become the hero of the third book in the trilogy. Himself the product of a reconciliation of opposites, Falk, the protagonist of *City of Illusions,* is inwardly divided into two opposed personalities. At the beginning of the novel he does not know it, nor does the reader, for he is introduced simply as a man without a mind, without memory, without a past. The psychological direction of the narrative is toward the unification of the new self, created *ex nihilo,* with the old self totally forgotten.

The striking opening sentence of the book initiates many levels of meaning in one image: "Imagine darkness." The pervasive darkness includes the darkness of the hero, whose mind has been eradicated; the darkness of the society, whose past civilization has been completely destroyed in interglobal war; the darkness of a country deeply forested and sparsely populated; and the darkness of reality in the grip of the illusory mode of life imposed by the ruling lords, the Shing. This dark world is not another world, however, but the land mass of the former United States. The year is 4370 A.D., and this country is largely wilderness, with only a few small and isolated settlements far apart from one another.

Out of this dark forest, into a clearing, steps a man without a mind. Not an idiot or an imbecile, not a lunatic, but a human being totally without mental awareness of any sort. This otherwise normal person, alien only in his yellow eyes, is adopted by the family of Zove who live in a rural commune of about forty people. Theirs is a closed and self-sustaining economy, partly primitive, partly sophisticated. They grow and make by hand whatever they need, yet they possess technological devices, including a "slider," a flying machine. They have a library of words, music, and images, but no communication with the outside world.

The family teach their adopted alien guest as they would teach a child, and he becomes one of them, eventually becoming the lover of the young woman, Parth. Inevitably he feels, however, that he must leave the security of this hospitable "chalet-castle-farmhouse" and journey westward in search of his lost identity. His theory is that the Shing—the enemy—had destroyed his mind in order to prevent his bringing a message to Earth from another planet, and it is only by going to their city, Es Toch, that he will be able to recover memory of his past.

Several chapters are devoted to his trip westward. He meets many unusual characters along the way and also acquires a companion-lover who stays with him all the way to Es Toch. He meets talking animals who remind him defensively of the Shing prohibition against taking life; he meets the misogynistic Bee-Keepers, the savage tribe of Bassnaska; and he meets two unforgettable individuals, the great listener, All-Alonio, and the Prince of Kansas. All of these encounters give rise to the same advice: go alone. "Go alone, Opalstone, said the Prince of Kansas. Go alone, said Hiardan, the Bee-Keeper. Go alone, said the old Listener in the forest. Go alone, my son, said Zove" (121).[8] But he travels with Estrel, the woman who helped him escape a vicious group of hunters, and trusts her completely, never suspecting that the supposed amulet she always wears and obviously treasures is actually a transmitting device.

Along with the fast-moving narrative of the journey, two cameo portraits of unusual characters add depth to the picaresque plot. The voluble old man who calls himself the Listener lives all alone in the midst of wilderness. All-Alonio, whose talk is mad, elusive, and profound, is not lonely: "I am no more lonely than the mill brook, or a weathercock, or the north star, or the south wind, or an April shower, or a January thaw, or the first spider in a new house" (55). He shares an important common heritage with Falk, for he is, as he puts it, a "thurro-dowist," or Taoist. One of the few objects that Falk took away with him from Zove's house is his copy of the Old Canon, the book of the Way, the *Tao Te Ching*.

Knowledge of the Old Canon also relates Falk to his other strange host, the Prince of Kansas. Ruler of a small but relatively sophisticated enclave in the wilderness, the prince has about 200 subjects. He also has a large library, including a copy of the Old Canon to spare for his guest who has lost his. He only plays the game of being prince yet his followers obey him without any need for enforcement: "His people chose to serve him, perhaps because they found, in thus affirming the innate and essential grandeur of one person, that they reaffirmed their own quality as men" (103). He is also proud possessor of Griffon, one of an almost extinct breed, the dog. To Falk the beast beside the throne seems mythological, something come to life out of the old legends. Along with the Old Canon, the prince possesses another object familiar to Falk, a patterning-frame, like the one at Zove's house but larger and much more elaborate. Falk spends thirteen days with the prince, then leaves for "the mirage and dust" of his westward trek.

When Falk and Estrel finally reach Es Toch, they see a spectacular city built on the two rims of a narrow canyon: "On the very edges of the facing cliffs the towers of the city jutted up, hardly based on earth at all, linked across the chasm by delicate bridgespans. Towers, roadways and bridges ceased and the wall closed the city off again just before a vertiginous bend of the canyon" (113). This awesome location (which Le Guin based on the Black Canyon of the Gunnison) is matched only by its eerie appearance. The descriptions of it are largely in terms of wavering and shifting light. Green towers shine as if "translucent" (113), helicopters have "diaphanous vanes" and sliders "flicker" along the streets. The room in which Falk finds himself is even more remarkable. The entire room is in fact translucent, with the room beneath it visible to him.

> Walls floor and ceiling were all of the same translucent stuff, which appeared soft and undulant like many thicknesses of pale green veiling, but was tough and slick to the touch. Queer carvings and crimpings and ridges forming ornate patterns all over the floor were, to the exploring hand, non-existent; they were eye-deceiving paintings, or lay beneath a smooth transparent surface. . . . Visibility without discrimination, solitude without privacy. It was extraordinarily beautiful, this masked shimmer of lights and shapes through inchoate planes of green, and extraordinarily disturbing. (116–17)

Most shocking of all, however, is Estrel's apparent betrayal. She seizes his laser and delivers Falk into the hands of the enemy, the Shing. But is it her betrayal or her loyalty which is illusory? In this city of illusions, Falk finds all experience a series of shifting realities. Even the physical presence of the Shing lords is illusory—seen and heard, they fade when approached, a screen image having substituted for a solid person.

The mediator between Falk and his captors is the boy, Har Orry, who convinces the former that they both came to Earth from another planet whose exact location is not known. Orry is too young to remember the name of that planet's sun, and the Shing are eager to restore Falk's memory of himself as the alien Ramarren so that he can communicate the name to them. In his dilemma the divided Falk-Ramarren realizes that he must submit to the mind-restoration surgery of the Shing in order to regain his identity as Ramarren but not at the expense of losing his identity as Falk. He succeeds in unifying his split selves with the aid of the inspiring little book, the Old Canon, and in a whirlwind conclusion he escapes his captors, taking both Orry and one of the Shing with him as he flies back to his native planet of Werel.

The Old Canon thus functions explicitly as a numinous object in *The City of Illusions* as well as a thematic device through its ideational content. Since the tenets of Taoism provide the underlying moral framework not only of the Hainish trilogy but also of much of Le Guin's later fiction, a basic understanding of them is essential to understanding her works. She was early influenced by Taoism and welcomed the opportunity to use her own translation of the *Tao Te Ching* in this novel.[9]

The Taoist ethic stresses the virtue of inaction, or what Lao-Tse called "wu wei," translated by Le Guin as "action through stillness." The value of nonaction is based on the recognition of a cyclical pattern in nature. This cycle is not the familiar western image of the wheel of fortune, which is governed by time, but rather a pattern of wholeness and balance, with every action followed by a compensatory reaction. Every challenge produces a response, every aggression a defense. "It succeeds by *being* rather than doing, by attitude rather than act, by attraction rather than compulsion."[10] Lao-Tse's favorite image for the power of inaction is water, which is soft and yielding but easily overcomes rock, which is hard and resistant. It is not a renunciation of power but a recognition of power within the balanced scheme of nature.

Moral relativity is an inevitable correlative of this balance. No action in itself can be "good" or "evil," but upsetting the balance in any way will cause further disturbance, perhaps pain and suffering, as nature acts to redress that balance. In terms of traditional Christian dualism, there is no "evil" as such. That is why Le Guin's fiction is singularly lacking in villains, and why her attempts to create an "enemy" result in either vagueness (as in the case of the Faradayans who remain unknown) or melodrama (as in the case of the Shing, who are unconvincing villains). The same relativity applies to races as to individuals. The farborns and the nomads are equally "good," and no moral judgment is exacted of the Fiia, the Gdemiar, or any of the other races in Rocannon's world.

A minor but subtle point in Taoist doctrine has special relevance to *City of Illusions*. Lao-Tse notes that "to tell a lie is impossible because every statement has a reason."[11] The underlying reason is, then, the deeper truth of the statement. (If a person lies about his age, it is because he sees himself as a younger person and wishes others to see him so. The "lie" represents a kind of spiritual, subjective truth.) Since in *City of Illusions* the Shing are indeed liars, the question of their personal truths becomes relevant. Here perhaps is the main flaw in this often brilliant book. The Shing are not fully developed, as Le Guin realized: "The Shing are the least convincing lot of people I ever wrote."[12] As a race, they are almost a caricature, complete with sneer, snarl, and black hats. The one individual among them who achieves some depth is Estrel, but ultimately even she baffles the reader. Part of the reason for this is Le Guin's technique of narrating from the protagonist's point of view. Estrel seems at first a model of courage and loyalty because she seems so to Falk, but when she abruptly turns on him, laughing as she delivers him to the Shing, the reader can only share Falk's dismay and astonishment. And since the reunited Falk-Ramarren sees her only once, and then in an ambiguous encounter, she must remain for reader as for protagonist, not merely an enigma but an irreconcilable contradiction.

Like its two predecessors, *City of Illusions* promises more than it delivers. But its limited achievement is the greater because of its greater potential. Not only does the moral position of Taoism add philosophical clarity to the work, but also in theme, setting, character, and narrative line it is a rich novel. The theme of a postholocaust world is of course a SF convention, but it is handled with originality. With the trained eye of an anthropologist, Le Guin sees the precise way in which a scattered and defeated human race reorganizes itself for survival. The drab but secure communal life in Zove's house is credibly presented. Its most striking feature, the patterning frame—a kind of occult abacus of destiny,—is a tribute to the author's inventiveness. It is at once "a fortune-teller, a computer, an implement of mystical discipline, a toy" (101).

The setting is remarkable in its contrasting scenes of a country retrogressed to a state of wilderness privation and a futuristic city filled with air traffic and illusory architecture. The American wilderness is both beautiful and pathetic: "The sense of time, but more than that the sense of space, extent, the wideness of the continent. The wideness, the wilderness. Prairie, forest; undergrowth, bushes, grass, weeds; the wilderness." But here and there "a buried supermarket or a ruined freeway made mysterious and pathetic as all things are by age."[13] The City of Es Toch, on the other hand, is a mockery. The city as goal and dream of civilization is perverted in the image of the lush yet shadowy capital of the Shing. Paradoxically, despite its bright lights, it represents darkness more than the wilderness does. The wilderness enfolds the direct darkness of nature, but the city offers a perversion of light as of truth. What seems real and solid is exposed as "a blur of lights . . . a flicker of color, fading" (119). The city is indeed a wilderness in yet another sense, for it is not a place of men. It has no history, no myths, no libraries or museums, no education or economy. And its location on the rim of a canyon hints visually at its profound hollowness. It is a lie. Both geographical settings, wild and urban, are moral settings as well, with the dark forest of the mind, in all its innocence and ignorance, pitted against the false luminescence of the human construct.

In the case of the divided hero, Falk-Ramarren, character is at one with narrative. At the start of the novel—"Imagine darkness"—he is mentally a newborn infant. His initial personality as Falk (i.e., "yellow" because of his eyes and skin color) is the product of his sojourn in Zove's house, and his individuation process is the equivalent of his westward trek to the city. The advanced stage in his individuation, the reconciliation of his opposed selves, is outwardly manifested in the restoration surgery performed by the Shing and the concomitant, unifying message to both selves from the Old Canon. The simultaneity of outer and inner action is the most sophisticated experiment yet for Le Guin. The narrative is also, in a sense, circular, for as it begins in one kind of darkness, it ends in another. At the end of the novel, Falk's ship enters the darkness of interplanetary space as he flies toward his home planet. "Home" is of course an ambivalent concept for the protagonist. "Was he leaving home or going home"? The question is a variation on the pervasive motif of "To go is to return."

The largely neglected early trilogy is thus in fact a substantial introduction to the fiction of Le Guin. It establishes several of her major themes, including the Taoist ethic of balance, the reconciliation of opposites, and the importance of cultural diversity, as well as several characteristic narrative techniques, such as the symbolic use of setting, the evolving point of view through the growing consciousness of the protagonist, and the circular structure of the archetypal journey to outer lands and return to inner self. It also sets the stage for two further Hainish epics, *The Left Hand of Darkness* (which takes place much later, 4870 A.D.) and *The Dispossessed* (much earlier, 2300 A.D.). Le Guin has created a universe.

Chapter Three

The Earthsea Trilogy

Le Guin's second trilogy, a fantasy set in the imaginary world of Earthsea, is a major achievement, considered by some critics her best work to date.[1] The first of the three books, *A Wizard of Earthsea*, was published in 1968, directly after the last work in the Hainish trilogy. The other two books, *The Tombs of Atuan* and *The Farthest Shore*, were published in 1971 and 1972, overlapping with *The Lathe of Heaven* (1971) and *The Left Hand of Darkness* (1969). Fantasy rather than science fiction, these new works explore inner lands rather than outer spaces. For Le Guin, fantasy is the medium best suited to a description of the journey to self-knowledge, as "only the symbolic language of the deeper psyche will fit [the events of that voyage] without trivializing them."[2] In each volume of the Earthsea trilogy the protagonist undertakes such a journey in an appropriately symbolic setting.

The fantasy trilogy continues to develop some of the themes and techniques of the earlier Hainish books, including the uses of cultural anthropology, symbols and archetypes drawn from Jungian psychology, the philosophical emphasis on the Taoist ideal of balance and the reconciliation of opposites, and the focus on narrative quest as circular journey. In contrast to the earlier books, they were written for children, but in their integration and internalization of plot, setting, and character, they become deeper works of fiction than the category of children's literature to which they belong.[3] Actually more suitable for adolescents than for children, these three books rank thematically and stylistically with great works of adult fiction.

Although the three novels can be read and enjoyed separately, they are a closely interwoven trilogy, unified through a common setting and protagonist. They are much more closely interdependent than the loosely related Hainish trilogy. As the title indicates, the setting throughout is a sea strewn with hundreds of islands. A few of the islands are portrayed in their disparate cultures in some detail, whereas many others are named but not actually introduced into the narrative. (A map is provided for the reader.)[4] The world of Earthsea is relatively primitive. There are no references to machines, and even the large merchant ships are powered by oars. It is also a world to which magic is central, and every island or town has its local mage to take care of problems concerning weather, medicine, war, and minor repairs. The protagonist is a mage, first introduced as a young boy named Duny and called the Sparrowhawk by his friends, but who matures to become ultimately both a dragon-lord and an archmage whose real name is Ged. In terms of this central character the overall plot of the trilogy recounts Ged's journey to self-knowledge, but the congruent patterns of narrative include on the social level, a movement from disorder to order; on the religious level, from transcendance to immanence; and on the metaphysical, from imbalance to balance in the natural and moral realms. Obviously such narrative and thematic complexity suggests fiction worthy of adult reading.

The secondary world of Earthsea was introduced to readers somewhat before the appearance of these three books. "The Rule of Names" and "The Word of Unbinding," seed stories of the later novels, appeared in *Fantastic* in 1964. "The Rule of Names" has direct bearing on *The Wizard of Earthsea*, while "The Word of Unbinding" foreshadows *The Farthest Shore*. The central character in the earlier story is also a wizard, an apparently inept one named Mr. Underhill who, however, turns out to be a dragon in disguise. He is actually the dragon Yevaud, whom Ged will eventually bind to the island of Pendor. The theme of the story is the vital importance of true names as opposed to mere use names. Knowing the true name of a person, be he wizard or dragon, confers power over him. To share one's true name with someone is thus to show absolute trust.[5] A light touch characterizes this humorous short piece which precedes the rather more somber account in the novel of Ged's quest for selfhood.

A Wizard of Earthsea

In *A Wizard of Earthsea* Ged's journey to self-knowledge is largely focused on his struggle to find and name the mysterious shadow which relentlessly pursues him. As Le Guin explained in her essay "The Child and the Shadow," the archetypal shadow in the Jungian sense—"the dark brother" of the conscious mind—is both a dangerous threat and a valuable guide on this journey. "It is inferior, primitive, awkward, animallike, childlike; powerful, vital, spontaneous. It's not weak and decent . . . it's dark and hairy and unseemly; but without it, the person is nothing."[6] Realized in this novel as a separate entity, the shadow is both cause and object of the hero's quest.

The hero is introduced as a young boy nicknamed the Sparrow-hawk. Motherless and neglected by his father, the lad is a mere goatherd, but he shows a remarkable talent for deeds of magic. When he succeeds in routing a barbaric invasion by his skill in fogweaving, the news of his gifted abilities spreads through the islands. On his thirteenth birthday, he is visited by mage Ogion, who confers on him his true name—Ged—and takes him away from his native village to become Ogion's apprentice in wizardry at Re Albi in his home, called the Falcon's Nest.

Life with Ogion is a meditative retreat for the impatient boy eager to perform great deeds of magic, but he learns much natural lore. It is also during his brief apprenticeship with the wise old man, and before Ged goes off to the College for Wizards, that the shadow appears for the first time. He sees it as he pores over a forbidden book of runes: "something was crouching beside the closed door, a shapeless clot of shadow darker than the darkness" (22).[7] His subsequent journey, to the island of Roke to attend the college, is on board a boat prophetically named *Shadow*.

On the island of Roke, an old Scottish word meaning mist or fog, Ged completes his training in wizardry and also his rites of passage to adulthood. Always proud as well as impatient, Ged lets the taunts of his fellow students prompt him to undertake a greater display of power than is either wise or safe. Chafing under the boasts of a rival student, Jasper, Ged foolishly summons from the dead the spirit of a legendary woman, Elfarran. In an awesome scene, he recites with more skill than wisdom the Spell of Summoning, and succeeds in invoking a fearful shadow-beast. The dreadful apparition turns with fury against its summoner. The young man's friends are unable to save him from its wild attack. Only the superior magic of the archmage Nemmerle can dispel the ominous shapeless thing, but the old man is utterly exhausted by the effort and dies shortly thereafter.

Profoundly humbled by this devastating experience, Ged accepts a professional post as mage in the modest fishing town of Low Torning, which has been under threat of a dragon attack. In this village Ged makes friends with a fisherman, Pechvarry, and his son, Ioth. They are the lonely wizard's only companions apart from the little wild animal, the otak, which he has adopted. When the boy becomes mortally ill, Ged tries unsuccessfully to save him, almost losing his own life as he pursues the lad's dying spirit close to the dry lands of death. In doing so Ged has violated the balance in the world, once more challenging the natural separation of living and dead, as he had when he summoned the spirit. This time Ged's life is saved by the loving intervention of the pet otak. In its instinctive wisdom the little beast licks his companion, thus summoning through his touch the lost spirit.

Although this attempt to save a child's life is a personal failure, Ged achieves a major success for the town. He seeks out the threatening dragon who has occupied the abandoned island of Pendor for four generations. He confronts it with knowledge of its name, Yevaud (the same dragon who appeared in the story "The Rule of Names"). Not only does Ged resist the dragon's tempting offer to him to reveal the shadow's name in exchange for betrayal of the town, but he actually negotiates with the wily dragon, binding him with an oath never to leave his own island of Pendor. Yevaud will never threaten the Archipelago again.

In spite of this success, Ged is continually plagued by dreams about the nameless shadow. Without knowing its name, he is helpless against it. He cannot even return to Roke by boat because the Roke wind is set against him. On the advice of a mysterious person he meets, he sails instead for the Court of Terrenon. This person is revealed later to be a "gebbeth," a body which "has been drained of true substance and is something like a shell or a vapor in the form of a man, an unreal flesh clothing the shadow which is real" (107). He is eventually driven by the pursuing gebbeth into the castle of Terrenon, where he encounters Serret, whom he had known earlier as the sorcerous daughter of the Lord of Re Albi but who is now the wife of Lord Benderesk. In this castle he faces one more severe temptation. The Stone of Terrenon carries the strong Old Power, which can reveal the name of the shadow to Ged but which also threatens to possess his soul. Ged rejects the offer of this power which would ultimately enslave him and escapes the castle by transforming himself into a hawk. In that form he returns to his master Ogion, who restores his body, renews his spirit, and shapes him a new staff of yew. Thus renewed he sets off to hunt the shadow which had been hunting him. The decision is a spiritual turning point in his journey to selfhood.

Among his adventures as he now heads eastward in pursuit, is an encounter with an elderly man and woman on a remote island. Marooned there since early childhood, the two people have little to communicate, but the woman gives the wizard a mysterious half-ring. This talisman will be the focus of his quest in the next volume of the trilogy. Also on this journey, Ged meets his old friend from Roke, Vetch, who is now a mage on the island of Ismay, and Vetch decides to accompany Ged in his boat, the *Lookfar*.

The quest culminates at an ultimate point in the east, where the sea turns to sand and no wind stirs. "There were no directions here, no north or south or east or west, only towards and away" (178). There Ged finally confronts the shadow and learns its name. Identifying it raises this unconscious horror over the threshold of consciousness even as the sea has given way to land.

Aloud and clearly, breaking that old silence, Ged spoke the shadow's name and in the same moment the shadow spoke without lips or tongue, saying the same word: "Ged." And the two voices were one voice. (179)

The hunt is over; the quest is completed. All that remains is for Ged to accept and integrate the shadow which is a part of himself after all:

Ged reached out his hands, dropping his staff, and took hold of his shadow, of the black self that reached out to him. Light and darkness met, and joined, and were one. (179)

This climactic episode, which occurs near the end of the book, is a major event on Ged's journey to self-knowledge and to adulthood. The newly integrated shadow will continue to be his guide on the journey toward light.

Throughout *A Wizard of Earthsea* the narrative structure of the quest is thematically enriched by Le Guin's skillful interweaving of symbols and motifs. In addition to the shadow as central symbol she incorporates birds, dragons, and stones for their symbolic suggestiveness. Birds are representative of the soul in folklore and legend all over the world. Separation of the soul from the body at death has been traditionally enacted as the flight of a bird from a cage,[8] and becoming a winged being denotes the process of spiritualization. Ged as wizard is a spiritual figure, identified from the start with the sparrowhawk, a bird consecrated to the sun by the ancient Egyptians, Greeks, and Romans, who attributed to it all of the powers associated with the sun. The mountain home of the mage Ogion is also called the Falcon's Nest. The elderly mage Nemmerle keeps a pet raven, which disappears at the death of his master. When Ged wants to escape from the Castle of Terrenon, he transforms himself into a hawk in order to fly back to Re Albi to be restored by Ogion. On the other hand, the enchantress Serret transforms herself into a gull, only to be destroyed by pursuing winged black creatures, a negative and destructive form of spiritual power.

Le Guin also uses dragons and stones in both traditional and original ways to enhance her narrative. Her dragons are ancient and guileful beings, who speak the magically endowed Old Speech. No one dares look into the green eyes of a dragon, and his laughter is seen, rather than heard, as yellow smoke that issues from his nostrils. The dragon of Pendor is an impressive giant, "lean as a hound" and "huge as a hill" (89), and his scales are grey-black, "catching the daylight like broken stone" (89). Like dragons, certain stones are invested with the Old Powers. The Stone of Terrenon tests Ged even as the dragon of Pendor had done. Also like the dragon, which Ged binds to the island of Pendor forevermore, the Stone of Terrenon is bound to its location. We learn that it is so with the Old Powers; "being bound each to an isle, a certain place, cave or stone or welling spring" (123).[9]

The style of *A Wizard of Earthsea* is suitable to its subject of mythic magery. Artful yet simple, the language is largely Anglo-Saxon in diction, strongly alliterative, and suggestively resonant of an austere but heroic age. The alliteration is pervasive, recalling the oral tradition of the heroic poem *Beowulf*.[10] "The beasts began to bleat and browse. . . ." (3); "You witless woodenhead! . . . you spineless slave-sons!" (32); "the soft singing of spells" (129). And, like *Beowulf*, *Wizard* is also marked with gnomic formulas. ("To light a candle is to cast a shadow" (44); "Infinite are the arguments of mages" (161); "Only in silence of the word" (181). Above all, language is not merely a matter of style, but language is itself a subject of *A Wizard of Earthsea*. In the world of Earthsea, the word is creative. All spoken languages derive from Old Speech, which is now understood only by dragons and wizards. But the true names of everything are those of the Old Speech, which is the heart of a wizard's education. "Who knows a man's name, holds that man's life in his keeping" (69). This "rule of names" applies not only to men but to all created things. That is why magic is "the true naming of a thing" (46). It is also the magic of Segoy, Creator of Earthsea, "the language Segoy spoke who made the islands of the world" (47). For Earthsea, the beginning was the Word.

The Tombs of Atuan

The theme of names is also central to the second volume in the trilogy, *The Tombs of Atuan,* which in many ways parallels *A Wizard of Earthsea.* Like its predecessor, *The Tombs* is about coming-of-age, but focused on a girl rather than a boy. As Le Guin put it, "The subject of *The Tombs of Atuan* is, if I had to put it in one word, sex. . . . More exactly, you could call it a feminine coming of age. Birth, rebirth, destruction, freedom are the themes."[11] In this treatment of female coming of age, not only the rule of names but also several other themes recur but from a contrasting point of view to that of the male-centered *Wizard.*

The island of Atuan had been introduced fleetingly but significantly into the narrative of *A Wizard.* We learned in the opening chapter of the earlier book about the Kargish empire, of which Atuan is one of four islands. We learned also that the Kargs are a fierce, even savage people, white-skinned and yellow-haired, given to raiding and violence. They apparently worship twin masculine deities, for they rush into battle crying the names of the White Godbrothers "Wuluah" and "Atwah." It is an attacking band of Kargs that Ged dispels with his magically produced fog. Near the end of *A Wizard* Ged finds the broken ring of Erreth-Akbe which will eventually lead him on his quest to find the other half in the tombs of Atuan.

Although the presence of Ged unifies the three works, the young wizard does not actually appear until the middle of the *Tombs of Atuan.* The first half of this book is exclusively concerned with introducing the female protagonist, Tenar, and with developing the exact nature of the feminine religion which is observed in the symbolic setting of the ancient tombs of Atuan. This religion is dedicated to the worship of the Nameless Ones, dark and destructive forces which exist far underground, "the ancient and holy Powers of the Earth before the Light" (107).[12] Ged's sudden appearance in these mysterious tombs thus has a very different meaning for him than it has for Tenar.

A series of complex symbolic polarities surrounds the very birth of the girl-child Tenar. It is believed by those who follow the religion of the Nameless Ones that its high priestess is repeatedly reborn in the body of a girl baby born close to the time of the former priestess's death. It is Tenar's awesome but grim destiny to be thus chosen as the incarnation of the recently deceased priestess. She is introduced to the reader as a lively, healthy child of three with black hair and white skin (in obvious contrast to Ged's dark skin.) The polarities of dark and light are intensified when, in spite of her mother's frantic attempts to rescue her from her destined role, she is duly initiated at the age of six. Clad in a black robe in a ceremonial enactment of the conflict between the forces of light and darkness, she enters the dark Place of the Tombs and surrenders her old identity as Tenar. Now in the service of the Nameless Ones she adopts the new name of Arha, which means the Eaten One. Her individual identity is thus sacrificed to her assigned role as priestess of the ancient underworld powers. Her supposed rebirth as a priestess represents her death as an individual.

For the next eight years, until the age of fourteen when she makes her crossing into womanhood and becomes formally acknowledged as the highest priestess of the tombs, she remains in this remote and sterile location, surrounded by women and engulfed in ritual.[13] During this period of training her life consists almost entirely of ceremonial details and traditional womanly skills such as weaving and spinning. Her training is thus the opposite of Ged's. Whereas Ged attended a college for wizards and gained much knowledge about the nature of the world, Tenar learns only about rituals and the unexplorable world of the dark tombs where no light ever appears. Furthermore, while Ged erred in the direction of too much consciousness, Tenar's problem is that of almost total unconsciousness. The solar oriented Sparrowhawk was guilty of pride and ambition, while the lunar priestess remains entombed and enslaved to an endless round of ritual:

Nothing happened. Once the ceremonies of her consecration were over, the days went on as they had always gone. There was wool to be spun, black cloth to be woven, meal to be ground, rites to be performed; the Nine Chants must be sung nightly, the doorways blessed, the Stones fed with goat's blood twice a year, the dances of the dark of the moon danced before the Empty Throne. And so the whole year had passed. . . .(24)

Arha's life is thus virtually limited to an unconscious level, as she moves through her daily round of prescribed and habitual religious duties. Unlike the young Sparrowhawk, who chose unwisely and acted rashly, Arha has no opportunity for either personal choice or voluntary actions. Her development as a conscious individual is totally stultified. She is indeed "eaten."

Her relationships with other people are also extremely limited in both number and depth. The matriarchal community is, of course, limited by definition to females and eunuchs. Arha's closest friend is the gentle eunuch, Manan, who provides an element of almost maternal love in his care of her. His affection is not so much returned as taken for granted by Arha, who enjoys teasing her rather pathetic "potato-faced" guardian. Her closest friend of her own age is Penthe, a cheerful, sensuous girl, completely unsuited to her life in training as a priestess. "I'd rather marry a pigherd and live in a ditch," she complains. "I'd rather anything than stay buried alive here all my born days with a mess of women in a perishing old desert where nobody ever comes" (40). Her frank admission of doubts about the Nameless Ones puzzles Arha, who is not sufficiently free from the control of her dark masters to sense the sheer vitality implicit in that sunny skepticism. Arha's other close associate is Kossil, the grim, older woman who has hardened in her years of service to the Nameless Ones so that she no longer feels warmth toward anyone. Her harsh life is an image of futility. As Ged later explains, "I think [the Nameless Ones] drove your priestess Kossil mad a long time ago; I think she has prowled these caverns as she prowls the labyrinth of her own self, and now she cannot see the daylight anymore" (107).

Arha's first conscious act in her role of head priestess occurs at age fifteen, when she orders the death by starvation of three male prisoners who have defiled the tombs. For any male to enter the secret underground precincts is of course a symbolic rape, and the ritual sacrifice of the male intruder is standard practice for this matriarchal cult. This destructive action has its negative effect on Arha, however, and she faints, falling into an illness that lasts for several days. During her illness she has several dreams, one of which is particularly rich in its imagery of the feminine archetype: "She dreamed that she had to carry a full bowl of water, a deep brass bowl, through the dark, to someone who was thirsty. She could never get to this person" (38). Since nourishment is the primary function of the great mother archetype,[14] this dream clearly reflects the tension in Arha between the positive and negative manifestations of the mother image. The dream is also prophetic, for she will have a literal opportunity to provide or to deny nourishment, to sustain life or to destroy it.

Part of Arha's training in the hands of the older women is an inculcation of hatred for the wizards of the Inner Lands, regarded as masters of deception and trickery. The wizards admittedly work magic, but Kossil tries to denigrate their achievements as products of deception. The conscious action, based on knowledge of the words of power, seems to her a matter of subtle trickery, quite unlike the more profound spiritual power of the Nameless Ones. Her vehement rejection of the superior rational powers of wizards is also linked with her rejection of the masculine world, and its corresponding worship of the Godking in neighboring lands.

This quiet, empty world of feminine mystery is interrupted by the unexpected appearance of the wizard Ged, whose werelight Arha detects in the undertomb near the entrance to the labyrinth. Ged, who has violated the sanctity of the tombs in his effort to recover the missing half of the Ring of Erreth-Akbe, is trapped underground and finds himself completely at the mercy of the young priestess. Her dream of the cauldron is realized in her immediate situation, as she must now choose between leaving the intruder to die of thirst or helping him to survive by bringing him food and water.

Her first impulse, dictated by the Terrible Mother element in her own unconscious, is destructive.[15] "She would not give him any water. She would give him death, death, death, death, death" (74). But this negative impulse is suppressed by an even greater one—curiosity. Her prisoner may be blasphemous, but he is also interesting, and she decides to bring him the food and water necessary for his survival if only to permit her to learn more about him. Her eagerness to learn about life proves to be on the side of life itself.

Before her encounter with Ged, the tombs represented for Arha an undifferentiated unconsciousness, deep, demanding, and dumb. With his sudden challenging appearance, she must for the first time act. She must now find within herself the counterpart of the rationality that the wizard represents for her. Her unreasoning devotion to the terrifying nameless gods has kept her existence almost entirely on the level of intuition. Psychologically, as well as literally, she has been living out her years underground. But it is also in the underground— at once womb and tomb—that the transformation begins.

In her talks with Ged, as she brings him "water and bread and life" (84), she begins to discover herself. She is astonished to find that the wizard knows her real name, and it is through him that her first sense of self-knowledge comes. She has been, as her name indicates, "eaten," with her individuality totally consumed in the dark, meaningless round of her ritualized existence. But Ged leads her to rediscover the individual Tenar. "You must be Arha, or you must be Tenar. You cannot be both" (113).

She also learns that he is the possessor of the broken fragment of a sacred ring. When Ged explains to her that he has come to his holy place to investigate the hitherto undisturbed treasure room in order to search for the missing half, she reveals to him that as priestess, she has in her possession a sacred semicircle on a silver chain around her neck. In a climatic moment of illumination for both of them, Ged places in Tenar's hand the other half of the fabled ring which once belonged to the legendary hero, Erreth-Akbe, and she places it next to her half on the silver chain. The new totality of the ring is matched by her new awareness of totality in herself. The ring newly made whole is obviously a symbol of totality, and it represents for her the birth of the ego, much as the integration of the shadow-beast had meant for Ged. On the social level the ring, marked with a bond-rune, signifies peace and unity for Earthsea.

Now that Ged has, in effect, restored her true name, Tenar casts aside the role of Arha, instinctive votary of the destructive gods of darkness. She is now able to choose freedom. No longer enslaved to unconscious obedience, Tenar is free enough inwardly to decide in favor of undertaking a dangerous escape. "You have set us both free," Ged exalts, and the two set out on the dark and labyrinthine path that leads to daylight (115). As John Layard has pointed out, "the labyrinth always has to do with death and rebirth, is almost always connected with a cave, and is always presided over by a woman, though it may be walked through by men." The labyrinthine way represents part of the individuation process. Like Kossil, Tenar "prowls the labyrinth of her own self" (107).[16]

But freedom does not come all at once. There will be moments when Tenar temporarily regresses, succumbing to the pull of the consecrated Eaten One. The first such moment occurs at the entrance to the tombs when Ged's staff and voice force the rocks blocking their escape to break open for them. Under the starry sky just paling toward dawn, Tenar falls to the ground and refuses to follow Ged, who suddenly appears to her like a black-faced demon. He persuades her to come with him by reminding her of the ring, and as the two move away from the ominous opening to the tombs, an earthquake shakes both the huge tombstones and the Hall of the Throne: "a huge crack opened among the Tombstones. . . . The stones that still stood upright toppled into it and were swallowed" (123). Tenar then realizes that Ged's work held back the earthquake long enough for them to escape; his magery subdued the anger of the dark powers. Ged's mentor Ogion, the reader recalls, was famed as the mage who held back an earthquake.

Tenar suffers one more relapse. One more time the Nameless Ones reach out to recapture their lost votary. As she looks at Ged, finding him momentarily abstracted, deep in his own thoughts, she suddenly feels an unreasoning fear, and reaches for a knife. "The little blade was sharp enough to cut a finger to the bone, or to cut the arteries of a throat. She would serve her Masters still, though they had betrayed her and forsaken her. They would guide and drive her hand in the last act of darkness. They would accept the sacrifice" (140). But as she turns on him with the knife poised, his expression clears and he addresses her softly, trustingly, seemingly not even noticing the weapon. Her rage dissipates, and she is again ready to join him in their journey back to civilization.

Tenar's story ends with their arrival in the port of Havnor. Hand in hand with the wizard, she enters the white streets of the city. Only sixteen years of age, she is alone and somewhat afraid but free to grow. She is ready to face her future. Tenar does not reappear later on in the trilogy—a disappointment to some readers—for her coming-of-age story is completed here. We hear of her only once more, when Ged refers to her in *The Farthest Shore* as "The White Lady of Gont" (8). *The Tombs of Atuan* thus parallels *A Wizard of Earthsea,* with its focus on the adolescent rites of passage of a female rather than of a male. Whereas the wizard must cope primarily with the problem of an inflated ego, the priestess must deal with the threatening power of the unconscious. Ged's shadow was separated from him and needed to be reintegrated, but Tenar's shadow is not merely within her but overflows her whole psychic being, so that her feelings like her body have been entombed. In Havnor, with the completed silver ring about her wrist, she is liberated from the darkness.

This story of feminine coming of age has its parallels in myth as in modern life. Le Guin uses two myths as implicit structural motifs, that of Theseus and the Minotaur and that of Demeter and Persephone. With her close knowledge of the maze of paths in the tombs, Tenar is like Ariadne leading Theseus out of the labyrinth. She is also like Demeter, whose devotion to the underworld powers is a blight but whose reappearance in the world heralds a new spring. But these experiences are universal and immediate as well as mythic. The en-

slavement to the Nameless Ones, to the dark forces of the unconscious, is in fact reflected in the lives of all adolescent females who
bear the burden of past tradition and feel compelled to accept a traditionally imposed identity. As one critic put it, the contemporary
young woman must break away from "the accumulated demands and
expectations of mothers and grandmothers and great grandmothers."[17]
Like Tenar, she must consciously choose her own identity and not
simply accept herself as a reincarnation of a past role.

The tombs, along with the worship of the Nameless Ones, have
represented a collective religious shadow for the islands of Earthsea.
Another form of the collective shadow appears in the final volume of
the trilogy, *The Farthest Shore,* where the vitality of Earthsea is endan-
gered by the loss of distinction between life and death.

The Farthest Shore

The Farthest Shore is about the theme of death, which is also about
coming of age—as Le Guin pointed out—"in the largest sense," for
the final stage in this process is the acceptance of one's own mortality.[18] It also implies the moral and social integration of the fact of
death. In this volume Ged has become an aged wizard, grey-haired
and contemplative, but he is accompanied by a young man, Arren,
who awaits fulfillment of his noble destiny as king of all Earthsea.
The paths of the old man and the young—wizard and prince—meet
at the rowan tree, the center of the island of Roke and, by extension,
the center of the world.[19] There they agree to undertake together
their quest to free Earthsea from the mysterious evil which has upset
the equilibrium between life and death.

The world of Earthsea has been afflicted with a devastating spiritual plague of joylessness, together with a failure of magic, blurring
of distinctions, and loss of meaning. "There is a hole in the world
and the sea is running out of it. The light is running out" (154).[20]
The evil seems to be associated with a widespread rejection of mortality, and there are ominous whispers and mutterings about the
opportunity to live forever. Ged sees in this apparently unmeasured
desire for life on the part of human beings a threat to the balance of
nature. As he sees it, death is "the price we pay for life," and he sets
out with Arren on the journey westward in an effort to restore the
balance of nature by reestablishing mortality.

As they move westward, the direction of the setting sun and the opposite of the eastward quest recounted in the opening volume, Ged and Arren reflect on the differences between age and youth and between magery and kingship. As Ged explains to his young companion, "When I was young, I had to choose between the life of being and the life of doing. And I leapt at the latter like a trout to a fly. But each deed you do, each act, binds you to itself and to its consequences, and makes you act again and yet again. Then very seldom do you come upon a space, a time like this, between act and act, when you may stop and simply be. Or wonder who, after all, you are" (34–35). Arren is impatient for action, but Ged compares himself to the ancient dragons, who are both the oldest and the wisest of all beings, who have stopped acting in favor of simply being. "They do not do; they are" (37).

Although Ged may in theory ally himself with existence as opposed to action, in fact he is at once both active and contemplative, both involved and detached. He acts many times in the course of their adventurous journey westward. He acts decisively, he acts courageously, and he acts imaginatively. He dons a disguise in order to go about asking questions undetected; he risks ambush in a lonely room on a dark night in a dangerous part of a drug-ridden town; he daringly rescues his young companion who is captured by brutal slave traders. Such exploits are scarcely those of a person who has entirely given up on activity.

Arren also plays an active part in these adventures. A young man with a regal heritage, he is destined for heroism as well as kingship. The name Arren means "sword," and he carries an enchanted sword, which cannot be used except in the service of life. It is a sword which cannot be drawn for revenge or aggression. Arren is also born to fulfill the prophecy made by the last king who reigned 800 years ago. *"He shall inherit my throne who has crossed the dark land living and come to the far shores of the day"* (17). Arren agrees to accompany Ged on the quest as they stand beneath the rowan tree, and we learn later that the prince's real name is Lebannen, which means "rowan tree."

In the pride of his youth and ancestry, Arren is confidently eager to help Ged find the source of the mysterious evil. He learns, however, that he is subject to temptation and that he is capable of failure. In the episode which takes place in Hort Town, where many inhabitants are victims of the drug Hazia, Arren fails in his duty as guard. While Ged attempts to enter in spirit the drug-induced dream world of the former sorcerer Hare, Arren stands guard. As the lad watches

the two men, he finds that he cannot resist following the lord of
shadows who beckons him with a tiny flame, no larger than a pearl,
offering eternal life. Because of this lapse of attention, Ged is
knocked unconscious and Arren himself hauled off by slave traders.
Later, when Ged has regained consciousness and also managed to find
Arren and free him from his captors, the young man is chagrined
with the sense of his own failure.

In a subsequent episode, Arren experiences an even greater spiritual failure. They are at sea. Ged has been wounded, their companion
Sopli has drowned, and Arren surrenders to a feeling of despair about
his own survival. He tends Ged's wound listlessly, and instead of
trying to sail their boat to a port, he simply lets it drift aimlessly
through the open sea. Having lost faith in magery, he "looked at
[Ged] with the clear eyes of despair and saw nothing" (108). From
this dark night of the soul, Arren is rescued, together with the
scarcely conscious mage, by the Raft People, a community who spend
their entire lives on rafts, floating on the open sea. Their stay with
the Raft People is a dreamlike experience, a time of rebirth. It is also
a time for Arren to recognize his own shadow, his fear of death. He
admits that he neglected Ged out of fear of death. A boy of seventeen, he has not yet been able to accept the fact of mortality. His
own weakness thus reflects the very evil that is the object of his
quest. But he has now learned that "to refuse death is to refuse life"
(121).

When Ged recovers, the companions continue their westward
quest. The climactic events occur when they complete their journey
in the "dry land" of the dead. At the very edge of that grim, grey
landscape they meet their enemy, the source of the evil which has
brought Earthsea into a state of despair. There, before the stone wall
which separates the living and the dead, they meet the former sorcerer, Cob, who has surrendered his humanity to his overpowering
urge to cling to fleshly existence. It is Cob's magic which has opened
the door between life and death, turning the living world into a
world of living death, where the sun is dimmed and life is joyless.
Cob's body is killed in a self-sacrificial attack by a dragon, but Cob's
spirit climbs over the wall into the land of shadows, where Ged and
Arren must follow. It is a dismal journey through that land where
stars shine but do not twinkle, where shadows meet but do not
speak, and where there is only dust to drink.[21] But the old man and
the boy persist until they come to the fatal door that Cob's misguided

magic has opened between that world and ours. Ged then uses all the magic he can muster, asserting a superhuman strength in the weakness of his age, to close that door. Shaky yet strong, he sways a little, then stands erect. He commands in a clear voice: "Be thou made whole! . . . And with his staff he drew in lines of fire across the gate of rocks a figure: the rune Agnen, the Rune of Ending, which closes roads and is drawn on coffin lids. And there was then no gap or void place among the boulders. The door was shut" (184).

In their long and difficult journey back to the world of the living, Ged and Arren need each other. The aging wizard is able to act as guide, but his physical strength is unequal to the challenge. The young prince, however, musters an endurance even beyond hope, and he is able to carry his mentor safely over the edge of darkness and back to the light. Although Arren carries Ged to safety over the wall, both are at that point totally stranded on a deserted beach far west of the nearest human habitation. Left to themselves, they would perish. But there on the beach they encounter a superbly ancient and wise dragon, Kalessin, who addresses them in the Old Speech and offers to fly them back to civilization.

As the companions mount the dragon, Arren suddenly sees the wizard's staff lying on the beach, half-buried in the sand, and reaches down to get it. The wizard stops him, however, explaining that he has spent all of his powers in the dry land of the dead. The staff can no longer help him: "I am no mage now" (193).[22] But the loss is also a gain. Although Ged as mage has lost the ability to perform feats with his staff, he has gained a higher form of wisdom. The staff served as a kind of medium between the wizard and the things of the earth, between spirit and matter. Now Ged is closer to the airborne dragons. In his eyes there is now "something like that laughter in the eyes of Kalessin . . ." (196). This is not to say that he has lost all contact with human responsibility. He is yet to undertake the important duty of establishing Arren on his rightful throne. But in his more transcendental nature, he influences human behavior without actually being part of it. Ged's spiritual guidance has made possible the fulfillment of the prophecy: *"He shall inherit my throne who has crossed the dark land living and come to the far shores of the day."* His physical presence is also necessary to inaugurate the reign of the new king.

Ged acknowledges the new king by kneeling in homage and wishing him a long and successful reign. He then takes his own departure from the scene of human activity. He flies off in an easterly direction on the neck of the great dragon, Kalessin. As does the *Odyssey,* this last volume of the Earthsea books offers alternative endings.[23] In one version, Ged attends the crowning of Arren in Havnor, after which he sails off in his boat *Lookfar,* never to be seen again. In another, Ged does not come to the coronation, although the young king has sought him. Hearing rumors that Ged has gone alone and afoot into the forests of the mountain, the new king does not search further for the wizard but acknowledges that "He rules a greater kingdom than I do" (197).

Ged's final, mysterious flight into the unknown on the back of a winged dragon is an apotheosis appropriate to a mythic hero. Throughout the Earthsea trilogy Ged as protagonist has exemplified the paradigmatic career of the mythic hero. From the first book, in which he demonstrates the divine signs of talent characteristic of the childhood of mythic heroes, Ged has moved through the other traditional stages, including trial and quest, periods of meditation and withdrawal, symbolic death and journey to the underworld, and, finally, rebirth and apotheosis. Interwoven with Ged's complete career are the partial careers of Tenar and Arren, both richly indebted to mythic motifs. Tenar is the priestess of the underworld, devoured by forces of darkness until her rescue through the light of wizardry. Arren is the young prince destined to fulfill an ancient prophecy and restore peace and unity to his fragmented kingdom.

Along with the mythic roots of character and narrative, Le Guin also endows the landscape of her imaginary world with mythic features rich in suggestiveness. The name Earthsea in itself suggests a reconciliation of opposites, a balance of conscious and unconscious. The sea is associated not only with the unconscious but also with death, so that the sea journey to an island is at once expressive of a new level of self-consciousness and of resurrection. Ged's integration with the shadow thus occurs at the point where land and sea meet and are one. An important part of this mythic cosmology is the world tree at the center. Like the tree Yggdrasil in Norse mythology, the Immanent Grove is the center of Earthsea.

The center of it is still, and all moves about it, but the grove itself often seems to the confused viewer to be moving. "And they consider—the novices, the townsfolk, the farmers—that the Grove moves about in a mystifying manner. But in this they are mistaken, for the Grove does not move. Its roots are the roots of being. It is all the rest that moves" (9).

Integrated with the mythic patterns that infuse setting as well as plot and character in the trilogy are patterns of imagery. The central image is that of the spider weaving a web. We learn early in the first book that Ogion watches the spider weaving, and in the last book Ged describes the spider as a patterner. The web images both creation and destruction. The world of Earthsea is a web, with the Master Patterner at its center in the Immanent Grove. But the web is at once light and dark, a black center filled with silver threads catching the sunlight. Evil in this world is the web woven by men. The name of the magician who opens the door between life and death is Cob, an archaic word for spider (as in cobweb). Although the spider image is both central and recurring, the most pervasive imagery is that of light and darkness. There is scarcely a chapter in the trilogy without a pattern of light and dark images, in continual movements of conflict and reconciliation, ranging from Tenar's white skin and Ged's dark to the bright yellow star over the dark waters of the South Reach.

Both myth and image are successfully integrated with theme in these artfully written books. Like the patterned web, all is part of the whole. No symbols are imposed and no episodes introduced that are not integral to the world of Earthsea and the story of its master wizard who maintains the balance, restores a king, and finds himself. Earthsea is a convincingly authenticated world, drawn with a sure hand for fine detail. A mature narrative about growing up, a moral tale without a moral, a realistic depiction of a fantasy world, the trilogy is also a paradoxical work, but the paradox is at the heart of its inherent Taoist view of life. One of the many gnomic sayings in the work, "To light a candle is to cast a shadow," is a metaphoric summation of this view.

Chapter Four

The Left Hand of Darkness

The Left Hand of Darkness, winner of both the Hugo and Nebula awards for 1969, established Ursula Le Guin as a major science fiction writer. Critical recognition of her work actually began with the publication of this novel, for the earlier Hainish trilogy had received almost no attention from the critics or even the reviewers, and *A Wizard of Earthsea* was still relegated to the category of children's literature. Chronologically and thematically, *The Left Hand of Darkness* takes its place as one of six books in the Hainish series.[1] In terms of their interior chronology, the Hainish novels are in the following order: *The Dispossessed* (published last, in 1974) comes first, taking place in 2300 A.D., followed by *The Word for World Is Forest,* set in the year 2368. Then comes the trilogy, with *Rocannon's World* taking place in 2684, *Planet of Exile* in 3755, and *City of Illusions* in 4370. Farthest of all into the future, the events in *The Left Hand of Darkness* occur in 4870.

This chronology also reflects successive stages in the development of an interplanetary league. *The Dispossessed* concerns an early successful settlement of a new world, and *The Word for World Is Forest* a failure in colonizing efforts. At the time of the latter story the league of worlds is in existence, but references to it are minimal. In *Rocannon's World,* the league is a major theme. The titular world here is in the early stages of involvement with the league. *Planet of Exile* concerns a world which has lost its former ties with the others, and *City of Illusions* deals with a world which has been separated from those ties but is trying to return. By the time of *The Left Hand of Darkness,* there are eighty-three habitable planets in the league, now in terms of its own calendar in the year 2520. The league at this advanced stage has in fact been supplemented by yet another formal organization in the interplanetary community. This organization, known as the Ekumen, is concerned primarily with educational and cultural communication among the planets rather than merely with political and military relationships. What are its purposes? "Material profit.

Increase of knowledge. The augmentation of the complexity and intensity of the field of intelligent life. The enrichment of harmony and the greater glory of God. Curiosity, Adventure. Delight" (34).[2] That the Ekumenical year is already 1491 suggests that this new group has already been successful in its efforts to unite the various human races scattered over light years in space.

Narrative Structure

On the objective level, the plot of *The Left Hand of Darkness* recounts the mission by an envoy of the Ekumen who attempts to bring the planet Gethen into that group. In this account Le Guin develops the theme of cultural diversity through use of an outside observer, as she had done in the earlier Hainish works, but with notable differences. The most important difference is the use of a first-person narrative, which maintains a subjective level of development parallel to the objective one. Most of the narration is told directly by the envoy, Genly Ai, and reflects his own slowly evolving consciousness. The reader thus sees the events on Gethen from Genly Ai's at first naïve and egotistic point of view, then gradually discovers with him a series of profound errors in judgment. The novel is thus a *Bildungsroman* in that the reader shares in the central character's growth process. His fragmentary and evolving perceptions condition the reader's response.

In addition to the ten chapters of the envoy's first person narrative five chapters are told in the third person and five are related in the first person by other characters. What is important to remember here is that all of the twenty chapters are chosen by Genly Ai. His is the overall structuring consciousness of the book. He selects and arranges all of the material including that which is told by someone else. At the very beginning of the novel he explains to the reader: "The story is not all mine, nor told by me alone. Indeed I am not sure whose story it is; you can judge better. But it is all one, and if at moments the facts seem to alter with an altered voice, why then you can choose the fact you like best; yet none of them are false, and it is all one story" (1–2). The narrator is thus neither a static nor an omniscient voice nor even a solitary one, but nevertheless the story is all one.

Although the story is one, however, the unity is diffused through a multiple structure.[3] Along the central plot line, several separate narratives thread their simultaneous ways. The primary narrative is, of course, Genly Ai's running account of his Ekumenical mission. His minor successes and failures along the way are interspersed with his reactions to the planet and to the usual anthropological data written up by the professional cultural observer. Thus we learn almost tangentially about the formidable climate of Gethen, which translates as winter, and about the remarkable ambisexuality of the native Gethenian population. The diplomatic mission is also a travel narrative, culminating in an adventurous and prolonged flight to escape over a glacier.

Along with the elements of travel and anthropological observation, a narrative of political intrigue insinuates its way into the action. Although Genly Ai is too politically naïve to understand the forces at work, he is drawn into the often puzzling and sometimes dangerous currents of local politics. Through him the reader learns about the political and religious institutions of Gethen's two major countries, Karhide and Orgoreyn, direct opposites in most ways, and about the subtle Gethenian code of behavior known as "shifgrethor," an elusive but all-important attitude underlying all human relationships.

A scientific narrative accompanies the political one. Genly Ai has landed on Gethen with the aid of a spaceship which continues to orbit the planet awaiting his signal to return and pick him up on the completion of his mission. The people of Gethen, although technologically advanced, have no concept of interplanetary travel and react with mingled skepticism and fear to his report of a ship awaiting him in what they consider the void. Genly Ai also possesses an instantaneous communicator, called the ansible, which is regarded with derision. The ansible serves to objectify Genly Ai's challenge in carrying out his mission, for his ultimate problem is a matter of communication.

Finally, infusing the other levels of narration and ultimately transcending them is the growing personal relationship between Genly Ai, the outsider, and Therem Harth rem ir Estraven, the Karhidish politican who ultimately brings the mission to a successful conclusion through his own personal sacrifice. By the end of the novel the large scope of historical movement recedes in the light of personal triumph and tragedy. Like Genly Ai, the reader comes to refocus his attention on the individual and feels deeply moved by the profound devotion achieved at the price of death. The vastness of the Ekumenical ideal fades before the immediacy of one person's sacrifice. Yet at the same time the reader comes to realize that cosmic unity depends on personal relationship. It is "all one story."

The Winter Journey and the Myth of Androgyny

Of the many themes explored in this thought-provoking book, one of the most central and pervasive is that of winter. Le Guin had introduced the permanently freezing planet called Winter in the short story "Winter's King," written shortly before the novel.[4] On Gethen the only living beings able to survive the extreme cold are humans. No other large biological species exists there. As a result, Gethen is an object world, essentially irrelevant to human life, but thereby affirming its very uniqueness. In this bitter cold, the human is alienated but autonomous. Human life does not merge with the environment as it does in temperate climates, nor does it surrender to the enervating effects of the climate, as is the moral and physical danger in the tropics. Instead man is insulated against his hostile environment, alone and independent.

Le Guin authenticates life on Winter in fine graphic detail. Layers of clothing, "woven plant-fiber, artificial fiber, fur, leather," provide armor against the cold, and since there are no large meat animals, the limited diet of fish, nuts, and grain necessitates eating several times a day. A common table implement is "a little device with which you crack the ice that has formed on your drink between drafts" (12). Breathing in double-digit below zero temperatures is hazardous: "if you didn't look out, your nostrils might freeze shut, and then to keep from suffocating you would gasp in a lungful of razors" (244). It is not surprising that in such a frigid climate, there are many words for snow: "sixty-two words for the various kinds, states, ages, and qualities of snow; fallen snow, that is. There is another set of words for the varieties of snowfall; another for ice; a set of twenty or more that define what the temperature range is, how strong a wind blows, and what kind of precipitation is occurring, all together" (168–69).

Underlying these vivid surface scenes of winter is the rich substructure of the winter mythos. As David Ketterer has pointed out, the novel enacts a mythic journey through winter both spatially and temporally.[5] The book begins and ends in late spring. The journey across the planet moves north and east in a clockwise direction from the nation of Karhide to Orgoreyn and back to Karhide by way of the glacier. The action thus takes place both during winter and across Winter. Furthermore the pattern of the action moves through destruction and disintegration toward unity, following the movement

from the winter mythos of satire toward romance as formulated by
Northrop Frye in his consideration of the seasonal archetypes.[6] The
ecology of winter is, therefore, no mere trapping but is close to the
thematic center of the book.

Also close to the center is the androgyny theme. When Le Guin
published her story "Winter's King," she did not yet see the Gethenians as androgynous. The winter theme preceded and in a sense
produced the androgyny theme. Just as the movement through the
divisive destructiveness of winter leads to unity in rebirth, so the
movement from one sex to another among the Gethenians leads to a
new unity in respect to sexuality. Because of their androgyny the
Gethenians are less prone to dualistic perceptions than are men from
earth. As Genly Ai observes, they are even obsessed with wholeness,
as perhaps we are with dualities.

The precise physical nature of Gethenian androgyny is carefully delineated in the report from an earlier expedition to the planet. The
sexual cycle averages twenty-six to twenty-eight days. During
twenty-one to twenty-two days of this cycle the individual is in *somer,*
sexually inactive. On about the twenty-third day, the individual enters the phase of *kemmer,* produced by hormonal secretion. In this
phase the sexual impulse is extremely strong, but which gender will
be assumed is unpredictable, depending on available relationships. As
the report notes, "Normal individuals have no predisposition to
either sexual role in kemmer; they do not know whether they will be
the male or the female, and have no choice in the matter" (91). No
physiological habituation is achieved during kemmer, and the same
individual may be at times female and at times male. Many mothers
are at differing periods fathers.

But the unique physiology of Gethenian ambisexuality is subordi-
nate to the larger myth of androgyny which it so strikingly embod-
ies.[7] Le Guin was drawn to the archetype of the androgyne which she
found "alive now and full of creative-destructive energy."[8] In myth
and literature androgyny has traditionally implied a condition of lost
primordial unity. Separation into male and female, as in the creation
myth of Genesis and in Aristophanes' story in Plato's *Symposium,* for
example, marks the end of mythic time and the beginning of real
time. This nostalgia for former wholeness is reflected in the writings
of the alchemists and in Jungian psychology. Jung postulates the unconscious as the opposite gender to the conscious. The anima, or feminine archetype, is manifest in men, while the animus, or masculine

archetype, is present in women. The androgyne image is also relevant to Taoism, where it is not static but dynamic in function. In Taoism the wholeness of androgyny derives from the creative tension of opposites. Wholeness does not result from the incorporation of the opposite but from a continual, vital state of tension with it.

Genly Ai's first person account traces the evolution of his own response to androgyny. From the first, he feels an uneasiness about the dual sexuality of the Gethenians, who regard him as a pervert. "Though I had been nearly two years on Winter I was still far from being able to see the people of the planet through their own eyes. I tried to, but my efforts took the form of self-consciously seeing a Gethenian first as a man, then as a woman, forcing him into those categories so irrelevant to his nature and so essential to my own" (12). His sense of alienation is intensified in the case of the Karhidish prime minister, Estraven, whom he positively dislikes. The source of his antipathy is clearly implicit in his perceptions of Estraven's femininity. He first notices Estraven as "the person on my left," identifying him with the feminine side. When Genly is invited to dinner by Estraven, his host impresses him as "womanly, all charm and tact and lack of substance," and the envoy admits that he mistrusts this "soft, supple femininity" (12). The envoy's words betray his own limited sense of the feminine, and accordingly his sense of his own masculinity is self-conscious, justifying, and highly stereotypical.

It is not until the two companions undertake their epic flight across the glacier at the end of the novel that Genly comes both to accept the feminine side of Estraven and to recognize his own. When they first harness themselves to the sledge, Genly jokingly describes himself and his partner as "a stallion and a mule," but he eventually recognizes that the slighting reference to the neuter animal is far off the mark. During their journey Estraven goes into kemmer as a woman. Only then does Genly completely accept his friend. Through their shared hardships they have become close, and Genly confesses that "I had not wanted to give my trust, my friendship to a man who was a woman, a woman who was a man." But now because of the sexual tension provoked by kemmer, their friendship is confirmed and elevated to the relationship of love. They do not, however, surrender to the sexual urge: "for us to meet sexually would be for us to meet once more as aliens" (248–49). Their love is deeper than sexual union, for it is based on the continuing creative tension of opposites. The journey on the ice is thus a "journey into each other's heart."[9] It is fitting that the chapter in which the two companions realize their profound love is told from both of their points of view. It is the only episode in the book told this way.

As an expression of their new intimacy Genly Ai attempts to teach his friend the art of mindspeech, that long lost art introduced centuries ago from Rocannon's world. Estraven is able to learn the skill but finds that he hears only his dead brother's voice when Genly Ai bespeaks him. Estraven and his brother had vowed kemmering many years ago; the brother is long since dead, Estraven banished from his domain, but a son born to them still resides in their family hearth. The silent communication between the two fugitives, the exile and the envoy, further deepens their love.

The winter journey and the myth of androgyny thus join to reinforce the central theme of the book: unity through the creative tension of opposites.

Political and Religious Themes

This creative tension of opposites also pervades two other themes of the book, the political and the religious institutions of the planet Gethen. Politically the two countries of Karhide and Orgoreyn are polar opposites. Karhide, where Genly Ai resides when the book opens, is a feudal society, ruled by a mad king, Argaven XV (descendant of the titular ruler in "Winter's King"). Genly's mission to persuade Karhide to join the Ekumen is inevitably undermined by the instability of the king, who is by turns canny and superstitious in his madness. The country itself reflects the confusion at the top. The parade that Genly watches in the opening chapter is a masterpiece of disorder. No one marches in step, the music is discordant, and the flags are tangled. Disgruntled with his host country, Genly grumbles, "Karhide is no country for comfort" (51).

When Genly decides to pursue his mission in Orgoreyn, however, he finds that the totalitarian oppression in that state is an even more formidable opponent to the alliance than is the feudal chaos of Karhide. Genly is betrayed and mistreated in Orgoreyn. Seized by the Orgota police, he is imprisoned first overnight in jail, then forced into a sealed van with other prisoners and transported to a work camp, ironically called a Voluntary Farm. The truck journey is nightmarish; the Voluntary Farm is worse. The inhumane treatment that Genly receives there differs painfully from the often baffling but fundamentally tolerant treatment he had received from the Karhidish. When Genly is eventually rescued from the farm by Estraven, he realizes more than ever the importance of his mission. His rescue, which takes the form of a mock death and rebirth (his unconscious body is carried out as a corpse), is entirely engineered by Estraven.

Orgoreyn is a bureaucratic society with tendencies toward aggression. In this totalitarian country the people are trained from birth in a "discipline of cooperation, obedience, submission to a group purpose ordered from above" (173). Unlike the Karhidish, they tend to disrupt the ecology and even try to modify their ambisexuality through drugs. At this point their aggressive imperialism thus needs to be offset by the larger view of Ekumenical cooperation, for at the time of the novel Gethen faces a turning point in its history. So far it has been characterized by an absence of war. Thirty centuries of advanced technology on Gethen have failed to produce a single war. In spite of the many profound differences between Karhide and Gethen, their languages share an important feature: there is no word for war. At this moment, however, a border dispute between the two countries hints at a possible large scale fight. Because of their organization and "submission to a group purpose" the Orgota may be capable of starting war. This Genly learns during captivity.

One reason that war has never developed on Gethen is that the natural competitiveness of the inhabitants is channeled into shifgrethor. As Genly learns, it is a very elusive concept. Although he never fully understands its subtle workings, he calls it "prestige, face, place, the pride-relationship, the untranslatable and all-important principle of social authority in Karhide and all civilizations on Gethen" (14). Derived from an old word for shadow, shifgrethor as ritual behavior pertains only to an individual person—as does a shadow—and cannot be translated into an impersonal abstraction. Although the basis of all social and political actions, it is limited to individuals. Genly often finds that he has said or done the wrong thing at the wrong time in violation of the code of shifgrethor. Based on such a stylized and sophisticated concept, politics on Gethen is virtually unintelligible to an outsider. But shifgrethor has so far completely supplanted organized aggression.

The religions of Karhide and Orgoreyn are as different as their political systems. The major religious group in Karhide is called the Handdara, or the Foretellers, because of their ability to prophesy. Theirs is a mystique of darkness. In their holistic vision darkness is

emphasized over light, and things are known in terms of their opposites. For them the highest goal of knowledge is thus to "unlearn,"
and Estraven, who has had Handdara training in Karhide, calls Orgoreyn his "uncountry." It is a religion "without institution, without
priests, without hierarchy, without vows, without creed,"(55) based
on "an old darkness, passive, anarchic, silent, the fecund darkness of
the Handdara" (60). Genly visits the Foretellers, who are led by Faxe
the Weaver, in order to investigate reports of their ability to prophesy. He learns that their predictions are often paradoxical, but his
own question about Gethen's future acceptance of the Ekumen is an-
swered unequivocally in the affirmative. The mystic "untrance"
which produces the prophecy is, however, a harrowing experience for
him to participate in.

In contrast to the mystic Handdara is the positivistic Yomeshta
sect, the dominant religion in Orgoreyn. This highly rational religion
suits the commercial and bureaucratic society of Orgota. Committed
to the proposition that truth comes only from the light, the Yomeshta, or followers of Meshe, totally reject darkness. "There is neither darkness nor death," reads the Yomesh Canon (164), a view
lacking in the creative duality of opposites. The danger inherent in
denying the dark, a theme pervasive in the Earthsea trilogy as well as
in this novel, is revealed in the behavior patterns of the Orgota people. They pervert their potential for darkness into the furtive ways of
political treachery and impersonal cruelty. Genly finds them "insipid"
and "not quite solid." It is, he thinks, "as if they did not cast shadows." Even their sturdily constructed buildings seem to him lacking
substantiality, recalling the shadowy city of the Shing in *City of
Illusions*.

The relationship of light and darkness, central to both religions, is
expounded in the poem from which the title of the novel is taken.
Here is the complete verse:

> *Light is the left hand of darkness*
> *and darkness the right hand of light.*
> *Two are one, life and death, lying*
> *together like lovers in kemmer,*
> *like hands joined together,*
> *like the end and the way.* (233–34)

The interdependence of light and darkness, and of life and death, as
expressed here, recalls a similar verse in the Earthsea trilogy which

includes the line: "only in dark the light." The darkness that is essential to light is reinforced in the imagery of the novel. During the flight across the glacier, Estraven falls into an unnoticed crevasse in the ice because there are no shadows to guide his steps. "It's queer that daylight's not enough," he remarks, "We need the shadows, in order to walk" (267). And in response to this observation, Genly Ai draws the yin-yang symbol to show his friend, explaining its meaning in terms of the vital interaction of opposites. "I drew the double curve within the circle, and blacked the yin half of the symbol, then pushed it back to my companion. . . . It is yin and yang. *Light is the left hand of darkness* . . . how did it go? Light, dark. Fear, courage. Cold, warmth. Female, male. It is yourself, Therem. Both and one. A shadow on snow" (267).

The shadow image also functions to unite the political and religious themes. As already explained, the basis of political behavior is shifgrethor, which comes from an old word meaning shadow. The basis of religious beliefs is the attitude toward darkness, positive in the case of the Handdara and negative in the case of the Yomeshta. The titular image is thus a unifying element, incorporating both the theme of androgyny and the theme of the relationship of light and darkness in politics and religion. The overall theme of the creative tension of opposites is thus reinforced at all levels.

The six nonnarrative chapters interpolated into Genly Ai's account of his mission all contribute to the organic unity of the book. Myth, scripture, scientific report, and hearth tale all weave continuity into the intricate narrative pattern of the whole. The most straightforward and objective of these chapters is "The Question of Sex," written in the form of field notes by an investigator on Gethen fifty years prior to the action of the novel. Here the writer speculates about the origins of the ambisexual population and its implications for social customs. Observations are made concerning the equalization of maternal obligations, the absence of rape and of the Oedipus complex, and the even more striking absence of war. The writer suggests a theory relating war and rape. Perhaps war is "a purely masculine displacement-activity, a vast Rape," that cannot, therefore, occur without strictly separated masculinity and femininity. Piqued by these suggestive notes from an outside observer, the reader is not told until the last paragraph of the chapter that the reporter is a woman, "no expert on the attractions of violence or the nature of war" (97).

The scriptural chapter, supposedly taken from a book composed 900 years ago, is called "On Time and Darkness." This brief selection concerns the god Meshe and represents the Yomeshta point of view as opposed to the Handdara. It begins "Meshe is the Center of Time" and maintains a gnomic style throughout. The text rejects darkness: "Darkness is only in the mortal eye, that thinks it sees, but sees not" (164). And it scorns the followers of the Handdara cult, "those that call upon the darkness" (164). A footnote at the end of the chapter ingeniously parallels the religious point of view toward time and light with the theory of the expanding universe that accounts for the appearance of the stars in the sky at night. Religion and science thus comment obliquely on each other.

The mythic chapter relates a prehistorical Orgota account of the creation. The opening sentence, "In the beginning there was nothing but ice and the sun" (237), echoes the glacial flight of Genly Ai and Estraven, who find their world reduced to those two elements. After the creation the sun gradually melts three ice-shapes, each of which interprets its melting differently: "I bleed," "I weep," and "I sweat." The one that says "I bleed" creates the hills and valleys of the earth, the one that says "I weep" creates the seas and the rivers, and the one that says "I sweat" creates plants, animals, and humans. The human beings do not awaken directly after their creation but need the milk melted into their mouths by the three ice-shapes. The first one awakened soon kills all but two of his brothers. One other runs away but is pursued and killed. The last left alive escapes successfully, only to return and mate with the killer of his brothers. They produce offspring, each of whom has a piece of darkness that follows him about in the daylight. The shadow is thus created as part of the initial conception of the human being. We learn further that the creation takes place on the Gobrin ice, which is traversed by Genly Ai and Estraven, who also see it when "there is nothing but ice and sun," and who fall because there are no shadows to guide them in the daylight.

The other three interpolated chapters are "hearth tales" or folk stories from the past that parallel events taking place presently in the novel. The first of these hearth tales is called "The Place Inside the Blizzard," and is recounted directly after the opening scene when Genly watches the parade and the keystone ceremony in Karhide. It also takes place on a glacial sheet, this one contiguous to the Gobrin glacier of the main action. The substance of the tale is in effect a condensed and displaced version of the main action. In the story an exile encounters his dead sibling-kemmering in "a place in the blizzard," a place literally and metaphorically apart from the society that made both of them outcasts. The dead brother has committed suicide, an act that is never on Gethen considered justifiable or forgivable. When the dead brother tries to seize his living sibling by the hand, the latter flees and after an almost fatal struggle across the ice sheet finds his way back to civilization. The "place inside the blizzard" is also a mystical place, a point where space and time meet.[10] The mythic situation obviously mirrors the main action of the novel in many ways. Genly Ai and Estraven also meet at a "central" place, far from human society, where each is unique. Estraven's death is also a kind of suicide, which functions to preserve the life of his companion. The center where time and space meet also recalls the scriptural chapter about time and darkness, where Meshe is seen as the Center. And it is inside the blizzard where the bright whiteness functions as darkness to blind the travelers.

The second hearth tale is called "The Nineteenth Day." It concerns the Foretellers who are asked by a wealthy lord when he will die. He is enraged by their paradoxical answer, "on the 19th day." The story culminates ironically in murder and suicide—on the nineteenth day of a month. The tale exemplifies the point insisted upon by the foretellers that there are no right answers to the wrong questions. "Ignorance is the ground of thought" (71) they argue although their direct answer to Genly's question about the alliance with the Ekumen implies that there are legitimate questions.

The third story, called "Estraven the Traitor," concerns a forebear of the major character in the book. In this earlier time a feud is raging between the domains of Estre and Stok. Two young men of the rival domains, Arek of Estre and Therem of Stok, meet accidentally but become kemmerings. Arek is subsequently murdered by irate members of the Stok domain, but Therem later bears his and Arek's child. The child is named Therem, and when he becomes an adult history repeats itself. He encounters Therem of Stok and the two become friends. Their personal fidelity to each other as friends transcends the feud between their families, and peace ensues. Because of his healing the feud, however, Therem of Estre, or Estraven, is called a traitor by his relatives who wish to continue the traditional antipathy between their houses. Obviously in this context the title "traitor" becomes an ironically complimentary one. The supposed traitor to the limited group in the local domain becomes on the higher level of human society a heroic figure. His larger sense of humanity replaces the petty and bloody feud with a civilized relationship.

This story serves as an ironic paradigm to that of the Estraven in the novel. From the moment early in the action where Estraven is banished from Karhide by the mad king, he is known as a traitor. It becomes gradually clear to the envoy, and to the reader, that he is a traitor only in the most limited and idiosyncratic sense, for he is loyal to a much higher concept of humanity. The irony also extends to the narrator at the end of the book. Like his dead friend, Genly Ai betrays a lesser cause in favor of a greater. He has promised Estraven not to let his ship arrive until the exile's name has been cleared of the charge of treason. Genly is forced to recognize, however, that to wait would be to lose the alliance for which his friend actually gave his life. He breaks his word and summons the ship in order to be true to the purpose of Estraven's sacrifice.

All of these six extranarrative chapters thus comment on the events and themes of the main story. They all represent tangential versions of episodes and characters involved in the narrator's account of his mission. The mythic mode functions as mirror.

As Jean Murray Walker has pointed out, the mythic materials also represent the collective thought of traditional Gethen societies.[11] Their main concern is the mediation of opposites, which takes place through kinship exchange, both on the personal and social levels. Social and individual exchange is essential to the continued existence of the Hearth, the basic community unit on Gethen, for without it social groups are not possible. Such exchange is absent only at the beginning (when the first individual is created), but is subsequently repudiated through suicide and incest, which are therefore condemned. In "The Place Inside the Blizzard" the rule of exchange is broken, and a Hearth group suffers famine until the surviving brother admits his incestuous guilt and accepts his responsibility. In the tale of Estraven the Traitor, the concept of exchange is demonstrated positively rather than negatively. Therem of Estre mediates, through his name as well as his deeds, the antipathy between his domain and that of Stok. He is ironically labeled a traitor, however, indicating the need for personal sacrifice in achieving a positive exchange between competing groups. Like the Therem of the myth, who loses his own status in both societies when he reconciles them, Estraven must sacrifice himself in order to achieve the exchange with an outsider. His willingness to join the Ekumen is analogous to Therem's acceptance of the rival domain. Estraven is also parallel to the brother-figure in both tales in that he has vowed in intention, although not in words, his lifelong fidelity to his own brother. He is thus guilty of an incestuous commitment contrary to that law of exchange which makes social groups possible. Near the end of the novel Estraven hears his brother's voice when Genly Ai bespeaks him, and it is only through the myths that the meaning of this identification becomes clear to the reader. The myths and the mythic Hearth tales thus further confirm the central theme of the reconciliation of opposites.

Critical Reception

Critical reception of *The Left Hand of Darkness* displayed a tension of opposites appropriate to the novel. Winner of both the Hugo and the Nebula awards and reviewed in major journals, it was clearly acknowledged as a major work. At the same time, however, a debate raged as to its overall success. Central to the debate from the beginning was the issue of whether the ambisexuality of the Gethenians was actually organic to the book or whether it was in fact an element extraneous to the plot. Polish science fiction writer Stanislaw Lem argued that a plot summary of the book need not even mention the theme of sexuality. Furthermore Lem criticized what he considered Le Guin's inadequate handling of the psychological problems deriving from the ambiguous gender of the Gethenians. According to Lem the intense uncertainty as to future sexual identity would produce an anxiety syndrome leading to serious psychological malaise: "Although her anthropological understanding is very good, her psychological insight, on the other hand, is only sufficient and sometimes insufficient." Lem also charged that the portrayal of the feminine side of the Gethenian nature was totally ineffective. He notes that the Gethenian are really masculine in "garments, manners of speech, mores, and behavior.[12]

Le Guin responded vigorously to Lem's challenges. In her view Estraven neither says nor does anything that only a man would say or do. Instead the fault is the readers' for our stereotypical assumptions. "Most of us are unwilling or unable to imagine women as scheming prime ministers, haulers of sledges across icy wastes, etc."[13] As for the Gethenian garments, she points out quite logically that they are based on the typical Eskimo attire of tunic and trousers, adding that skirts are scarcely appropriate to the subzero climate of the winter planet.

A similar challenge came from Canadian critic, David Ketterer, who focused on the underlying mythic structure in his interpretation of the novel. Like Lem he finds that the Gethenian sexuality is independent of the plot, but the reason for this he finds in the author's conscious use of a mythic-apocalyptic structure. In her answer to his reading, Le Guin admitted the difficulty in giving proper aesthetic form to the myth of the Androgyne. Several feminist critics added their voices to those of Lem and Ketterer in complaining that Estraven seems more like a man than a manwoman. Le Guin's most formal reply to this chorus of complaint took the form of an essay, "Is Gender Necessary?" In this thoughtfully prepared statement Le Guin admits certain flaws in the book but also points out certain failures on the part of the readers. "For the reader, I left out too much. One does not see Estraven as a mother, with his children, in any role which we automatically perceive as 'female': and therefore, we tend to see him as a man. This is a real flaw in the book, and I can only be very grateful to those readers, men and women, whose willingness to participate in the experiment led them to fill in that omission with the work of their own imagination."[14] The word "experiment" is important here. Le Guin sees her science fiction as "thought-experiment," as she explains in her introduction to the paperback edition of the book, and a thought-experiment is neither predictive nor polemic. A literary thought-experiment is a metaphor.

More recent criticism of the book, such as Martin Bickman's perceptive essay "Le Guin's *The Left Hand of Darkness*: Form and Content," has concentrated on the artistic unity of the work. Bickman usefully points out to readers what should already be familiar to readers of her earlier works, that is, the point of view of the narrator controls the perception implicit in the narration. As we have seen in the case of both the Hainish trilogy and the Earthsea trilogy, the reader learns through the controlling point of view, which is not omniscient. In *The Left Hand of Darkness* Genly Ai's point of view develops slowly, so that his own discovery of the feminine nature of Estraven does not come until close to the end of the novel, and the reader has no basis for getting ahead of the narrator.

Since Le Guin has exploited the word play on "eye" and "I" elsewhere, it is probably not at all amiss to detect it in the narrator's name.[15] Genly Ai is at once both the outside structuring consciousness of the book and a central figure inside its action. He is thus both the observing "eye" and the participating "I." The gap between what the "eye" sees and what the "I" understands is notably wide at the beginning but narrows considerably as the book progresses. In the final pages, when Genly visits the Estraven family, the two are finally joined into one, although ironically now that the "eye" can see, the "I" can no longer act. The situation recalls that of Rocannon and Falk-Ramarren, both of whom must leave their newly won planet just as they come to understand and identify with it, one through death, the other through flight. In Genly Ai's case, the "eye" has also been overwhelmingly masculine in what it sees, while the "I" grows slowly in feminine self-awareness.

Unity is also achieved through the subtle web of language in this book with its many disparate uses of style and tone. One such example carefully frames the whole. The public ceremony which Genly observes in the opening chapter is the completion of an arch at the River Gate. The king personally sets the keystone in the arch, explaining as he does so that the red cement used symbolizes the blood-bond necessary to sustain the arch. In the past human blood was added to a mortar of ground bones. Now animal blood is used. Near the end of the novel, as Genly Ai contemplates his duty to fulfill the mission which his friend has given his life for, he expresses his decision metaphorically: "I must set the keystone in the arch." This time the blood is human.

The Left Hand of Darkness is a major achievement. In its unity of style, structure, and content, and in its holistic vision of unity through diversity, it is an artistic triumph. The central theme of the creative tension of opposites is fulfilled through its many subthemes of androgyny, winter, religion, politics, mythology, science, and communication. To the extent that it is flawed—and every work of art is—the flaws are by-products of the complex vision it presents. Unlike much science fiction which can come closer to perfection by dint of its more restricted aims, this novel transcends the genre by attempting to do much more, perhaps too much. It has been suggested that the novel itself expands the limits of science fiction as a medium. In any case, *The Left Hand Of Darkness* ranks with the Earthsea trilogy as an artistic achievement, and it surpasses most contemporary science fiction in its range and complexity of purpose, technique, and thematic concern.

Chapter Five

The Lathe of Heaven, "Vaster Than Empires and More Slow," and *The Word for World Is Forest*

The novel *The Lathe of Heaven* and the short story "Vaster Than Empires and More Slow" were published in 1971, followed by the novella *The Word for World Is Forest* in 1972.[1] These three works demonstrate a continuity with the Hainish and the Earthsea trilogies, but at the same time they also reveal strikingly new themes and techniques. Central to the continuity they represent is the prevailing Taoist vision of life. *The Lathe of Heaven* is, in fact, the most explicitly Taoist work in the Le Guin canon. The predominantly new themes, on the other hand, are essentially two: the dream in *The Lathe of Heaven* and *The Word for World Is Forest,* and the vegetable world in *The Word for World Is Forest* and "Vaster Than Empires and More Slow." The new techniques, involving both style and narrative structure, are evident only in *The Lathe of Heaven.*

The Lathe of Heaven

What is most familiar about *The Lathe of Heaven* to the Le Guin reader is the philosophical perspective of Taoism. Each of the eleven chapters in the book is introduced with a quotation, seven of which are taken from the writings of Chuang Tse and Lao Tse. The title is taken from Chuang Tse: "To let understanding stop at what cannot be understood is a high attainment. Those who cannot do it will be destroyed on the lathe of heaven" (25). Both the plot and the characterization in the book function as realization of this precept. What is new to the reader of this book—and there is much that is—distinguishes it not only from the preceding works but also from those which follow. *The Lathe of Heaven* remains somewhat of an anomaly in the fiction of Le Guin.[2]

To begin with, unlike the earlier novels *The Lathe of Heaven* is set in this world. Specifically the setting is Portland, Oregon, in the apocalyptic year 1998.[3] The descriptions of Portland throughout the novel are a compound of realistic precision and satiric exaggeration. The rainy weather, the view of Mt. Hood, the Willamette River, and Reed College all help to authenticate the location. But the Portland of 1998 is drastically changed in many ways. Like most American cities at that time, it has suffered irrevocably from the greenhouse effect. The skies are no longer blue, and the snows have disappeared from the mountain peaks, here, as everywhere else in the world. Portland has also become a densely populated city, where food supplies are short, bureaucratic procedures are long, and where "undernourishment, overcrowding, and pervading foulness of the environment were the norm" (26).

In the larger world at this turn in the millennium a war is in progress. The exact alignment of nations is not clear, but one of the involved countries is "Isragypt," a new Arab-Israeli amalgam. Into this grim, futuristic world Le Guin introduces her perturbed protagonist, George Orr, a very ordinary young man in every way but one. George has one extraordinary ability: his dreams materialize in the real world. His dreams come true not only for himself but for the whole world, in effect altering all human history. This uncanny gift for what he calls "effective" dreaming sends George to a psychiatrist for help, after his experiments with dream-suppressing drugs have failed. The confrontation of patient and psychiatrist establishes the dialectic of character and theme which shapes the structure of the book.

George the dreamer is in every way the opposite of Dr. Haber the psychiatric dream specialist. Whereas George is the perfect, passive Taoist hero, Haber is a Faustian figure, driven by a ruthless ambition for power. When the psychiatrist first meets George, he sums up his new patient somewhat contemptuously as "unaggressive, placid, milquetoast, repressed, conventional" (6). He soon learns, however, that the young man's unaggressiveness does not mean a milquetoast personality. George Orr possesses the strength of a Taoist ideal: "the natural integrity of uncarved wood" (*Tao,* 28). And, as Haber discovers, "though the uncarved wood is small,/ It cannot be employed (used as vessel) by anyone" (*Tao,* 32).[4] George ranks "right in the middle of the graph" (17) in regard to all of his physical and mental attributes, in no way unbalanced, extreme, or outstanding. Above all, he does not want to change anything, either himself or the world.

In sharp contrast Dr. Haber sees the young man's ability to dream effectively as an opportunity to reshape the world and to alter the human condition. He interprets man's purpose on earth "to do things, change things, run things, make a better world" (81). Although his own purposes are ultimately humanitarian, when he tries to induce specific dreams in his patient through hypnosis, the results are often catastrophic. When he asks George to dream of a world free from the problems of overpopulation, what results is a carcinomic plague which wipes out six billion people. As he becomes more and more intensely involved in his determination to "improve" the world by controlling George's dreams, Dr. Haber inevitably takes the final leap into assuming the role of effective dreamer himself. He is able to do so because of his careful study of George's dream patterns as recorded on the electroencephalograph, or Augmentor. Having started out as a bluff, hearty, outgoing psychiatrist, who feels superior to his quiet and unassertive patient, Dr. Haber becomes transformed into an almost parodic "mad scientist" in his megalomaniacal desire to change the world. His last appearance in the novel shows him as a patient in an insane asylum, staring silently, mindlessly, into the void.

Ironically it is George's one real action which ultimately reduces Haber to total and permanent inaction. Initiating action is not Orr's natural bent: "He had never known what to do. He had always done what seemed to want doing, the next thing to be done, without asking questions, without forcing himself, without worrying about it" (73). But although by temperament a born victim, Orr is never a willing tool. The necessary action he will and does perform. What it is the reader must find out for himself. Suffice it to say that it is an action which saves the world.

Only two other significant characters appear in *The Lathe of Heaven*, a woman and an alien race. The woman is a young black lawyer, Heather Lelache, who falls in love with George and shares some of his dream existences. Her personality, like her racially mixed ancestry, is paradoxical. She is at once "fierce" and "fragile," brave and frightened, tough and soft. Her first reaction to George is negative: "If she stepped on him he wouldn't even crunch" (41). Sensing his vulnerability, she imagines herself a black widow spider about to consume her victim. Neither passive like George nor power-hungry like Haber, she is an active person willing to go out on a limb to help her lover. She even undertakes to direct one of his effective dreams.

The other major character, an alien race, is the result of this dream. In an earlier dream, aliens had landed on the moon; in this one, they come to earth. These Aldebaranians, as they are called, represent even more than George the Taoist ideal of inaction. Completely unaggressive, they arrive on Earth unarmed. They are also sensitive dreamers, with a deeper understanding of what dreaming means in the universe as a whole than Haber, the supposed oneirologist, can recognize. As George explains, "Everything dreams. The play of form, of being, is the dreaming of substance. Rocks have their dreams, and the earth changes" (168).

In appearance the Aldebaranians are very strange indeed. One is described in this fashion: "it was encased in a suit of some kind, which gave it a bulky, greenish, armored, inexpressive look like a giant sea turtle standing on its hind legs" (121). At several points, individual aliens are likened to giant sea turtles. When George meets the alien store proprietor, Tiua'k Ennbe Ennbe, "the right hand, a great, greenish, flipper-like extremity" (154) comes forward for an introductory handshake. The voices of the aliens are metallic and toneless, emanating from the left elbow joint. What they speak, however, is always conciliatory and often platitudinous. With fine irony, the first words spoken by an invading alien—the invasion has, of course, terrified the entire human race into a state of hysteria—are a paraphrase of the golden rule: "Do not do to others what you wish others not to do to you" (121). Throughout the book they show a fondness for uttering proverbial wisdom. When George attempts to question one of them, the response is charmingly irrelevant: "One swallow does not make a summer. Many hands make light work" (155). Eventually George accepts employment with an alien merchant, who obligingly murmurs, "To go is to return."[5]

The narrowly focused dialectic between the passive patient and the assertive psychiatrist widens into a larger dialectic involving all four characters. Like George, Heather and the aliens see themselves as parts of the whole. George is not only a patient, he is also a draftsman, a designer, who likes to fit things together. The balance he has achieved within himself he likes to find in things as well, as when he browses in an antique shop and picks up a hammer, admiring its balance. Heather, too, believes in the whole of which she is a part, "and that in being a part one is whole: such a person has no desire whatever, at any time, to play God" (108). And the aliens, congenial and unaggressive, flow with the world, making no attempt to impose their own will on it or to change its direction. George, Heather, and the aliens all agree that "What does matter is that we're a part. Like a thread in a cloth or a grass-blade in a field. It *is* and we *are"* (81). All oppose Haber's willful determination to change the world, to play God.

Supplementing this thematic structure, based on a dialectical tension of opposites, is a complex and dynamic narrative structure. The narrative movement of the book offers a continually shifting continuum of present events, along with their related pasts. In one continuum, for example, Heather exists; in another, she does not. In one, racial problems are eliminated by turning everyone's skin grey, but in a subsequent one, color variations return. Each dream which alters the reality of the present shifts the past accordingly. Although these startling shifts in the continuum are clearly delineated, they can be confusing to a careless reader, for the pace is fast and each word counts. Both "sure-handed" and "beautifully wrought," as one reviewer described it, *The Lathe of Heaven* demands an attentive and concentrated reading.[6]

Along with the unusual narrative time scheme, the tone of the novel is also a new feature to the reader who comes from the more solemn speculative worlds of Earthsea and Hainish high fantasy. *The Lathe of Heaven* is a satiric work, and its tone is frequently sardonic, colloquial, breezy, with occasional sentence fragments, conversational incoherence, and stream-of-consciousness. As the time shifts with the dreams, so the point of view shifts with the characters, often resulting in subjective distortions. When George is regaining consciousness after an overdose of drugs, for example, he hears voices "through the roar of breaking seas," and when he tries to hold onto the wall, "there was nothing to hold on to, and the wall turned into the floor" (2). Similarly, Heather's waking up during the alien invasion reflects a slowly growing awareness: "Cold, cold. Hard. Bright, Too bright. Sunrise in the window through shift and flicker of trees. Over the bed. The floor trembled. The hills muttered and dreamed of falling in the sea, and over the hills, faint and horrible, the sirens of distant towns howled, howled, howled" (111).

The objective satirical style blends humor with incisive exaggeration. The hero's ride on a crowded subway is described this way: "The headline . . . stared Orr eye to I for six stops. The newspaperholder fought his way off and was replaced by a couple of tomatoes on a green plastic plate, beneath which was an old lady in a green plastic coat, who stood on Orr's left foot for three more stops" (25). The disappearance of American forests is wryly lamented: "Van Duzer

Forest Corridor, ancient wooden road sign: land preserved long ago from the logging companies. Not quite all the forests of America had gone for grocery bags, split-levels, and Dick Tracy on Sunday morning. A few remained" (94). But at times the humor gives way to nightmare in this millennial world: "This was Thursday; it would be the hand-to-hands, the biggest attraction of the week except for Saturday night football. More athletes actually got killed in the hand-to-hands, but they lacked the dramatic, cathartic aspects of football, the sheer carnage when 144 men were involved at once, the drenching of the arena stands with blood. The skill of the single fighters was fine, but lacked the splendid abreactive release of mass killing" (134).

The diction of the novel is also influenced by its scientific subject matter. Although *The Lathe of Heaven* is a satiric vision of the future with a strong undercurrent of Taoist philosophy, it is fundamentally a classic work of "what-if" science fiction. The book offers a speculative answer to the question: What if dreams could change reality? Le Guin's handling of the question is not irresponsibly speculative but is based on a solid knowledge of both recent dream research and other sciences. Theodore Sturgeon noted the scientific integrity of the book: "The author has done some profound research in psychology, cerebro-physiology and biochemistry, and is familiar with some very recent findings in the field of dream research. In addition, her perceptions of such matters as geopolitics, race, socialized medicine and the patient-shrink relationship are razor sharp and more than a little cutting."[7] When Dr. Haber discusses the pioneers in dream research—Dement, Aserinsky, Berger, Oswald, and Hartmann—his list is an accurate one. When he explains that alcoholism can cause "central pontine myelinolysis" the terms are precisely accurate, based on the anatomical words "pons" and "myelin," referring to connections between the encasings of nerve fibers in the spinal column.

On the other hand, Le Guin invents suitable phrases for the aliens' references to dreaming. The aliens immediately recognize the ability of George Orr (whom they call JorJor) to dream effectively. They realize that he is capable of what they call "iakhlu." They also use the mystical phrase "Er Perehnne," which is never defined but which should be spoken before dreaming. Scientist Haber, typically, does not follow George's advice to speak the phrase prior to entering the dream state.

Along with the subjective, satiric, and scientific uses of language, a strain of poetic imagery is also found in the finely crafted prose of *The Lathe of Heaven,* as well as recurring images of the sea and of sea creatures. From the start, George is identified with the jellyfish. On the most obvious level, his unassertive nature makes him seem a moral jellyfish to more aggressive people. When Heather first sees him, for example, she compares his soft skin to a fish's belly. But, as the opening words of the book make clear, the jellyfish adrift in the ocean is also a paradoxical image of strength. "Current-borne, wave-flung, tugged hugely by the whole might of ocean, the jellyfish drifts in the tidal abyss. . . . Hanging, swaying, pulsing, the most vulnerable and insubstantial creature, it has for its defense the violence and power of the whole ocean, to which it has entrusted its being, its going, and its will" (1). The jellyfish image also serves subtly to connect George with the aliens who so nearly resemble sea turtles. Near the end of the book, Orr's first noneffective dreams are compared to waves of the sea far from shore: "profound and harmless, breaking nowhere, changing nothing." And as the alien E'hememen Asfah watches over him, he dreams of sea turtles diving and swimming, with "heavy inexhaustible grace through the depths, in their element" (179).

The words of a popular song also function as a thematic motif in the book. When the alien proprietor gives George a record of the Beatles' song, "With A Little Help from My Friends," he borrows his friend Mannie's old phonograph in order to hear it. Along with Heather, George listens to the "nutty and subtle" song eleven times and falls asleep. From the moment he wakes up, many things have changed. Heather notices that he seems much more relaxed, as if a burden had been removed from him. Then, when he visits Haber's office for one more dream session, he wakes up while still supposedly under hypnosis and attached to the Augmentor. His dream has told him that he is normal again.

The refrain "a little help from my friends" also intimates the theme of relationships that is important in the novel. Haber and Orr are the opposite in respect to their attitude toward others. Haber avoids human involvement: "He had never wanted marriage nor close friendships, he had chosen a strenuous research carried out when others sleep, he had avoided entanglements. He kept his sex life almost entirely to one-night stands" (114). Orr, on the other hand, seeks intimacy. Not a reasoner like scientist Haber, he feels connections, both in his work as draftsman and in his personal life. When he first meets Heather, he immediately and intuitively likes her, and their handshake becomes the inauguration of a close bond between them. He also likes the aliens, finding them agreeable and easy to talk to. The gift of a record from one of them touches him deeply. For George as for Heather, love means sharing. When they find one morning that they have only five eggs, they decide to scramble them as the only equitable basis for sharing. The friendly gesture of the handshake closes the novel, as George shakes the alien's big green flipper and joins Heather in a coffee break.

With help from his friends, George is finally able to "enter the eye of the nightmare" and save the world from dissolution, in one of the most vividly exciting scenes in science fiction. Not only is the world thus restored to normal after a succession of nightmares, but the entire story comes full circle, with the ending recapitulating the beginning. "To go is to return," murmurs the alien, reiterating the theme of the circular journey that Le Guin introduced in the Hainish trilogy. The end is a new beginning, at least for everyone but Haber, and George sets out to win Heather once more as if for the first time.

The Lathe of Heaven was successfully produced on public television in 1979. The screening of the spectacular shifts in reality was convincing without being melodramatic, and the acting was effective. Sleep-researcher William C. Dement participated in the production. Commenting on the challenges of filming the book, Le Guin explained that the greatest problem was in deciding how to film the dream sequences. Fortunately the decision was to present them exactly the same as the waking scenes, an approach in keeping with the book.[8] The apocalyptic mood, however, was less successfully communicated than on the printed page, where the reader's imagination is free to play a larger role.

The Word for World Is Forest

The novella *The Word For World Is Forest* has two features in common with *The Lathe of Heaven,* the theme of dreaming and the dialectical structure based on diametrically opposed characters. In spite of these major similarities, however, the two works are drastically different in conception. Whereas *The Lathe of Heaven* is set in Portland only a generation from now, *The Word for World Is Forest* takes place on a distant planet in 2368 A.D.[9] While *The Lathe of Heaven* is breezy and often comic in tone, *The Word for World Is Forest* is both a serious and an angry work. And while *The Lathe of Heaven* concludes on a positive note, with the continuing existence and restored balance of the world confirmed, at least for the time being, *The Word for World Is Forest* ends in a stand-off of futility and despair.

The dialectical structure is the central feature of *The Word for World Is Forest*. In a large sense it represents the conflict between the natives of the heavily forested world Athshe and the Terran colonists who invade and despoil this world. More narrowly, it is focused on one of the Athsheans, Selver, and one of the Terran humans, Captain Davidson. Davidson is a military man, coldly rational and pragmatic, motivated by an arrogant conviction of human superiority to the natives, whom he scornfully calls "Creechies." Selver, on the other hand, is an intuitive being, a dreamer, neither scientist nor soldier, but highly sensitive and perceptive in nonrational ways.

The struggle between Davidson's aggressive colonists and the gentle natives is manifested initially in their differing attitudes toward the forest. For the natives the forest is the world. In their language the same word serves for both. The title is literally true. These people see themselves as extensions of the forest; their various family clans are named after kinds of trees, like the ash and the oak. To be related by blood is to be of the same tree. They also internalize their forest landscape through their language. Words describing mental states are taken from words referring to trees. Their word for dream, for example, is also the word for a tree root.

For the Terrans, on the other hand, trees are merely objects. The dense dark forest seems alien and frightening to them, and is valued only as a source of wood. At this future time, the earth has virtually run out of trees, and the purpose of this colonization is to exploit the vast resources of the forest. The trees which have such subjective spiritual value for the Athsheans have for the Terrans merely political and commercial value as products.

The Terran name for this world is New Tahiti; and Davidson, like most of the other colonists, envisions it as a potential Eden. Ironically, however, his ignorance of ecology has already totally defoliated one area of it, now called Dump Island. He sees the environment as an object to be tamed and cannot therefore understand why a soybean farm should need to "waste a lot of space on trees" (2). He also regards the native population as a subhuman species worthy only of enslavement as forced labor. His own image of ideal manhood reflects with telling irony on this warped perspective; "the only time a man is really and entirely a man is when he's just had a woman or just killed another man" (81).

What are the Athsheans really like? A diminutive people, only about a meter high, they are lightly covered with green fur. Naked human skin accordingly seems repulsive to them, and one female remarks sarcastically that nursing a "yumen" child must be "like trying to suckle a fish" (136). In their emphasis on the inner life, the Athsheans somewhat resemble the Fiia of *Rocannon's World*. They are also a totally nonaggressive people: "rape, violent assault, and murder virtually don't exist among them" (61). To achieve this state they have cultivated certain aggression-halting postures and procedures. To assume a prone position on the back, with head turned and throat exposed, for example, is absolutely effective in turning away any attack. Another universally recognized procedure among them is ritual singing. The Athsheans have learned to sing competitively as an artistic substitute for and sublimation of warfare. When Selver has an opportunity to kill Davidson, whom he has learned to hate, he stays his hand and sings instead.

Another distinctive trait of the Athsheans is their remarkable dreaming ability.[10] As mentioned before, their word for dream is also the word for root, and this attitude toward the dream is the key to their behavior. Dreams are the roots of their waking activities. Dreaming is not an exclusive feature of sleeping, however. These people, especially the more gifted dreamers among them, follow a polycyclic sleep pattern, quite unlike the alteration of sleep and waking accepted by the Terrans. A 120-minute cycle is the unit of rhythm necessary to them for both day and night, which is why they cannot be conditioned into an eight-hour work day without suffering severe psychological damage. "Once you have learned to do your dreaming wide awake, to balance your sanity not on the razor's edge of reason but on the double support, the fine balance, of reason and dream; once you have learned that, you cannot unlearn it any more than you can unlearn to think" (99). Furthermore their periods of peak energy are at dawn and dusk, not at midday which the Terrans regard as the appropriate time for activity.

Among the Terran colonists is a scientist, Raj Lyubov, who, although a Captain like Davidson, is interested in studying rather than exploiting the native people. Both humane and sympathetic to unfamiliar behavior patterns, Lyubov saves Selver's life after a vicious attack on him by Davidson, and he admires the nonviolent social order achieved by the Athsheans. Although he tries to study their dreams with an EEG rather like Dr. Haber's, he is unable to understand fully the "extraordinary impulse-patterns" (101) of their brains in dream-state. Lyubov's role is that of the anthropologist, committed to bridging the gap between differing cultures, to establishing communications between differing species of the genus Man.

The dream visions of the Athsheans influence their religion as well as other facets of their lives. As their leaders are the best dreamers, their gods are those who can translate the dream vision into experience. Their word for god is "sha'ab" which also means "translator." The god is thus a link between the two realities of dream-time and world-time, one who can speak the perceptions of the unconscious. "To 'speak' that tongue is to act. To do a new thing. To change, or to be changed, radically, from the root" (106).

Selver the dreamer becomes such a god, but the new thing he speaks is a bad dream. He speaks killing. Selver has suffered even beyond the exploitation he has shared with his fellows, for his own wife was raped by Davidson and died either in the act or immediately thereafter. Selver had then attacked Davidson physically, in itself an unheard of action. Rescued by Lyubov, Selver recovers from the brutal blows sustained in the fight, only to dream and to translate for his fellows the idea of killing members of one's own species. Needless to say, the colonists suffer the consequences of this new dream-reality.

The conclusion of this short novel confirms the dialectic. Selver is alive but has taught his people the new act of killing, which has in turn resulted in the deaths of several colonists. Davidson is also alive but is captured and sent to desolate Dump Island, where he must remain alone and unable to escape, for there is not a tree left with which to build a boat. Lyubov is dead, but his death is at least in one sense a positive factor. His death has a profound effect on his friend Selver, who feels that the spirit of Lyubov lives on within him, "a shadow in the mind" (163). The humans have in fact represented the collective shadow of the Athsheans, rather as the Clayfolk did for the Fiia in *Rocannon's World*. Selver absorbs this shadow from the dead Lyubov, thereby accepting the responsibility for his own actions. His introduction of violence into his own world has represented his and his race's acceptance of the "other," the human race.[11] The ending is thus, on the whole, a grim one from the view point of the characters. Only for the planet itself is it a happy one, for the beautiful forested world is saved and will remain safe from exploitation by Terran colonists, who will never return.

A Hugo and Nebula award-winner, *The Word for World Is Forest* is deftly written and imaginatively conceived, but its polemic style and purpose make it fall somewhat below the level of literary achievement in the books discussed so far.

The major characters, Davidson and Selver, exist only on the level of their dialectical positions. Unlike George Orr and Dr. Haber, who take on a complex individuality, these antagonists function only in respect to each other. Although convincing within these limitations, the two men are essentially one-dimensional. Similarly the style, although at times both moving and hard-hitting, is limited by its polemic purpose. Written in a mood of protest against the American military action in Vietnam, this novella is not meant to be entertainment.

"Vaster Than Empires and More Slow"

As in *The Word for World Is Forest,* the theme of a symbiotic relationship with the landscape is central to the short story "Vaster Than Empires and More Slow." The title is taken from Andrew Marvell's poem "To His Coy Mistress": "Our vegetable love should grow/Vaster than empires, and more slow." In her brief introduction to the story, as reprinted in *The Wind's Twelve Quarters,* Le Guin stresses the psychological dimension of this image: "We all have forests in our minds. Forests unexplored, unending. Each of us gets lost in the forest, every night, alone" (166). The "vegetable love" in the story refers to the absorption of the protagonist Osden into the forest world of the planet he is investigating.

The story occurs in the early years of the Hainish league, when spaceships are sent out to investigate possible life on unknown planets. One such survey team of investigators sent to World 4470 includes among its personnel an empath, Osden, who has an extraordinary ability to sense the feelings of others. This remarkable knack of empathy combines with a thoroughly antagonistic personality, so that Mr. Osden insults and alienates all of his fellows on the expedition. When they land on the unknown uninhabited world, most of the surveyors feel an uncanny fear when they enter the forests, almost as if living beings were there. They attribute their fear to the alien environment and to their own anxiety about surviving their mission. Osden, however, decides to spend several days alone in the forest in order to learn if there is anything there with which to establish empathy. When his experiment proves positive, the others speculate

whether something sentient might be produced by the interconnect-
edness of the root-nodes. But what Osden has sensed from the forest
is a mutual terror. Attacked by one of his teammates, he has bled on
the tree roots, and in response the forest has transmitted its terror
back to him. He blames his fellows: "Can't you see that I retransmit
every negative or aggressive affect you've felt towards me since we
first met? . . . The forest-mind out there transmits only terror, now,
and the only message I can send it is terror" (192). Osden is thus in
somewhat the same position as Selver, having introduced a new idea
of violence into the forest world, to which it has reacted with total
fear. Also like Selver, Osden decides to accept this fear, this Other.
"He had taken the fear into himself, and, accepting, had transcended
it. He had given up his self to the alien, an unreserved surrender,
that left no place for evil. He had learned the love of the Other, and
thereby had been given his whole self" (199). When his shipmates
leave the planet, Osden, whose mind has achieved unity with the natural landscape, stays behind to become part of the vegetable world.

Osden's empathic unity with World 4470 is contrasted sharply
with the total inability of his shipmates to achieve empathy either
with him or with each other. From the start the crew are presented
as a neurotic lot. One is autoerotic; one sleeps most of the time,
thumb in mouth; all are misfits of one sort or another. Inevitably
their ability to cooperate on the survey is limited, and their anxiety
produced by the sentient vegetation succeeds in further alienating
them from each other. They argue aimlessly and withdraw further
into their psychotic symptoms. One is dead from fear when the time
comes for the return flight. In the limited compass of the story, they
are one-dimensional characters. Only the empath is convincingly
developed.

Le Guin once described herself as one of the most arboreal of
science-fiction writers.[12] The vegetable world stories illustrate this
tendency, which is apparent elsewhere but to a much lesser extent.
In these two works the forest functions both literally and metaphorically, establishing a dialectic between rational and intuitive in a new
way. The Athshean forest is perceived as a literal forest by the rational soldier Davidson, whereas for the intuitive Selver it is metaphorically an extension of his own mind and being. Similarly the
forest on World 4470 remains for most of the surveying team an
objective literal forest which they try, without success, to analyze ra-
tionally. For Osden, in contrast, the forest is not an object distinct

from himself but rather man and forest merge into a unified whole. Osden's arboreal identity with the landscape is foreshadowed in his oblique reference to another Marvell poem, "The Garden." Referring to the planet as "one big green thought" Osden eventually becomes "a green thought in a green shade."[13]

Chapter Six

The Dispossessed
and Related Stories

The Dispossessed (1974) is both an end and a beginning. Like *The Left Hand of Darkness* a winner of both the Hugo and the Nebula awards for science fiction, it represents the culmination of the Hainish series of interplanetary works and is, in fact, the last of Le Guin's science-fiction novels to date. It is also the culmination of her Taoist vision, this time with an emphasis on a different feature of that philosophy, namely anarchism. *The Dispossessed* begins a new phase in Le Guin's writing with a focus on political ideas and a tendency toward both utopian and mainstream fiction. After this work the outer spaces are largely abandoned in favor of earthbound societies, and the inner spaces of the private world are relegated to the context of political systems.

Le Guin stated that her purpose in writing this novel was to embody an anarchist society. Her interest in the subject had grown initially out of her Taoism: "I think it's a perfectly natural step to go from Taoism to anarchism. That's what I found myself doing. They are definitely related, they appeal to the same type of person, the same bent of mind." Although she was already familiar with the Taoist roots of anarchism in the writings of Chuang Tse, disciple of Lao Tse, she turned to modern writers for further extensive study: "It took me years of reading and pondering and muddling, and much assistance from Engels, Marx, Godwin, Goldman, Goodman, and above all Shelley and Kropotkin."[1] The conception which developed out of all this reading, and which underlies both the novel and its short story prologue, "The Day Before the Revolution," is an idealized anarchy, "not the bomb-in-the-pocket stuff, which is terrorism, whatever name it tries to dignify itself with."[2]

The anarchistic society depicted in *The Dispossessed* is based on the theories of its imagined revolutionary founder, Odo, a woman whose story is told retrospectively in "The Day Before the Revolution."

Odonian anarchism, expounded in her two works *Analogy* and *The Social Organism,* is based on a total rejection of the authoritarian state and a corresponding emphasis on solidarity and mutual aid. It is, as Le Guin comments, "the most idealistic . . . of all political theories."[3] Odo's theories are translated into practice after her death, when the revolution that she inspired results in a colonization of the moon. The moon world is named Anarres, that is, "without things," as its society denies the principle of private ownership of property.

The Dispossessed is thus partly science fiction—with its setting alternating between the planet Urras and its moon Anarres, and its protagonist a physicist who travels between them—and partly utopian fiction, with its thematic focus on the contrasting political systems of these two worlds.

Narrative Structure

The structure of *The Dispossessed*—like that of *The Left Hand of Darkness*—is a function of theme and character. Based on alternating scenes set in two worlds, the structure here is contrapuntal. After the opening chapter in which the scientist hero Shevek takes a spaceship from his own world of Anarres to visit Urras, the even-numbered chapters are set on his home planet and the odd-numbered ones take place on Urras. At the end of the thirteenth and last chapter, Shevek takes ship again, this time to return home to Anarres. His voyage is thus circular, as has been the case with most of Le Guin's protagonists. The narrative is related in the third person, but the viewpoint throughout is Shevek's. Unlike the earlier Hainish novels in which we encountered two contrasting views of the same world, here we have one consistent view of two very different worlds.

Along with the settings, the time patterns alternate. After the initial airport scene, the chapters which take place on Anarres move from the past up to the present, beginning with a scene from Shevek's infancy and ending with his decision to travel to Urras. The events on Urras, on the other hand, are all taking place in the present. The final chapter in which Shevek decides to return home intersects the final Anarres chapter in which he decides to leave. This alternation of time schemes ingeniously reflects the theme of Shevek's interest in temporal theory. It is the aim of his life work in physics to reconcile sequence and simultaneity, linear and circular time, being and becoming. "Time has two aspects. There is the arrow, the running river, without which there is no change, no progress, or direction, or creation. And there is the circle or the cycle, without which there is chaos, meaningless succession of instants, a world without clocks or seasons or promises" (180).[4] The pragmatic result of his unified theory will be the ansible, the instrument of simultaneous communication which figures so importantly in the earlier Hainish books. Rocannon, Falk-Ramarren, and Genly Ai all use the ansible.

The double narrative of the book, unlike its predecessors, offers little in the way of adventure or suspense. Plot and protagonist are essentially one, for through the *Bildungsroman* of Shevek's development we learn of his perceptions of two societies on his home and host planets. An intellectual and a keen observer, for him perception is development.

The narrative line on Anarres is based on sequential time. It begins with Shevek as a child of two, gazing at the sun which he wants to claim as his own. "Mine sun," he cries, only to be reprimanded by his nurse who explains to him in simple language that nothing is to be owned, all is to be shared. This minor episode exemplifies the author's method of equating Shevek's development with an exposition of the Odonian philosophy governing the world of Anarres. At age eight, the child Shevek has a dream in which a wall, frightening as an obstacle, gives way to the discovery of a primal number which reconciles unity and plurality. Although he does not quite understand it, the dream excites the youngster and foreshadows the later discovery of the unified temporal theory which will overcome walls. At age twelve, Shevek and some friends play a game involving imprisonment, a concept which is not enacted on Anarres but which they have read about, and the sensitive boy becomes sick with revulsion.

The boy grows up to become a physicist, encouraged and supported by two of his teachers, both women—Mitis and Gvarab—but exploited by Sabul, a top physicist to whom he is later apprenticed. Sabul, a male, is quite un-Odonian in his desire for power and prestige. The only way that Shevek can eventually publish his important book is to list Sabul as coauthor. During his early manhood Shevek also meets Takver, the woman who will become his partner for life. Although marriage does not exist on Anarres, some sexual partners prefer to be pair bonded for life. In this choice Shevek is different from his parents, for his father had remained with him but his mother had drifted away, preferring to follow her own work.

Shevek and Takver have two children, but they are separated when a vast famine afflicts the planet. Both are posted to emergency jobs, and four years pass before Shevek is able to rejoin his family. On a personal level the prolonged separation is painful for both of them, but on the social level their willingness to accept it testifies to their belief in mutual aid. Only through individual sacrifice can the colony survive.

Shevek also continues to experience frustration in respect to his scientific research. Not only does his acceptance of jobs doing manual labor detract from his work, but also he encounters bureaucratic obstacles. He undertakes to learn Iotic, the language spoken on Urras, and plans eventually to journey to that planet in order to communicate personally with the scientists there with whom he has corresponded about his theories. Their interest encourages him to pursue his temporal theory in spite of the apparent neglect and indifference of the Anarresti. When he finally arranges the space flight, his departure is met by crowds protesting his action as traitorous.

In this scene at the airport, the most important symbol in the novel is introduced: the wall. It is first mentioned as simply a stone wall surrounding the port, but with this suggestive comment: "like all walls, it was ambiguous, two-faced" (1). After this episode, walls are referred to repeatedly in the novel, both as literal and metaphorical structures that separate. Shevek makes it his purpose in going to Urras "to unbuild walls." Since his own world was settled in revolt against Urras, the two planets have had very limited communication, and their peoples share a mutual dislike and mistrust. Shevek's success in removing the wall that keeps them apart is ambiguous, but when he returns home he brings along an Urrasti scientist, Ketho. To that extent at least the wall is diminished.

Shevek's adventures on Urras, recounted in the odd-numbered chapters, are designed to illustrate life on that planet as well as to illuminate his own development. He finds life at the university in the country of A-Io luxurious and attractive, and he enjoys the attention showered on him by his colleagues. He discovers evidence of an underside to his bright view of this society in such disturbing details as the wire-tapping device in his room, in the revelation that a fellow physicist is a police spy, and in the intimation that the poor are kept out of his sight. He visits the home of a friendly colleague and is favorably impressed with the family life he encounters there, but when he converses with his servant he finds that life is very different among the lower classes. Gradually he becomes aware of a disparity between appearance and reality in this new world.

The crisis in his growing perceptions occurs at a cocktail party given by the vivacious sister of a colleague. Having had no experience with the effects of alcoholic drinks, Shevek becomes drunk. Under the combined influence of his own intoxication and his hostess's blatant sexuality, he tries to seduce her and later becomes sick. Overcome with guilt about his disgraceful behavior, he comes to realize his own alienation from the ways of this rich society. He then decides to investigate the part of Urras that he has not been permitted to see. He slips off to the poor section of the city and contacts some anarchists whose names he acquired from his servant. There he finds himself participating in a mass demonstration, but when police fire on the crowd he is forced to take refuge in a cellar with a man dying of a gunshot wound.

After this tragic initiation into the deep-seated political problems of the world he had so misjudged, Shevek reaches two major decisions. He decides to take refuge in the Terran embassy, from where he plans to return home to Anarres. He also decides not to let the country of A-Io have his temporal theory because they want to own it in order to advance their own national power. Instead he will publicly broadcast his theory to the whole world, so that all humanity can benefit from the interstellar communication which it will make possible. When he returns to his own world, he will take with him a man from Urras. Shevek has not given up on his desire to unbuild walls.

Themes

Since Taoism provides the base for Le Guin's anarchistic ideal as explored in the novel, it is useful to consider the specifically Taoist influence on her views before moving on to other themes. As Elizabeth Cummins Cogell has pointed out, the basic principles of Odonianism are congruent with those of Taoism.[5] The unity of nature and the eternality of change are precepts underlying both. Odonianism follows the model of nature, which offers an undifferentiated society. There are no unequal classes in nature. Balance and harmony predominate in nature, not hierarchy. The Odonian social practices of sharing, cooperative labor, and mutual aid grow out of this vision of nature. Furthermore, since human evolution has produced a predominantly social species, it follows that the most social humans are the strongest. Strength lies in social cooperation. The Taoist theory of "wu wei," or letting alone, also influences the Odonian society. No aggressive action is sponsored on Anarres, a fact which leads a sarcastic Urrasti physicist to call the Anarresti "womanish." Finally, recognition of the eternality of change is implicit both in the social structure based on revolution, as is the case of the Anarres colony, and of the unified theory of time with which Shevek is concerned.

Although Le Guin feels that the Taoist theory of anarchy is the social system most in keeping with nature, she does not make the utopian mistake of depicting a society which has attained that ideal. The subtitle of her work is "an ambiguous utopia," and although her sympathies are clearly on the side of the new world rather than the old, that new world is a thought-experiment rather than a visionary success. In the alternating chapters, the reader learns the strengths and weaknesses of both the anarchistic and the propertarian systems of Anarres and Urras. The resulting comparative vision favors the anarchistic experiment but not without recognizing its problems and even admitting some advantages of the contrary system. "To light a candle is to cast a shadow," as Ged learns in Earthsea, and Anarres has its shadow side.

The advantages of the world founded by revolution over a century ago are obvious. Like most conventional utopias, Anarres has no government, no law, no class distinction, no large cities, and no money. Since Anarres is also a harsh world, with an environment hostile to human habitation, sharing and mutual aid have become practical matters of survival rather than vague ideals. As is also true in many traditional utopias, living arrangements are communal, with dormitories and refectories the rule. Private rooms are allowed only for paired couples.

On the other hand, the goal of social harmony creates tensions with the demands of the individual. Society does not cultivate or even understand genius. The individual with an outstanding talent may be discouraged by the group who show no interest in his work, not being motivated by respect for personal achievement. Shevek is a case in point. As a child in school, he is reprimanded by an insensitive teacher when he presents a challenging paradox to his classmates. The mathematically minded youngster is told that he must stop "egoizing," which is the Anarresti word for placing individual interests above those of the group. Since the educational system cannot deal with individual creativity it tends to foster mediocrity and conformity. On the adult level, Shevek encounters the same problem when he tries to publish his highly original theories and is stopped by Sabul, whose own ambition and pride lead him to stifle his young colleague's accomplishments.

The case of Shevek's friend Tirin also illustrates the dangers inherent in the system. Tirin is a gifted writer who composes and produces a dramatic comedy which is misinterpreted as an attack on Odonian principles. As a result of this unfortunate reaction to his sophisticated but innocent play, he is punished by being posted to a series of jobs at hard labor in remote locations. He eventually loses his mind. Absence of repressive laws does not protect from the equal tyranny of social approval and disapproval. Similarly, when Shevek is planning his voyage to Urras, several of his countrymen interpret his decision as treason. As a result, he and his partner are subjected to derision and even threats, and his children are mistreated in the dormitory where they sleep.

Although there are no rulers, there are administrators, and Anarres is beginning to have a problem with burgeoning bureaucracy. In a world where the economy is handled through a central agency, the danger is perhaps inevitable although the use of computers ensures certain kinds of impersonal justice. Every personal name, for example, is generated by a computer and assigned to one living person. There are no inherited or chosen names. But the growing bureaucracy threatens to become a power structure of the sort that Odo rebelled against in the first place. Shevek's friend Bedap explains the source of this negative kind of power exerted by such mediocrities as Sabul: "Public opinion! That's the power structure he's part of, and knows how to use. The unadmitted, inadmissible government that rules the Odonian society by stifling the individual mind. . . . The social conscience isn't a living thing anymore, but a machine, a power machine, controlled by bureaucrats" (134–35).

Although Shevek is incensed at Bedap's attack, later in the book, shortly before his decision to visit Urras, he arrives independently at the same disparaging point of view. He laments to Takver: "We don't cooperate—we *obey*. We fear being outcast, being called lazy, dysfunctional, egoizing. We fear our neighbor's opinion more than we respect our own freedom of choice" (265).

It is thus a somewhat disillusioned Shevek who travels to Urras. At first that world impresses him both with its natural beauty and with its human achievement. He hears the birds sing for the first time, plays with a child's pet otter, and marvels at the colorful foliage in autumn. He is also astonished to find the people apparently all well dressed, well fed, industrious, and content. Perhaps, he feels, Urras is not the abode of misery, injustice, and inequity that he had been taught to believe. He does, however, feel a certain unease at the emphasis on excess, for Odonians believe that "excess is excrement." In an elegant shopping street he is dismayed at the world of "excremental" things: "coats, dresses, gowns, robes, trousers, breeches, shirts, blouses, hats, shoes, stockings, scarves, shawls, vests, capes, umbrellas, clothes to wear while sleeping, while swimming, while playing games, while at an afternoon party, while at an evening party, while at a party in the country, while traveling, while at the theater, while riding horses, gardening, receiving guests, boating, dining, hunting" (106). He is further shocked to learn that one fur coat costs 8400 "units," while the average living wage is 2000 "units."

What comes into focus gradually for the visitor is the disturbing picture of a two-class society. Whereas on Anarres a marginal existence is shared by all, on Urras the upper classes enjoy an enviable prosperity while the lower classes suffer poverty and neglect. Through his servant Efor, Shevek learns about the deprived segment of society which he has not been permitted to see. Determined now to discover it, he takes a subway to what is obviously the slum section of the city. "The lampposts were there, but the lights were not turned on, or were broken. Yellow gleams slitted from around shuttered windows here and there. Down the street, light streamed from an open doorway, around which a group of men were lounging, talking loud. The pavement, greasy with rain, was littered with scraps of paper and refuse. . . . People went by, silent hasty shadows" (233). There he learns about an impending strike on the part of the city's four hundred thousand unemployed. When he makes himself known to the strikers, he is viewed as a symbol of their own revolutionary purposes: "To know that there is a society without government, without police, without economic exploitation, that they can never say again it's just a mirage, an idealist's dream!" (237). He joins them, knowing the danger to himself if violence erupts.

Le Guin thus sharpens the vision of her opposed worlds through contrast from within as well as without. Although Shevek believes in the Odonian revolutionary ideal of anarchism, with its substitution of

mutual aid and solidarity for government and authority, he also discovers its weaknesses, such as bureaucracy and the tyranny of public
opinion. Similarly, although he believes that propertarianism and
class structure are essentially vicious social systems, he also finds that
in such a society art and culture can thrive, and the gifted individual
can be nourished. Unlike most Utopian works, *The Dispossessed* maintains a dialectic throughout.

Characterization

In *The Dispossessed* Le Guin does not quite maintain the perfect balance of form and content that distinguished both the Earthsea trilogy
and *The Left Hand of Darkness.* Although a brilliant book, it is somewhat flawed by the tone of polemic in some of the dialogue, where
character and plot are subordinated to the ideological perspective.
The conversation occasionally turns to speechifying, and the long par-
agraphs signify political positions rather than personality. Many of
the peripheral characters tend to be spokesmen for points of view.
Shevek's colleagues, for example, represent differing facets of society:
the socialist sympathizer, the over-polite government spy, the par-
venu professor. The affected socialite and temptress, Vea, is also only
superficially realized.

On the other hand, the characterization of the central figures is
quite successful. Takver, the partner—spunky, loving, gentle,
sturdy—is a memorable portrayal. A fish geneticist by profession, she
is passionately concerned with all living creatures and all features of
the landscape. When she holds a leaf or a rock, she becomes an extension of it. She heroically bears her first child at home with little
assistance, and she endures famine and hard labor without complaint.
Yet she is no patient Griselda, but a lively, vehement, even assertive
woman.

Shevek is also complex and convincing.[6] A mixture of naïveté and
brilliance, he feels himself an alien on both worlds. A misfit among
the Anarresti for his individualistic ways, he is even less at home on
luxurious Urras where the possessors are really the possessed. He recognizes his isolation and regards himself as doubly exiled, both from
his own society and from his hosts. Critics are by no means unani-
mous in their assessment of Shevek's characterization, however. One
reviewer finds him "a complex human being and believeable scientist;"[7] another regards him as "the paradigm of the ideal voyager—

always willing to learn and change, confident of his movement because it is based on an emotional and logical understanding of the self."[8] In total contrast, a third complains that it is Shevek's "failure to conceive of the possibility of such a transformational change *in himself* that makes him seem to me such an awful schlemiel."[9]

Since the utopian themes of the novel dominate the science-fiction elements, there is not much stress on the distinctive planetary features of the two worlds. The main impression communicated is the contrast between the dryness and barrenness of the Anarresti landscape and the rich fertility and foliage of the Urrasti. The authenticating details of life on the two planets are focused on the social rather than the geographical dimension. Urras is not earth, in spite of certain obvious similarities, and its social customs combine the familiar with the dramatically different. Urrasti women shave their heads, and Vea's formal evening wear consists of "a full-length pleated skirt draped from the hips, leaving the whole torso naked. In her navel a little jewel glittered" (176). The children of Shevek's colleagues come to dinner dressed in "blue velvet coats and breeches" (118). The starkly contrasted austerity of life on Anarres is captured in a variety of revealing details. At a young people's party the refreshments consist of fried bread and pickles. There are no alcoholic drinks, and there is no meat. The first room that Shevek and Takver share has but a bed and two chairs, of which one is decrepit. When it is repaired, the room is considered completely furnished. Shevek brings with him an orange blanket that someone had left behind, an item that labels him a propertarian among his friends who have no personal possessions.

The richness and complexity of this novel unfortunately worked against its immediate recognition. *Time,* for example, allotted it a short paragraph in a composite review of several science-fiction works.[10] Neither wholly SF, nor utopian, nor mainstream, it is all of these and more, as critics have come somewhat belatedly to recognize. It also bears a significant relationship with three major short stories which combine the utopian and SF modes of fiction.

The thematic point of departure for the short stories is the speech of the Terran ambassador at the end of the novel. Although earth is not depicted in the book, its ambassador represents its circumstances in a devastating speech to Shevek. She explains to him that Urras seems like a paradise because her own world has been destroyed: "My world, my Earth, is a ruin. A planet spoiled by the human species.

We multiplied and gobbled and fought until there was nothing left, and then we died. We controlled neither appetite nor violence; we did not adapt. We destroyed ourselves. But we destroyed the world first. There are no forests left on my Earth. The air is grey, the sky is grey, it is always hot. It is habitable, it is still habitable, but not as this world is. This is a living world, a harmony. Mine is a discord" (279).

The Terran ambassador's passionate outburst is in a way irrelevant to the novel in that it does not contribute to the dialectical exploration of the two worlds Urras and Anarres. It does serve, however, as a useful introduction to the three closely related short works written about the same time.

"The Ones Who Walk Away from Omelas" and "The Day Before the Revolution"

Le Guin published "The Ones Who Walk Away from Omelas" in 1972. A Hugo winner, it is based on the myth of the scapegoat as she found it expounded in a William James essay.[11] James raises this question in "The Moral Philosophy and the Moral Life": "if the hypothesis were offered us of a world in which . . . millions kept permanently happy on the one simple condition that a certain lost soul on the far-off edge of things should lead a life of lonely torment, what except a specifical and independent sort of emotion can it be which would make us immediately feel, even though an impulse arose within us to clutch at the happiness so offered, how hideous a thing would be its enjoyment when deliberately accepted as the fruit of such a bargain?" (251).[12]

In this story Le Guin depicts a beautiful and joyous city, Omelas, whose well-being depends on the suffering of "one lost soul," a child living in utterly degraded and bestial circumstances in the basement of a public building. The people of Omelas are aware of this situation, but for the most part they accept the unalterable fact that to improve the lot of the child would be to throw away the happiness of the remaining thousands. A few people, however, cannot live with this fact without feeling overcome with guilt, and these few choose to leave the city. The ones who walk away from Omelas exemplify the revolutionary individual who cannot enjoy a prosperity dependent on the suffering of others.

One such revolutionary is Odo, theoretical founder of Shevek's society on Anarres. Since Odo lived several generations before the novel, she is referred to there as a semilegendary figure, but in "The Day Before the Revolution" (1975) Le Guin gives us a highly personal portrayal of Odo as an old woman on the eve of the revolution that she has inspired. At the time of the story, the revolution which will produce the anarchist settlement of Anarres is about to take place, and Odo, its spiritual mentor, is a woman of seventy-two.

The old woman is introduced to the reader as a young woman in her dream. Odo dreams of her former lover and "partner" (in Odonian revolutionary parlance marriage gives way to partnership) only to waken and rediscover her aged body as if it were a deteriorating possession. "Disgusting. Sad, depressing. Mean. Pitiful" (262).[13] Her waking thoughts are spasms of contradiction, as she vacillates between past memories and present observations. As the woman whose theories have given her name to a revolutionary movement, she sees herself as both a part of and apart from that movement. As a good Odonian, for example, she should say "partner" not "husband" as she recalls him in a dream, but she asks, "Why the hell did she have to be a good Odonian?" (264). Her attitude toward her own radical political system is at once one of participation and antagonism.

Odo is similarly ambivalent toward her activities. On the one hand, she wants to dictate letters to her secretary, Noi, in order to show that she is still in full control, but at the same time she repeatedly leaves the decisions concerning exact wording to him. When Noi reminds her of a scheduled meeting with a group of foreign students, she is at once pleased and dismayed:

She liked the young, and there was always something to learn from a foreigner, but she was tired of new faces, and tired of being on view. She learned from them, but they didn't learn from her; they had learnt all she had to teach long ago, from her books, from the Movement. They just come to look, as if she were the Great Tower in Rodarred, or the Canyon of the Tulaevea. A phenomenon, a monument. (271)

She resents being a monument, yet not without certain satisfaction in this passive new role. The revolutionary has become a "dear old lady" (272).

Throughout the story the use of graphic physical detail vivifies the fact of old age. When Odo gets out of bed in the morning, she looks down at her feet with loathing:

The toes, compressed by a lifetime of cheap shoes, were almost square where they touched each other, and bulged out above in corns; the nails were discolored and shapeless. Between the knob-like ankle-bones ran fine, dry wrinkles. (262)

But even this description of aged skin is marked by ambivalence:

The brief little plain at the base of the toes had kept its delicacy, but the skin was the color of mud, and knotted veins crossed the instep. (262)

Similarly, the effects of a stroke are clinically delineated to show the ways in which Odo's body has deteriorated and the ways in which it has not. Only the right side is afflicted:

Her right hand tingled. She scratched it, and then shook it in the air, spitefully. It had never quite got over the stroke. Neither had her right leg, or right eye, or the right corner of her mouth. They were sluggish, inept, they tingled. They made her feel like a robot with a short circuit. (267)

Most of all, however, the dynamic ambivalence of Odo's characterization is reflected in her relationship to her own role in the impending revolution. Odo has been the center of political activity all of her adult life and now fears becoming peripheral to it. " 'It's not easy,' she said to herself in justification, laboriously climbing the stairs, 'to accept being out of it when you've been in it, in the center of it, for fifty years' " (265). To her devoted followers she is still in the center of it, at least as a symbol, or a model, but for her the laborious stairs pose a threat to that centrality. Her own self-image is strained in opposite directions by self-pity and self-esteem.

The tension of opposites within Odo is focused on her role in the precise moment of time referred to in the title. She has worked her whole life to bring about a world revolution. She has worked and fought and written books. She has spent years in jail and has become the guiding spirit of the revolution which is just now about to take place on a large scale. Tomorrow. But her opposed feelings concern her own part to play on the eve of that crucial event. She feels both involved and detached. She surrenders to a deep but irrational desire to walk out into the streets although she knows that she is physically too weak to do so. Her recent stroke has debilitated her to the point where her own body seems to flop about her like a ragged garment. When she takes the walk, her fatigue forces her to sit on a doorstep in the slum, too weak to go on. As she sits there, inert, she wonders at her own identity. Who am I? she asks. She answers herself:

> She was the little girl with scabby knees, sitting on the doorstep staring down through the dirty golden haze of River Street in the heat of late summer, the six-year-old, the sixteen-year-old, the fierce, cross, dream-ridden girl, untouched, untouchable. She was herself. Indeed she had been the tireless worker and thinker, but a blood clot in a vein had taken that woman away from her. Indeed she had been the lover, the swimmer in the midst of life, but Taviri, dying, had taken that woman away with him. There was nothing left, really, but the foundation. She had come home; she had never left home. "True voyage is return." Dust and mud and a doorstep in the slums. (275–6)

With the help of an acquaintance who happens to walk by, Odo is able to go home, but once there her attitude toward her companions seems suddenly aloof, and her response to their questions cryptic. She is asked by them to speak on the morning of the revolution, but she asserts simply that she will not be there. The remark has a deeper meaning than they realize. As she sardonically puts it to herself, with a grim private joke, the "general strike" must yield to the "private stroke." Her laborious climb upstairs to her own room is in reality an ascent to her own death. "She was dizzy, but she was no longer afraid to fall" (277).

Odo will not see the revolution she has brought about. But the irony without reflects the tension of opposites within. Capable both of self-pity and self-praise, she has vacillated between action and surrender, between aggressive involvement and passive detachment. She is not as many people see her, merely a dead monument, nor is she altogether as people have known her to be in the past, a hard, fighting rebel. She is neither because she is both, at one and the same time, her stroke-ridden body declines, yet mounts the stairs; and her rebellious spirit soars, yet savors rest. The irony of this double vision of herself does not escape her own mordant awareness: "a drooling old woman who had started a world revolution" (265).

"The New Atlantis"

Odo will not see the revolution she brought about, nor will Belle, the narrator of "The New Atlantis" (also written in 1975) see the new world she has intuited through her music. Like *The Dispossessed* this

short story is structured in two alternating narratives which depict
contrasting worlds. In this case, however, one world is dying, the
other coming to life. The old world—focused on a future extrapola-
tion of the United States—is subsiding underwater, a victim of eco-
logical breakdown and political crisis, abetted by violent earthquakes.
The new world is emerging from the sea, a product of geological
pressures and creative energy. But the new world, the new Atlantis,
is also old, for it is reborn from the depths where the towers of the
old Atlantis still stand. And the old world is about to become the
"new" continent sinking beneath the sea, as the old Atlantis had
done so long ago. The irony intimated in the title is thus reflected in
the interlocking structure. Which is the "new" Atlantis?

The story is related in six sections, each with two parts. In each
section a first-person narrative about the events in Portland, Oregon,
alternates with an italicized passage representing a collective narrative
about the slowly emerging continent. There are parallels between the
two narrative parts in each of the six sections, and in the fifth, there
is even a slight communication between the two worlds. The six sections are also analogous in that they represent six stages in the re-
spective decline and elevation of the two separate worlds.

The two segments of the first section serve to introduce the opposed worlds. The individual narrator of the American narrative is a
woman returning from her vacation by bus. From her account we
learn about the degradation of the country at this unspecified future
time. (She later reminisces about the "dear old 1970s" when there
weren't any problems and life seemed simple.) The American mania
for hyperbolic rhetoric has lost all contact with reality. The "super-
sonic, superscenic, de luxe" bus breaks down when the driver tries to
go over thirty, and passengers eat a meatless hamburger at the Long-
horn Inch-Thick Steakhouse. The country has by then become a totally
corporative state, integrating all the existing bureaucracies—credit
cards, unions, mass media, health, education, and welfare—into a
totalitarian system. There are so-called rehabilitation camps for dis-
sidents, and universal compulsory employment which has produced
for the narrator (we learn later that her name is Belle) a deadening
job inspecting recycled paper bags four hours daily. When she returns
from her vacation to her dark apartment, where a three-week old
power outage continues, she finds a strange man sleeping in her bed.
On closer inspection by candlelight, he is revealed to be her own husband, recently released from his long incarceration in one of the rehabilitation camps.

While still on the bus, the narrator had heard rather vaguely about the emergence of a new continent from the sea. The collective voice of this new world is introduced in the first italicized passage, describing its inception and gradual movement toward self-awareness. "It was dark for so long, so very long. We were all blind. And there was the cold, a vast, unmoving, heavy cold" (400).[14] The evolving perception of time, space, and number is communicated through the appearance of tiny fitful lights. As in the myth of Genesis, time begins with the first appearance of light in the darkness. The appearance of another light stirs memories on the planets, and finally seven lights appear, then merge into one streak, and vanish.

In the second section we learn more about the American couple. The husband, Simon, is a mathematician, whose arrest resulted from one of his research papers being illegally published abroad. The wife, Belle, is a violist. Since marriage is also illegal at this time, they are in violation of the law in more ways than one. Their apartment is bugged and searched, and they must hire a black-market doctor for Simon, who has been almost crippled from his brutal treatment in the camp.

The idyllic tone of the italicized passage which follows is broken by the recognition that the lantern creatures who produce the bright lights are actually all mouth, and eat each other whole. "Light swallowed light, all swallowed together in the vaster mouth of the darkness" (404). Perhaps, as one critic suggested, the rapacious lights are analogous to the ideological movements in human history which swallow each other and are in turn lost in the vaster dark of the past. At any rate, the recognition of the predatory nature of the lights makes the otherwise lyrical account of the new creation rather ambiguous.

In the third section we get a clearer picture of a world on the edge of collapse, as the radio newscaster reports on wars raging in Liberia and Uruguay, and on police action in Arizona against the combined insurgent forces of the Neo-Birch and the Weathermen, both armed with nukes. The radio battery dims, as the announcer's fading voice mentions something about a new continent emerging. Near the end of this short section, Belle goes to sleep, hearing the sound of the waves in the distance, as she used to do in childhood. The dark sea seems to call her. In the next relatively long italicized passage, the collective voice continues its progress toward awareness, this time realizing the nature of space and of sound. The perception of sound requires proximity of space, as sight does not. But the newly emerging life is vaguely aware of a sound calling from the old world, a sound of yearning music.

Section four develops the theme of Simon's mathematical equations which have theoretically achieved direct conversion of solar energy. His scientist friends have worked out a practical application of his theory which would enable the world to tap the sun for power in a direct and efficient way. Simon's joy in the discovery makes him euphoric, but ironically he cannot implement it because he is not a government employee. The state has a monopoly on power sources, and there is continuing power shortage, as the recurring outages in the story remind us. The new discovery would make it possible for anyone to build a roof-top generator that would furnish the whole city with power, thus obviating any need for the state to deal with power at all. The entire episode is an ironic perversion of the creation motif: let there be light.

In the creation which is actually taking place in the italicized portion of the story, there is now a genuine dawn with a real sunrise. Unlike the dawn we know, however, it is cold and blue, the color farthest removed from the golden rays of the sun.

As the fourth section presented the climax of Simon's joy in mathematical discovery, the fifth section offers the joyful improvisation of Belle's music. While the others are staring in mingled admiration and frustration at the newly built solar cell, which they can do nothing with, Belle is practicing playing her viola in the bathroom where she won't disturb them with the sound. She abandons the printed music in favor of improvisation just in time, for another power outage leaves her completely in the dark. Her music soars sublimely in the dark, drifting out over the world and to the dark sea. The intense music brings about an almost mystical experience for the scientists, who suddenly hear the voices of the emerging continent. One of them sees the white towers, with the waters streaming down their sides. Simon realizes that they could theoretically raise the towers with their new power.

The italicized passage reveals that the emerging city has heard the music. As it breaks through the brightness into life, and the water streams down the white towers as envisioned by the scientist, the voice proclaims: "We are here. Whose voice? Who called to us?" (415).

The final section completes the double movement of creation and destruction. The narrator's world is coming to an end. Simon is arrested again, and the radio news reports major earthquakes and rising land masses in both the Atlantic and the Pacific. The breakthrough of the new Atlantis comes with a call for the Americans to answer: "Where are you? We are here. Where have you gone?" (416). But there is no answer.

The story is artfully unified through the combined motifs of music and number. The narrator Belle, whose very name is musical, is also a violist. When she first hears about the Atlanteans and tries to imagine what they look like, she envisions people in white ties and tails, carrying oboes and violas. Although she is forced to practice sitting on the toilet lid because her one-room apartment allows her no other privacy, she is fervent and committed to her musical career. During the course of the story she plays music of Schubert, Hindemith, and Berlioz, as well as that of her promising young composer friend, Forrest. Structurally in the narrative her own peak of musical creativity coincides with her husband's invention of the solar cell. The realization of her musical numbers matches the fulfillment of his mathematical equations.

Like the voices from Atlantis, Belle prefers sound to light. She resents an audience who enjoys watching a musician perform, as if what they actually saw could have anything to do with music. Her description of performing musicians is mocking: "a fiddler rolling his eyes and biting his tongue," "a pianist like a black cat strapped to an electrified bench" (409). The voices recognize sound as both totally independent of sight and infinitely more delicate. Sound is "a fragile thing, a tremor, as delicate as life itself" (407). Belle enjoys playing in the dark, for without light the sound seemed "softer and less muddled" (413). And, of course, the reader never sees the Atlanteans; they exist merely as a collective voice which is heard.

The new world arising from the depths of the sea responds to Belle's yearning music. When she transcends the printed music and bursts into inspired improvisation, the music travels out over the dark sea and sings in the darkness. Not only does the emerging world hear her music, but at the same time Simon and his friends are enabled, through the music, to see that world. In a climactic moment the two worlds are in brief communication through the medium of music. Simon and his friends see the white towers of the deep even as the voices from the towers rise and answer the call of the music.

Harmony is a traditional metaphor for the act of creation, as writers from Milton to Tolkien have known and demonstrated. In traditional numerical symbolism, seven also signifies creation. Seven is the number of totality, completeness, of the macrocosm.[15] The number seven recurs several times in the story. In addition to the seven notes of the musical scale, the seven colors of the spectrum figure prominently into the account of the emerging world. In the opening section, the appearance of the lights indicates a progression up to the number seven. The six sections represent the six days of the creation of the old world.

"The New Atlantis" is a literal and metaphorical extension of the Terran ambassador's remark at the end of *The Dispossessed*. Contrasting her own ruined earth with the relatively new world of Urras, she remarked that, "This is a living world, a harmony. Mine is a discord" (279). The chaotic, polluted, totalitarian world of the brilliant inventor who suffers arrest for his dissidence and of the talented musician who must practice in the dark on a toilet lid is a discordant world while the newly emerging continent, with its white towers streaming with water and its voices growing in perception is in a state of creative harmony. Simon's solar cell is the new "let there be light" which is lost in the darkness, while the improvisations on the viola drift out to the sea of creation, whence comes all life.

A richly suggestive story, "The New Atlantis" has, not at all surprisingly, evoked contradictory responses from those few critics who have given it attention. Rollin Lasseter sees it as analogous to the shadow world of *The Farthest Shore* because all the characters are "caught in that shadowed fixity." Even worse than the negative image of the United States as a totalitarian prison "polluted and used up" is the image of the characters who do not even care, who find nothing wonderful, "not even the convulsion of the earth itself, and the sinking of the outworn continents beneath the sea."[16] Similarly, George Slusser interprets the vision of the story as an essentially pessimistic one: "the individual life ends in death, the collective existence in annihilation."[17] In contrast, Darko Suvin reads the story optimistically, interpreting the narrative as "a sketch of a new, collectivist, and harmonious creation."[18] Suvin's is the fullest analysis yet of the story, and he quite rightly recognizes both movements— creation and destruction, harmony and discord.

An ambiguous and contrapuntal work, this short story bears a close relationship to the ambiguous utopian novel which preceded it. It also indicates the double focus in Le Guin's fiction at this point in her career. On the one hand, it represents a continuing absorption in the mythic theme of death and regeneration. The Atlantean theme illustrates the need for a return to primordial unity in order to restore lost vitality.[19] On a different plane it thus repeats the narrative pattern of *The Farthest Shore*. On the other hand, it also demonstrates Le Guin's new preoccupation with the political implications of her subject matter. The individual voice is presented in terms of the collective.

Chapter Seven

The Wind's Twelve Quarters, Orsinian Tales, and Very Far Away from Anywhere Else

Le Guin's major publications in 1975/76 are in the area of short fiction. *The Wind's Twelve Quarters* (1975) contains seventeen short stories; *Orsinian Tales* (1976) is a collection of eleven tales; and *Very Far Away from Anywhere Else* (1976) is a short novel (eighty-six pages) intended for an adolescent audience.[1] The major differences among these works illustrate the multi-directional tendencies in Le Guin's work at this period. Fantasy, science fiction, and a mainstream combination of romance and realism all appear both separately and together in these three books.

The Wind's Twelve Quarters

The Wind's Twelve Quarters offers what Le Guin calls a "retrospective." The stories represent a chronological survey of her work in the twelve-year period 1962–1974. Most are in the category of fantasy or science fiction, and each is briefly introduced by the author. Seven of these pieces are the "seed" stories of later novels.[2] Since these have been discussed earlier in connection with their related novels, they will not be discussed in the present context. Although it is not the germinal story of a longer work, "Vaster Than Empires and More Slow" has already been discussed in the context of its similarities with *The Word for World Is Forest*. Of the remaining nine stories, two are essentially fantasy, six are clearly SF, and one combines science fiction with realism.

The two fantasy stories are "April in Paris" and "Darkness Box." Le Guin notes that "April in Paris" is the first story she ever got paid for. It is a delightful "time" fantasy, in which characters from four different periods of history converge on a room in Paris. Professor Barry Pennyweather, a lonely scholar is an unheated apartment on the Island of Saint-Louis, is poring over the book he is writing about François Villon, when he almost burns himself with a flare-up from his cigarette lighter. It is the night of 2 April 1961, and he cries out "Hell." Sitting in that same room on April 2nd in the fourteenth century, another lonely scholar, Jehan Lenoir, pores over a book called *On the Primacy of the Element of Fire* and also calls out "Hell" (in late medieval French). In a mood of despondency and frustration, he then utters an incantation intended to summon a devil. Instead the spell succeeds in transporting Pennyweather back in time to Lenoir's period. The two scholars, both lonely men and frustrated intellectuals, share their knowledge (Lenoir knew Villon personally and Pennyweather knows all the elements) and strike up a firm friendship.

In spite of their pleasure in each other's conversation, however, both men miss female company. They decide to test Lenoir's necromantic skill in the direction of summoning suitable companions of the fair sex. In response to these effective but totally unpredictable spells, two women appear: a Gaulish slave from the distant past and an interstellar archeologist from the distant future. A small white puppy also materializes somewhat irrelevantly from one of his spells. The lost puppy, the mistreated slave, and the alienated archeologist have shared a common loneliness. But now on a soft April night in Paris, four lonely people and their pet are no longer lonely.

The consistently humorous tone and the outrageous use of magic combine with imaginative details to make this a satisfying fantasy story. In spite of its romantically happy ending, it is comic rather than sentimental.

The other fantasy story, "Darkness Box," is quite different although time is also the central theme. The protagonist Prince Rikard is called upon to defend his father's kingdom against the threats of his exiled brother. The battle is fought over and over, however, because this is a world out of time, where the sun never rises or sets, and no one ever dies. The battles repeatedly take place under a sunless sky, and the fallen get up to fight again the next day. One day a witch's child delivers to the Prince a box filled with darkness. When Rikard opens the box, darkness flows out and the shadow of mortality is loosed on the world. The sun will shine on the next day's battle, and the fallen will never see it rise again. Rikard's longing for mortality somewhat anticipates the theme of *The Farthest Shore*.

The six science-fiction stories exhibit a wide range of subject and technique. Le Guin describes "The Masters" as her first "genuine authentic real virgin-wool science fiction story" (37). The unidentified setting evokes the period of the inquisition, and the narrative involves the condemnation for heresy of those scientific thinkers who compute numbers. One man is burned at the stake for trying to calculate "the distance between the earth and God." The protagonist Ganil, exiled and bewildered, foreshadows Le Guin's later solitary and alienated heroes.

One of the best pieces in the collection is "Nine Lives." The story was originally published in *Playboy* with many minor changes, but the version given here is the complete one. It is a hard-core SF story in the sense that it is extrapolated from a contemporary scientific discovery, that is, cloning. As always in the fiction of Le Guin, however, the scientific element serves as symbol of something deeper. The setting this time is the dead planet Libra, where a two-man team, isolated for several months, is joined by a "tenclone," ten identical people (five male and five female) all named John Chow (with differentiating middle names). The ten, who are superb physical specimens of humanity, are derived from an extraordinarily talented person—the original John Chow—who was a mathematician, cellist, and engineer, a "Leonardo" type.

The remarkable efficiency and obvious amiability of the ten make a firm if unnerving impression on the two other men, Martin and Owen, but eventually their overwhelming presence affects the friendship between the latter. They become edgy and snappish, largely because of their isolation from the homogeneous group. The climax of the story is precipitated by an earthquake. In spite of the valiant efforts of Martin and Owen, all of the clones but one are trapped and killed. The solitary survivor, Kaph, faces a severe psychological crisis. Since all his life he has in effect known only himself, albeit distributed among other physical presences, he suffers from total alienation from Martin and Owen. The outcome of the story involves Kaph's discovery and acceptance of the "other." Le Guin is more interested here in exploring the psychological implications of cloning than the scientific methodology. Kaph Chow's alienation becomes a symbol of the human lot, and it both affects and is affected by his relationship with Martin and Owen. His new awareness of the importance of relationships is expressed at the end of the story through an image that recurs in several of the novels: a human hand held out in the dark.

"Things" is an end-of-the-world story, originally published in *Orbit* as "The End." The new title equates the end of the world with the abandonment of all things, both leaving behind actual objects and realizing that there are no more roads to take. In the somewhat enigmatic conclusion to the story the main characters, none of whom is significantly individualized, take a step beyond mere things in order to reach the sailboats which will purportedly take them to the islands.

"A Trip to the Head," which Le Guin facetiously calls a "Bung Puller" (159), is either wildly funny and mildly alarming or wildly alarming and mildly funny, depending on the reader's reverence for the rational. It concerns identity. The central figure, who remains "Blank" until very near the end of the story, is trying to establish his location ("Is this Earth? [160]), his memory ("I do remember England" [164]), and his sex ("You mean it doesn't *matter* if I am a man or a woman?" [163]). The other person, who remains unidentified, assures him that it is indeed Earth (where the population increases by thirty billion every Thursday) but reminds him that England sank. His memory is not real. He copulates with Amanda (who suddenly appears from nowhere), but she tells him grimly that sex is also not real. As he is about to give up on identifying himself ("I might as well be a bristleworm or a tree-sloth" [165]), he suddenly decides that he is himself. At that point the other is gone, and only the forest remains. "Blank" plunges eastward into the dark world of the forest "where nameless tigers burned" (165). Le Guin explains the mood of frustration which gave rise to the story so that one might interpret it as a spoof; on the other hand, it also comes through as a suggestive parable about the quicksand theories on which identity is based. The forest as an image of the human mind occurs elsewhere in Le Guin, and the punning title intimates layers of meaning hinted at in this readable but puzzling piece.

"The Stars Below" is an excellent science-fiction story. In its concern with the freedom of scientific thought it resembles "The Masters," but it is a deeper and more polished work of fiction. In this story science becomes a synonym for art and for the creative mind. "What happens to the creative mind when it is driven underground?" Le Guin asks. The answer is derived from alchemy. The alchemical image used in the title is inspired by a relevant passage from C. G. Jung: "Star-strewn heavens, stars reflected in dark water, nuggets of gold or golden sand scattered in black earth."[3] Ultimately the image reflects the hermetical formula "As above, so below."

The astronomer Guennar is charged with heresy because of his work with the telescope. His friends rescue him from being burned at the stake. They do not understand his theories but in their simplicity want to protect the man they like and admire. They take their fugitive friend underground into the mines where they work, a safe but untenable location for an astronomer whose life work is studying the heavens. Guennar prays to be forgiven for his apparently heretical studies: "All I ever saw in my telescopes was one spark of your glory, one least fragment of the order of your creation. You could not be jealous of that, my Lord!" (205). He tries to adapt to the life underground, but "there is not much good spending twelve hours a day in a black hole in the ground all your life long if there's nothing there, no secret, no treasure, nothing hidden" (212). In his explorations, he eventually finds a treasure, however: a silver deposit in an abandoned part of the mine. But once more he is doomed to having his theories rejected, for none of the miners believe in him. One day he disappears. His friends search for him and almost give up, but a few persistent men eventually find him, and along with him the unsuspected vein of raw silver. At the same time they discover the resemblance between the stars above and the silver below: "the veins and branches and knots and nodes shining among broken crystals in the shattered rock, like stars and gatherings of stars, depth below depth without end, the light" (221). The creative mind of the scientist provided the imaginative incentive to make the discovery to which the miners had been blinded by their literalism and their unquestioning acceptance of authority.

"The Field of Vision," originally published in the same year (1973), is thematically related to "The Stars Below." Both stories concern science and religion, both use exploration of the heavens as the basis for the narrative, and both end in the death of the sensitive scientist-protagonist. "The Field of Vision" is, however, futuristic in its setting, and the scientist in this case is an astronaut. After some baffling responses to ground control in Houston, the spaceship *Psyche* returns with its crew of three astronauts seriously affected by their flight. One is apparently blinded, one is physically unhurt but dazed and bewildered, and one is dead. Dr. Hughes, who seems to be blind, reacts strangely to the tests he is subjected to in the hospital. Although his room is kept absolutely dark, he complains about the dazzling bright light. He insists upon wearing dark goggles all the while, for he apparently can see nothing precisely, with everything transfigured into brightness. His surviving fellow astronaut, Temski, has become completely catatonic, but testing also reveals that he has become deaf. The reason for the mysterious death, blindness, and deafness is slowly revealed but never with complete clarity. It appears that the three men have had a vision of divinity in outer space. They have seen the one "true God, immanent in all things" (243). For Dr. Hughes the experience has been a shattering one spiritually and psychologically as well as physically. He has learned that to see God is to be no longer able to see. He laments, "All I have to do is open my eyes, and I see the Face of God. And I'd give all my life just to see one human face again, to see a tree, just a tree, a chair—a plain wooden chair, ordinary—They can keep their God, they can keep their Light. I want the world back. I want questions, not the answer. I want my own life back, and my own death!" (243). Unable to find his life again, he takes back his own death, in suicide. Meanwhile Temski, who perceived God through hearing, makes a kind of recovery. As Hughes explains, those who hear the truth can translate it into words, unlike those who see it. Mystics cannot articulate their visions unless they have heard the Word spoken by the Voice. One day Temski will be able to relate his vision to others in words.

The story is framed by quotations from the seventeenth-century religious poet, Henry Vaughn. Like Hughes, the poet has had a vision described by the opening lines of Vaughn's poem, "The World": "I saw Eternity the other night, / Like a great RING of pure and endless light."[4] The astronaut, unlike the poet, prefers the dark night to the true light. On the day of Hughes's suicide, the *Psyche* (meaning "soul") returns with documents from Mars, constituting the first chapters of the sacred text later to be universally accepted as the "sole vehicle of the One Eternal Truth" (243). The vision of this story is thus doubly ironic, inwardly and outwardly. Like Hughes, Le Guin prefers questions to answers, and this story provides provocative questions, with no easy answers.

Not exactly fantasy or science fiction, "The Good Trip" was published in 1970, when the drug scene was still a popular subject. Although the story is, in a sense, about drugs, it is neither a justification nor a condemnation, but rather a gentle tale of a troubled young man who does not take a chemical trip but rather gets there on his own. Holding the pill packet in his hand and watering a seedling olive-tree, Lewis has the "good" trip in his mind, startled to find sometime later that the packet he holds in his hand is still sealed and he is still pouring the water over the roots of the tree. On the trip he encounters his estranged wife and climbs Mt. Hood, "the higher reality. Eleven thousand feet higher" (113). By no means a major achievement, the story does illustrate Le Guin's virtually unfailing knack for transposing states of mind into convincing literary symbols.

Reception of *The Wind's Twelve Quarters* was, on the whole, positive. Although reviewers largely agree that her short stories are not as impressive as the novels, most find at least a few of the pieces in this collection worthy of equally serious critical attention. One reviewer described Le Guin as "the ideal science fiction writer for readers who ordinarily dislike science fiction,"[5] a comment in accord with the author's interest in the ideas and psychological implications of science rather than its technology and hardware. Another reviewer finds the SF stories the most successful ones in the collection. Those which follow up a real scientific possibility, such as "Nine Lives" and "The Field of Vision," are effective where some of the other more surrealistic pieces, like "Things" and "A Trip to the Head," seem gimmicky because they are not based on a scientifically possible cause.[6]

Orsinian Tales

Orsinian Tales, a collection of eleven short pieces, was published just a year after *The Wind's Twelve Quarters.* The two anthologies have little in common, however. Whereas the earlier book is arranged chronologically, illustrating Le Guin's development over a given period of time, the later book combines her first published story (1961) with some very recently published and others written specifically for this collection. The tales included here are also loosely related to one another in a way that is not true in the earlier collection. Here the arrangement is based on internal factors rather than authorial chronology, and the tales are linked by common features such as setting, theme, and family names.

Furthermore, these are "tales" rather than short stories. As James Bittner has pointed out, the tale is a work of short fiction closed off from the real world, more like a fable or a legend than a short story.[7] It is distanced from the reader through techniques similar to those used by Isak Dinessen and Lord Dunsany, also writers of tales. Although set in an imaginary world, these tales are not fantasy or science fiction. On the other hand, they resemble those genres in their freedom from the limitations of specific time and place. They are not what would be called "escape" reading, for the characters suffer and die, but their suffering and death take place in a country that never existed. The reader's identification is thus distanced both historically and aesthetically.

Le Guin created her imaginary country of Orsinia in 1951, long before she had published anything. As her own given name is derived from "ursa," the Latin word for bear, the Orsinian country is her namesake. Although a product of her imagination, however, it is not a secondary world in the fantasy or SF sense. It is located somewhere in middle or eastern Europe, and the tales contain repeated references to real places like Paris. Each tale is dated at the end, placing the narrative at a definite point in history. As Bittner has pointed out, the final tale in the collection, "Imaginary Countries," is actually the chronological center, as five tales take place before it and five after it. The pattern of narrative movement combines the circular and linear, as it combines realism and fantasy.

"Imaginary Countries," dated 1935, is the central story thematically as well as chronologically in terms of occurrence. It is a strongly autobiographical story, focused on a family consisting of a professor, his wife and three children, two boys and a girl. The girl Zida is the youngest, as Ursula was. The family are about to end their three-month stay at their summer home, which they call Asgard. During the summer the professor has been working on historical research with the help of his student assistant, and the imaginative children have been acting out Norse mythology. The older boy, Stanislas, has found a huge oak tree which he calls Yggdrasil (although he knows that Yggdrasil is an ash) and named a wooded area Loki's Grove. Zida is busy with her unicorn trap (which has not captured one yet), and Paul is building a tunnel to be used in Ragnarok, the end-of-the-world battle which they will enact on the eve of their departure. The mythic role-playing includes the parents, for the professor calls his wife Freya, as they reluctantly conclude the sad business of closing up the beloved place for the long academic year.

The tale obviously reflects the Le Guin family's summers, and the characters' delight in playing mythic roles and creating imaginary countries clearly echoes the author's own interests. It is beautifully wrought, with a strong sense of immediacy combined with a nostalgic air of distance. A brief epilogue spoken in the first person confirms the sense of a far-away event: "all this happened a long time ago, nearly forty years ago; I do not know if it happens now, even in imaginary countries" (209).

Of the five tales taking place before 1935, the date of "Imaginary Countries," the earliest is "The Barrow," dated 1150. This grim narrative returns to the medieval past of the region near Lake Malafrena, a geographical location referred to elsewhere in the tales and later to become the title of a novel. Ostensibly Christian, the primitive people in this remote village actually worship an unspeakable ancient god. A visiting priest becomes the sacrificial victim of the local leader, a young Count who wishes, thereby, to ensure his wife's successful childbirth. Relentless in its inevitable violence, this brief tale is also heavy with irony. The Count's name is subsequently honored in the bad Latin of the church chronicles as a staunch defender of the Church of God.

Another tale from the distant past, "The Lady of Moge" recounts the siege of a castle and the events following it in 1640. The central characters are a princess and an army officer. Although their roles are romantic, theirs is an antiromantic love story in which neither passionate love nor heroic death is achieved. They meet for the first time when they are both nineteen, but pride and circumstances separate them repeatedly through the years until the final scene, when they meet again in their sixties. She has become stout and he skinny, their physical deterioration grotesquely reflecting their awareness of having missed what is worthwhile in life. A powerful sense of loss is imparted in their tale, but so distanced through both time and tone that the reader does not identify with their human failure. It is a poignant tale, heavy with thoughts of what might have been, but all perceived as through a mist.

The other three tales set prior to "Imaginary Countries" all take place in the early twentieth century. Setting figures prominently in all three, where landscape achieves a moral resonance that deepens the actual events of the plot. In the relatively long tale "Brothers and Sisters" (1910), the setting is the "karst," a limestone plain, contrasted with the mountains where "The Barrow" takes place. "In the mountains the streams ran noisy in the sunlight; there were waterfalls. Here on the karst the rivers ran underground, silent in dark veins of stone. You could ride a horse all day from Sfaroy Kampe and still not reach the mountains, still be in the limestone dust" (84). The characters are closely identified with the rock and dust of the karst. When one man is injured in a rockslide, his friend remarks, "So he got a couple of tons of rock in the face, it won't hurt him, he's made of the stuff. He wasn't born, he was quarried out" (84).

He later applies the image to himself: "Here we all are," he went on, "lying around each of us under our private piles of rocks" (86). The passions, ambitions, fears, loves of the characters all seem an outcome of the solid rock landscape, covered only by a couple of inches of dirt, and the overwhelming absence of trees signifies the spiritual vacuity of the thwarted people living on the karst. The deterministic vision of life presented here is depressing, but the image of bedrock which dissolves in water serves to distance the tale by removing its foundation in reality.

In "The Forest" (1920) the scene moves from the rocky karst to the forest, where a tale told in retrospect serves to demonstrate that there can, indeed, be a justifiable murder. Again setting is important, for a main character lives "in a half-ruined house at the end of nowhere," an overt symbol of something missing in his own nature: "a gap, a forgotten place, a break in his humanity" (28). Once again, distancing is a major factor, for the passions that provoke the homicide are removed by the third person narrative of a long-ago event.

"Conversations at Night" (1920) focuses on a decaying house and garden and concerns the love of a strong-willed young woman for a blind man. Resisting both parental opposition and the man's own bitterness, the woman, Lisha, finds the inner strength that will permit her to share his life. Her moral courage leads them away from "the silent garden with its beautiful, ruined, staring house" (70) and out into the city streets, where an unknown fate awaits them. This tale, like several others in this collection, is essentially a prologue to an unknown future.

The remaining five tales take place after 1935. "An Die Musik" (1938) was Le Guin's first published story, originally appearing in the *Western Humanities Review* in 1961. Concerned with the theme of art and the role of the artist, it celebrates the devotion of the musician Gaye to his own art of composition. A gifted composer, Gaye is also a trapped man. After his father's death, he has undertaken to support his mother, his wife, and their three children. He is forced to spend most of his time working in a factory and giving music lessons, so that he has little time or energy left for creating music. What little he has written has been judged by professionals as remarkably good, but he is caught in a moral dilemma. He cannot abandon his family, nor can be forsake his music. Unable to solve the practical problem, what he achieves is a new understanding of the validity of the creative process. He is spiritually strengthened by his ability to justify his

profound need to create music. What good is music, he asks. "None,
Gaye thought, and that is the point. To the world and its states and
armies and factories and Leaders, music says, 'You are irrelevant';
and, arrogant and gentle as a god, to the suffering man it says only,
'Listen.' For being saved is not the point. Music saves nothing. Mer-
ciful, uncaring, it denies and breaks down all the shelters, the houses
men build for themselves, that they may see the sky" (168). Le Guin
once remarked that the purpose of art is "to persuade us to rejoice
and to teach us how to praise."[8] This tale affirms that definition in
its celebration of Gaye's devotion to his art.

"The Road East" (1956) is a vignette, a sharply delineated portrait
of a woman who refuses to believe in evil and of her son, who makes
the crucial decision to become involved in dangerous political actions.
Mrs. Eray rejects the notion of all evil, even illness. Although her
husband died from cancer, she continues to believe that it was all in
his mind. She closes out the world, refusing to acknowledge the political turmoil and social suffering that exist outside her own serene
household. At the end of the tale her son leaves, about to risk his life
in the revolutionary events taking place in their city. She is left
alone, her denial of evil having become a denial of reality. Once more
we have a tale which is a prologue to an event. The end is a
beginning.

The other three tales of recent times are also political in implication. "The Fountains" (1960) concerns a dissident scientist faced with
a difficult moral decision. He finds himself in Paris where he is
tempted to seek political asylum. He defects without any effort to do
so, but finding himself a free man, chooses not to remain. The fountains of Versailles, which he feels are his, lead him back to his own
country. "Knowing now that he was both a king and a thief and so
was at home anywhere, what turned him to his own land was mere
fidelity" (5).

"A Week in the Country" (1962) shows a young couple in love
caught up in a world of political violence and betrayal. They are unable to protect or even to mourn their friend who is shot in the street,
but in a world that baffles and threatens them they cling to each
other in some sort of hope. "No good letting go, is there." (149).
"The House" (1965) also focuses on a couple, in this case long di-
vorced but still loyal to each other in an abiding love and in their
isolation from the political world about them. The house which has
been in the man's family for years has been taken over by the govern-

ment, and its empty appearance—locked gate, drawn blinds—asserts his own sense of alienation and fragmentation: "nothing holds together, everything is broken off, broken up—people, years, events. All in pieces, fragments, not linked together. Nothing weighs anything anymore. You start from nothing, and so it doesn't matter which way you go. But it *must* matter" (180). Their marriage offers them weight and stability, and they realize that their destination is simply each other.

The four most modern tales all have urban settings, as opposed to the earlier tales which take place in rural settings such as mountains, forest, and karst. Consonant with the city location is the pervasive yet somewhat elusive political milieu. The characters in these recent tales are caught up in a world which challenges their integrity and leaves them rootless. In the unspecified central European setting, these events find people adrift on tides of historical flux. James Bittner described these tales as "acts of imagination that transform the calamity of history that is Central Europe into a celebration of the individual's ability to survive bad times."[9]

Each tale also represents a moral turning point in the lives of its principal characters. Each introduces a relationship with an oppressive environment—social or geographical or both—which must be challenged in the name of spiritual freedom. Although the actual external events are often slight, they are crystallized into a series of spiritual crises which have universal meaning. Although these external events are also often depressing, the endings of the tales frequently imply new beginnings. Le Guin reveals a profound compassion for the poor, the trapped, and the disillusioned, but she also reveals a way out of their suffering. Love for another often proves to be the road to freedom for both.

The reader coming to *Orsinian Tales* from Le Guin's fantasy and SF will likely be startled by the difference in tone and substance, but their artistic quality deserves the close reading they demand. Not entirely mainstream fiction, they represent a kind of medium between realism and fantasy, with a base in an imaginary country where the pretended ash is really an oak. For Le Guin it is also a flowering of her interest in the moral meanings of history to the individual living through it.

Critical reception of *Orsinian Tales* was on the whole surprised but favorable. Most reviewers agree with the assessment of the collection as "at once timely and timeless, rich, intelligently peopled," and with the recommendation that "each evocative portrait is worthy of every reader's leisurely perusal."[10] One dissenting view complained that "in the end, the Esperanto speak names, the defamiliarized settings, the cerebral contrivedness of it all work too busily against the stories' would-be humane themes of love, freedom, and fidelity in the hostile world of anti-contingent politics."[11] The final statement of themes is certainly accurate, but the objections voiced here seem to reflect that reader's failure to perceive both distancing techniques which Le Guin uses here, fitting the notion of "tale" as opposed to "story," and the innovative combination of mainstream and science-fiction point of view. The best of the stories here rank with the best of Le Guin elsewhere.

Very Far Away from Anywhere Else

Very Far Away from Anywhere Else was published the same year as *Orsinian Tales*. A very short novel, it is aimed at an adolescent audience, which is at once its main strength and its principal weakness. The sound basis of its appeal to the young adult reader may well limit its attraction for a mature reading audience. The main characters are Owen Griffiths, a brilliant high school student, and Natalie Fields, a gifted musician of the same age. They are both outsiders, at odds with their families and their schoolmates. Owen relates the story, describing himself in a tone of ironic diffidence. He sees himself as "a bright little jerk" and an introvert, one who does not "belong."

When the story begins, he has just received an astonishing present from his father for his seventeenth birthday. That insensitive man has bought his son, at considerable personal sacrifice, an expensive new car. Owen, who likes to walk and bicycle, does not want a car and is, in fact, embarrassed by its presence in front of the house. Furthermore, he wants to go to MIT, and sees the car as a major expense virtually canceling out his college education.

In this quandary Owen, who is also an only child and in need of someone to talk to, meets Natalie on the bus, and the two strike up a conversation. It turns out that she, too, is an introvert, interested in further education and misunderstood by her well-meaning family. Owen is able to share his private dreams and ambitions with this young woman, who is totally dedicated to a career in music. He even tells her about his imaginary country, Thorn, which he has never been able to share with anyone else. The two young people spend time alone together, until on one occasion when they go swimming, Owen makes a sexual advance. Natalie rejects him—although she has just told him that she loves him—and Owen is momentarily angry about what seems to him a rebuff. He takes her home, then drives around for a while in his unwanted car, distracted and confused by the incident. Careless in his brooding state of mind, he has an accident in which the car is destroyed. Fortunately Owen is not hurt, and he quickly realizes that the insurance money could give him a start at MIT.

He does not see Natalie again for a few weeks, but one evening he drifts into a concert where some of her original musical compositions are being played. He is very moved by the music and sees her afterwards in order to tell her about his reaction. Meeting again as friends over a cup of "weird tea," they realize the importance of maintaining their unusual friendship. Natalie assures Owen of his ability to cope with his problems, in spite of his own assertions of doubt. She also persuades him that he must go to MIT in order to fulfill his outstanding abilities in science and mathematics. Her own quiet, firm faith in her musical future inspires him to a comparable feeling about his own career plans. She understands that they are both "different," both solitary individuals, that each must live in Thorn, but also that each must achieve self-fulfillment in this world as well. As a result of her influence, he gets all A's for the first time in high school ("If you are going to be an egghead, you might as well be a hardboiled one" [86]), and gets a scholarship to MIT to carry him beyond the insurance money. At the end of the story, he is ready to go to college in the fall. Perhaps they will meet again in the east, perhaps in Thorn.

This slender book will come as a surprise to Le Guin readers, for it is different from anything preceding it. As one reviewer put it, this is "a small jewel of a book."[12] It is a jewel for a limited readership, perhaps, but highly successful within that target group. The author has much to say here about subjects of importance to the high-school generation—conformity, hypocrisy, and differences between real and pseudointellectualism as well as outright antiintellectualism. Owen's voice is convincing, for what he discovers about himself is never filtered through an adult consciousness. His voice is that of a highly intelligent person, assailed by all kinds of self-doubts and painfully sensitive to his status as an outsider. Natalie's own fierce idealism and unswerving devotion to her music provide him with the much needed opportunity to communicate with a kindred spirit. Their friendship is one of equals, thriving on mutual need and fulfillment. Each fills a void in the life of the other.

One of the admirable features of the work is the fact that both Owen and Natalie go beyond both stereotypes and male-female role-playing. Their sexual attraction is admitted but subordinated to those concerns of much higher importance to both of them. They achieve a meaningful friendship, neither to be destroyed by easy surrender to passionate impulse nor maintained at the expense of denying sexual identity. It is one of those very rare adolescent books about a genuine, convincing, successful male-female friendship.

Although "more thought-provoking than moving" as one reviewer put it, this story of the conflicts of adolescence is very appealing.[13] The characterization is sensitive, the conflict between the need for love and the need for identity is well handled, and the message about the importance of creativity and purposefulness in life is unobtrusively communicated in the very natural dialogue of the two young protagonists. Owen's made-up country of Thorn, for which Natalie writes a Thorn quintet, adds an imaginative dimension to their relationship.

On the whole, these three works—the short novel and the two short-story collections—reveal Le Guin's talent in the medium of the brief narrative. The narrow range and focus of short fiction make demands on the writer that are quite different from those of the novel. Although some writers, like Henry James and D. H. Lawrence, have mastered both forms equally, not all novelists find themselves at ease in the more circumscribed structure of the short story. Le Guin's performance as demonstrated in these three works, however, is of consistently high quality. Some of the short pieces are seminal portions of later novels, and some are minor masterpieces in their own right. The variety in choice of subject demonstrates her interest in innovation and her versatility.

Chapter Eight

"The Eye of the Heron,"
Malafrena, and
The Beginning Place

"The Eye of the Heron"

"The Eye of the Heron" was published in a feminist science-fiction collection called *Millennial Women,* edited by Virginia Kidd.[1] The five other pieces included in the collection are short stories, but Le Guin's contribution is the equivalent of a full-length (178 pages) novel.

The setting is the planet Victoria, colonized by two groups of people from Earth. The original settlement took place a little over a century ago, when the government of Brasil-America sent several thousand criminals, most of them men, to establish a penal colony. They were sent to Victoria in a one-way spaceship to assure their permanent exile. The second contingent of colonists were the People of the Peace, sent by the government of Canamerica fifty-five years ago because of their refusal to help the war effort. These people banded together in a Long March which started in Moskva, crossed Europe, and ended in Lisboa where they took ship to the Free Land. Along the route of the march, they were joined by people from all over the world. When they finally arrived in the harbor of Montral, they were imprisoned and forced to labor in making weapons. Only 2000 were permitted to take the single remaining one-way spaceship to Victoria. There they established their own town, called Shantih.

The two settlements, Victoria City and the Town of Shantih, have since lived in a state of uneasy tension. For a time cooperation seemed possible because the two settlements complemented each other. The Shantih dwellers were good farmers and produced most of the food for all of the settlers, while the residents of the city were technologically advanced and manufactured the tools, clothing, and other necessary items. The city people, however, now feel superior to the others, whom they regard as peasants and whose community they insult by referring to them as Shanty-dwellers. The city has developed a hierarchical society controlled by bosses who rule like petty monarchs, while the town people have a working democracy.

In recent years the growing differences in ideology have intensified, and the People of the Peace have been searching for a new place to settle. Several of their men have explored and discovered a valley about twenty miles away, which they regard as their "promised land." When they ask permission of the city council to establish a new settlement there, however, they are rebuffed. One of the most powerful of the city bosses, Falco, does not want to lose his farm laborers and tries to discourage their move by imprisoning some of their leaders. Boss Falco, arrogant, strong-willed, and prone to violence, finds himself in direct opposition to the gentle, soft-spoken leader of the People of the Peace, Lev.

Such is the social conflict on Victoria. Parallel to it and exacerbated by it is the personal conflict within the mind and heart of Falco's daughter, Luz Marina. Although she has been reared in the aristocratic ways of her domineering father, she has also had contact with Lev and his people through her schooling, a fact regretted by Falco, who concludes that it is a mistake to send peasants and women to school: "peasants become insolent, the women become boring" (143).

Although Luz has learned to read and write, she has never touched a book. "Books were too precious to be used in school; there were only a few dozen of them in the world. They were kept in the Archives" (138). But one day Luz discovers the book left behind by a doctor at her house. A first-aid manual, it is full of words that she does not understand, but the title page clearly confirms what she has learned in school, namely that Victoria was settled by criminals. Her own ancestors were thieves and murderers. This discovery coupled with her admiration for Lev and his people leads her to defy her father, who is eager to marry her off to one of his most ambitious followers, Herman Macmilan.

Luz's conflicting loyalties are further intensified by her dislike of Macmilan, who is a handsome but unscrupulous ruffian. She has, however, always taken for granted that marriage is the only future possible for her. Her ideas on that subject are changed by her conversations with Vera, a middle-aged woman of the People of the Peace, who has been placed under arrest in the Falco home. Luz is surprised to learn that Vera never married, for she sees the scorned existence of an old maid as the only alternative to marriage. "You make bonnets for other women's babies. . . . You get laughed at" (198). Vera's passionate response reveals to the young woman that there are other choices, that other worthwhile lives are indeed possible for women whether married or not: "You know, if we sit in the back room, with babies or without babies, and leave all the rest of the world to the men, then of course the men will do everything and be everything. Why should they? They're only half the human race" (199).

Eventually Luz's rebellious spirit leads her to action when she overhears plans for a raid on the town. She slips away from Casa Falco to go warn the People of the Peace of the impending threat. At first Lev does not believe her account of a troop of armed men, trained by young Macmilan to capture Lev and a few other hostages and thereby force the People of the Peace to violent retaliation. When Luz explains that she is offering herself as hostage, however, he is convinced and accepts her as one of his group. He explains to her the four procedural steps followed by his people in dealing with their opponents. The first step is to try negotiation and arbitration of the problem. Step two is noncooperation and step three is issuing an ultimatum. The final step, if the others fail, is civil disobedience.

Lev's admirable theory of peaceful resistance does not work out in practice. When the people of the town face the people of the city, Macmilan's troops open fire, destroying all hopes for peace. Lev is killed in the volley of gunfire, along with fifteen other people of Shantih and eight men of the city. Vera is deafened, as she had been standing near Macmilan, so that when he fired his gun the explosion was right beside her head. After this tragic confrontation, Luz makes her final choice. She will go along with the People of the Peace as they move to their new settlement in the valley.

The planet Victoria, as the setting of this novel, is not delineated with the detailed immediacy of most of Le Guin's other imaginary worlds. Climate and geography are scarcely referred to at all, and the way of life of both settlements is scarcely distinguishable from what it would be on Earth. Only the unique flora and fauna figure into the narrative, and these function largely as symbols rather than setting. Three of these take on special significance: a tree, an animal, and a bird. The ringtree, the wotsit, and the heron (which is really not a heron, but is called so) are all closely associated with theme and character.

The ringtree is introduced surreptitiously in the opening sentence of the novel. "In the sunlight in the center of a ring of trees Lev sat cross-legged, his head bent above his hands" (124). What the reader does not realize until three chapters later is that the ring of trees is not a coincidental feature of the landscape, but a precise stage in the cyclic development of the ringtree. With strict botanical accuracy of style, Le Guin explains how the ringtree begins as a single, fast-growing seedling with red leaves, which in maturity flowers with large honey-colored blossoms. The fertilized flowers eventually are transformed into hard-shelled seeds, most of which drop off, leaving at last one single seed on a high branch. Then, some sunny afternoon, "the seed performed its extraordinary feat: time-ripened and sun-warmed, it exploded. It went off with a bang that could be heard for miles" (168). Around the remaining central stem, the several hundred seedlets exploded from the shell burrow into the ground. "Ten years later, and for a century or two after that, from twenty to sixty copper-leaved trees stood in a perfect ring about the long-vanished central stem" (169). In time the seeds of the fruit of these trees are dropped in a spot from which the single seed will germinate to produce a single tree, and it the single seed. Thus "the cycle was repeated, from ringtree to tree-ring, timelessly" (169).

The image of the cyclical reproduction of circle from center and center from circle is reflected in the characterization of both the individuals and the groups in the novel. Lev is the idealistic center of his peace-loving people, as his initial posture indicates. Falco as a leader is also a center, but his circle—his elaborate fortresslike house—has become his prison, so that he cannot move outside it. The spiritual center of his household is his beloved daughter, who rejects him and elects to join the group opposed to his tyranny.

The image of the center is also related to the concept of the feminine. As Vera explains to Luz in their conversation about the role of women in the world: "A woman has a center, is a center. But a man isn't, he's a reaching out. So he reaches out and grabs things and piles them up around him and says, I'm this, I'm that, this is me, that's me, I'll prove that I am me!" (199–200). The association of the masculine with both the aggressive and the acquisitive recalls the remarks about war in *The Left Hand of Darkness* and the attitude toward possessions explored in *The Dispossessed*. That the feminine focus on the center is not limited to women, however, is made clear by the character of Lev. The concepts of masculine and feminine transcend biological sex differences.

The wotsit is a diminutive creature, its amusing name derived from its transformational nature. Small enough to fit in the palm of a hand, it looks like a toad with wings and three gold eyes, one on each side of its head and one in the middle. It can change color, becoming blue at times and at times sprouting pinkish fronds that give it the appearance of a feathery ball. It can also assume a flat, mothlike appearance. When one takes flight from its perch on Lev's hand, its movement is described vividly: "The six tiny, warm feet gripped and released, delicate and precise. It paused on the tip of his fingers and cocked its head to look at him with its right eye while its left and central eyes scanned the sky. It gathered itself into an arrow shape, shot out two translucent wings twice the length of its body, and flew off in a long effortless glide toward a sunlit slope beyond the ring of trees" (125). At the end of the novel, Luz and her fellow settlers are delighted to find that their new home is graced by the presence of these lovely, fragile creatures.

Equally lovely and even more significant thematically are the herons. Actually they are not authentic herons, but the stilt-legged, pale grey fish eaters that live in pairs by the pool resemble the herons on Earth, and are therefore called herons on Victoria. They are silent creatures, not afraid of men but staring at them from a safe distance with their "large, round eyes as colorless as water" (170). This large round eye becomes the symbolic center of the book. When Lev retires for quiet reflective thought beside the pool, his moment of stillness is the gift of the heron. "One of the herons walked silently out into the water from the far side of the pool. Lifting its narrow head it gazed at Lev. He gazed back, and for an instant was caught in that round, transparent eye, as depthless as the sky clear of clouds; and the moment was round, transparent, silent, a moment at the center of all moments, the eternal present moment of the silent animal" (174).[2] After the death of Lev, Luz assumes the role of center, and the new camp built by the People of Peace is called Heron Pool. The novel ends with a description of the herons watched by Luz, who pauses in her work for a moment of stillness while she observes them.

Le Guin's symbolic association of her heron with the feminine and with the mystic center is based on traditional favorable religious symbolism of the bird. Both a solar bird and a bird of the waters, the heron has become a symbol of morning and of the generation of life. In Egyptian mythology the heron is the first transformer of the soul after death, thus associated with regeneration and renewal. A sacred bird also in Taoism, it is associated with vigilance and quietness and signifies the ability to enter into higher states of consciousness. Its very nature therefore suggests the quiet peaceful resolution of the People of the Peace as well as the spiritual qualities of Lev and Luz. Naming the new settlement Heron Pool is a hopeful sign for the future.

"The Eye of the Heron" has not been reviewed separately but only as the major offering in the collection called *Millennial Women*. Reviewers of the collection generally agree that, as one reviewer put it, this novel is "the real gem."[3] The one notable weakness of the novel is implied in the very praise given it by one reviewer who writes, "the style is polished, the story line compelling, and the struggle between good and evil—exemplified by the confrontation between a ruthless, brutal culture and a band of colonists with a tradition of peace and nonviolent resistance—is timeless."[4] Timeless but too explicit. All of the colonists are presented as gentle people, and all of the Falco contingent brutes. In this way, the conflict is more like the one in *The Word for World Is Forest,* where the Terran invaders are totally evil and the native Creechies all lovable, than that in either *The Left Hand of Darkness* or *The Dispossessed,* where ambiguity adds complexity to the portrayal of both opposed societies. Also rather like *The Word for World Is Forest* is the effectiveness of the natural symbols. The forest-mind of Athshe resembles the still center of the herons at the pool. One of the strongest features of "The Eye of the Heron" is the character of Luz, the strong-willed young woman who chooses to turn her back on her privileged role in a class-structured society in favor of joining the pacifist outcasts moving to a new settlement. Readers may not find this novel a masterpiece, but they will not find it a disappointment.

Malafrena

Malafrena (1979) returns to Orsinia. This substantial historical novel (Le Guin's longest, 343 pages) takes place in the country of Orsinia during the nineteenth century when most of Europe was in the grip of the Austrian empire. The specific setting alternates between the country estate, Val Malafrena, and the capital city, Krasnoy, which also figured in *Orsinian Tales.* The hero is a young man, Itale Sorde, heir to the estate and a political revolutionary who goes to the city to fight for freedom. After his experiences there, including imprisonment, he returns to his country home. The outline of the narrative thus repeats the familiar circular journey. "To go is to return," but the events on this journey are not at all familiar.

At first this novel reminds the reader more of Tolstoy or Stendhal than Le Guin. The vast European canvas with its complex political background and individual foreground is like the world of *The Red and the Black*, where the destinies of men are set against the destinies of empires. It is actually a *Bildungsroman* focused on the young idealist and his fortunes on the shaky stage of a corrupt and tyrannical government. The opening section establishes the almost idyllic atmosphere of the family estate which is placed a hundred miles from anywhere. The Sorde family are landed gentry, and although they work hard to maintain the estate theirs is essentially an aristocratic way of life. Rural, it is lacking in urban sophistication, but it is secure, and the family conversation typically runs to chores and gossip.

Itale is a student and an intellectual. When he dares to post an anti-Austrian poem on the chapel door at the university, he is put on probation and decides to leave home in order to undertake further political activism in the city. The family—including his ailing father and a younger sister—and the friends he leaves behind are thereafter in the novel the subject of alternating chapters. The sense of contrast between the sturdiness and sweetness of the *domey* and the bustle and danger of the city maintains a dynamic forward movement in the narrative.

In the large city of Krasnoy, Itale edits a liberal journal, establishes a close friendship with a writer whom he has always admired, and becomes the lover of a baroness. His life is full, and his reputation is made. But his idealistic career as political activist is abruptly cut short by his arrest and subsequent incarceration for two years in the notorious prison of St. Lazar. When he is eventually released through the intervention of the baroness, he is a broken man, racked by typhus and maltreatment.

Itale returns home to the family estate, where he is able to resume his life. He is eventually able to talk about his prison experience: "I couldn't think about much. My mind wouldn't hold. It was always dark. The closest I could get to God was mathematics. . . . It wasn't much good. Do you know what worked? Not very often, but the only thing that ever did. I wouldn't think of God's love. I would think about the water inside the boat house in afternoon in summer, when the light comes from underneath. Or the plates—the dinner plates, the ones we used last night. If I could see them I was all right. So

much for the things of the spirit . . . " (336).[5] His return heralds a
new beginning as well. Just before his departure, he had given his
friend Piera a copy of *Vita Nova*. At that time he thought his own
new life would begin in Krasnoy. Now that he is back, he knows
that beginnings are a matter of life itself. As he explains to Piera,
"I didn't know why I left till I came back—I have to come back to
find that I have to go again. I haven't even begun the new life yet.
I am always beginning it. I will die beginning it" (342).

Itale Sorde's circular journey is different from that of the other Le
Guin heroes in that it is more externalized in its presentation. It lacks
the introspective dimension of the Hainish/Earthsea voyagers. Itale is
affected by events, but he does not develop inwardly through them.
He is involved in the spectacular movement of history, but he is not
shaped by it. In this way he is more like the characters in *Orsinian
Tales* than in the science fiction or fantasy. And although Orsinia is
an imaginary country, it is not a secondary world. Krasnoy breathes
the same air as Warsaw and Paris, the vivid scenes in the political
assembly are authentic in style and vintage.

In short, *Malafrena* is an excellent historical novel about a real historical period, although set in an imaginary eastern European country. It is equally effective in offering public and private scenes. The
debate in the assembly, the mob violence on the streets, the jail cell
in St. Lazar are described vividly and movingly, as are the more quiet
scenes of a family dinner, of the aged aunt winding yarn into balls,
of a shy man's proposal of marriage. Lindsay Duquid, in a review for
the *Times Literary Supplement,* described it as "a remarkable feat of
imagination. Background, characters and dialogue all have a fully autonomous life: there is a minimum of 'period' writing and of intrusive
passages of historical information."[6] Perhaps the one fault of the novel
is a certain falling off near the end, when the strands of narrative are
described through letters rather than resolved in immediate scenes.
But this is by no means a major blemish, and the novel remains a
satisfying reading experience and a testimonial to the remarkable versatility of its author.

The Beginning Place

At the end of "The Eye of the Heron," Luz describes the new settlement as "a beginning place," and near the end of *Malafrena,* Itale
asserts that he is "always beginning" the new life. These remarks

foreshadow the appearance in 1980 of *The Beginning Place*. The striking originality and complexity of this new work prompted one reviewer to remark that although it could not be called science fiction,
nonetheless "mainstream" is "too colorless a word for the opaline literary waters Le Guin has chosen as her own."[7] Sharply juxtaposing
elements of fantasy and realism, *The Beginning Place* cannot be easily
categorized, although another reviewer suggested dismissing both SF
and mainstream in favor of allegory.

An initial look at the plot is useful, but the actual events in the
narrative do not carry the burden of meaning in this highly symbolic
novel. The surface story concerns two young people who seek to escape from the thwarting circumstances of life at home. Hugh, aged
twenty, works as a checker in a supermarket although his heart is set
on going to school to study library science. He is the victim of his
neurotic mother who insists that he stay home every minute when he
is not working because she is terrified at the prospect of being alone
in an empty house. Hugh's life is a meaningless round of routine job,
TV dinners, and petty arguments. Irene, about nineteen, is the victim of her drunken stepfather, who subjects her to continual sexual
harassment. Her own father is dead, and her remarried mother is too
preoccupied with her five younger children to notice or to care. Irene
has tried sharing an apartment with unmarried friends, but finds herself caught in the middle of their domestic squabbles.

Since she was thirteen, Irene has been escaping periodically to a
place she once discovered while trying to run away. It is a verdant
area across a river where it is always twilight. Time seems to stand
still in this strange place, but there is an inhabited village. One day
Hugh, also running away from his desperately frustrating existence,
discovers the same area and keeps returning to it for the serenity it
offers him. Since his watch always stops in the twilight realm, he is
not missed at home.

Eventually Hugh and Irene meet in this mysterious world across
the river, and Hugh learns that the villagers have been expecting the
arrival of a hero who will save them from some unexplained danger.
Although Irene does not like Hugh, whom she regards as an intruder
in her private dreamworld, she goes with him on this ominous mission. The source of danger turns out to be a hideous dragonlike
monster, which Hugh is supposed to slay with the sword given him
by the villagers. Although they are both sick with fear, Irene drives
the monster from its cave and Hugh kills it with the sword, becom-

ing seriously wounded in the attack. Irene helps get him to safety
and back to the daylight world, where she signals a passing motorist
who rushes them to the hospital. Hugh and Irene have now come to
love each other and begin to plan their life together.

The plot is a strange one, and the sheer suspense, particularly re-
garding the nature of the unknown evil which threatens the village,
enhances its effectiveness. More importantly, however, this entertaining but enigmatic plot is in itself but the literal manifestation of the
underlying symbolic structure which generates it. The quotation
from Borges which serves as an epigram to the novel points to a symbolic reading: "Que rio es esta por el cual corre el Ganges?" (What
river is it through which the Ganges flows?) Borges's question suggests that there is a difference between the actual physical river
Ganges and the conceptual river which contains its meaning. The
idea of a sacred river provides the metaphysical river bed through
which the literal waves of the Ganges flow. Similarly in this novel
the idea of a quest for a new beginning provides the conceptual passage through which the adventures in the two worlds work their way.

A narrative structure which juxtaposes two contrary worlds is a familiar device in Le Guin's fiction, but only here and in "The New
Atlantis" are the opposed worlds represented in different literary
form. The home lives of Hugh and Irene are described in realistic
terms while the twilight kingdom across the river is drawn in the
mode of fantasy. Life along the metropolitan freeway is in fact presented as a satirical vignette of sprawling surburban emptiness, while
life in the village of Tembreabrezi seems misty and remote. Walking
along the freeway, Hugh finds: "Rubbish of paper and metal and
plastic underfoot, the air lashed and staggering with suction winds
and the ground shuddering as each truck approached and passed, ear-
drums battered by noise and nothing to breathe but burnt rubber and
diesel fumes" (3).[8] On the other hand, in the forested world he finds
the fragrance of mint and the gentle sound of a stream: "At the root
of the quietness was the music of the water" (5). In temporal terms,
back home the oven timer is set to ring when the TV dinner has fin-
ished cooking, but in the "beginning place" all time pieces cease to
function. As in the pastoral world of Shakespeare's *As You Like It,*
"there are no clocks in the forest."

As in traditional myth and folklore, the river serves as a threshhold
between the two worlds. Each time that Hugh crosses the river, he
undergoes a ritual cleansing, leaving the moral as well as physical dirt

and grime of his urban existence behind him. Sometimes the path to the village is easy to find, sometimes it is quite obscure, and Hugh gets lost. Irene has learned that the "gateway" through the trees disappears for periods of time only to return again suddenly. The ambiguities of location and the shifting points of entry recall the double worlds of Celtic mythology.

The twilight world is referred to frequently by Irene as the "ain" country, from a line in an old ballad. "When the flower is in the bud/ and the leaf is on the tree/the lark will sing me home/to my ain countrie" (110). The mysterious landscape is not only Irene's "own" country, for it also becomes such for Hugh. " 'This is my home,' he said to the earth and rocks and trees, and with his lips almost on the water, whispered, 'I am you. I am you' " (55). For both of the young people, the country across the river is also the terrain of their own psyches. In that twilight realm they journey deep within themselves.

Just as the river has a traditional mythic meaning as a point of entry to another world, so the twilight has the connotation of an "in-between" world. The region between one state and another, twilight suggests ambivalence, the blurred dividing line between the end of one cycle and the beginning of another. For Hugh and Irene the twilight world across the river signifies a transition, with the uncertainty that characterizes the meeting point between ending and beginning. The half-light of this mysterious kingdom is clearly not Edenic, as some reviewers have thought. It is by no means a paradisal state with but one serpent to be disposed of. Although the young visitors feel a sense of rebirth in the natural environment, their encounters with the inhabitants reveal a strained atmosphere of fear, danger, and tension. Local conversation tends toward gloom and anxiety. Furthermore the total lack of music is a portentous feature of this world. No one sings, not even the children. The complete absence of melody hangs heavy in the air, making the silence oppressive.

The journey across the river and into the twilight also represents a quest for both Hugh and Irene. Both are moving from adolescence to maturity, a journey so far deeply troubled by their unhappy experiences with their parents of the opposite sex. Hugh's nagging mother and Irene's vulgar stepfather are distorted images of the feminine and the masculine in the lives of these young people. Their escape to—and then from—the "ain" country brings about for both of them a normal, wholesome awareness of the opposite sex. Hugh is freed from his "devouring mother" and Irene from her "ogre" stepfather as a result of their adventures there. The twilight world becomes for them a "beginning place" of adult sexuality.

Hugh's quest is inaugurated in his need to escape from his mother. His futile and frustrating way of life is a trap devised by this paranoid selfish woman who has virtually enslaved him to her own neurotic routine. Since her separation from her husband, she has been restless, insecure, and terrified at the prospect of being alone. In the past seven years she and Hugh have lived in five different states. She insists on his coming home directly after work although she frequently calls him up to say that she is visiting friends and will be home late herself. In these cases she orders him to watch the first part of the evening TV program that she will miss so that he can report it to her. When they are together their evening meals consist of TV dinners and banal conversation, much of it spiced by her snide remarks about his irresponsibility, his overweight, his many other flaws of character and physique. There is always a knife's edge in her nagging voice.

At work Hugh meets a mother surrogate in the person of Donna, a vivacious and somewhat maternal woman who befriends him. Donna is forty-five, with "a lot of dark red hair, which she had recently got made into a fashionable mane of curls and tendrils that made her look twenty from behind and sixty face on" (15). Hugh's need for a mother is reflected even in his sexual daydreams, where he imagines himself suckling the breasts of a waitress he remembers from years past. In a moment of bitterness Hugh concludes that he was "born without parents" (107).

When Hugh first sees Irene in the twilight world he does not even recognize her as a female. Clad in jeans and white shirt, Irene has removed his sleeping bag and tried to scare him into never coming back to her world. He identifies her jeering voice telling him to get out as that of a small black-eyed and black-haired boy. Later, however, when he returns to find his way to the village, he meets a local girl whose beauty wins him. Allia, daughter of one of the local leaders, Lord Horn, is a pale, fragile girl whose wan fairness catches his fancy. She seems to him a realization of his idealized feminine nature, his anima. Her blondness makes all blond women attractive to him, and her delicacy makes him a champion of all that is delicate. He surrenders to the fascination of this archetypally feminine figure. She is described in numinous language: "Beneath every word he said or heard, within everything he saw or did, lay her name, and around her name like a halo, an armor of light, the unshaken joy" (101). His deepest desire is to have the opportunity to die for her. "He felt in himself the longing, the yearning to give so greatly to the beloved that nothing was left, to give all, all. To protect and guard her, to serve her, to die for her—the thought was unendurably sweet" (101).

In the grip of this idealized woman (what Goethe called the "ewig-Weibliche" or eternally feminine), Hugh is ready to accept the challenge laid on him by the leaders of the village. He is able to take on the role of savior although he is not at all sure what it is that he is to save them from. Allia ceremonially presents him with the sword to use against this evil, whatever it turns out to be, and the lumpish twenty-year old grocery checker sets off on his strange knightly quest. Although Allia knows the way, she is too weak in flesh and spirit to accompany the hero. Irene sees this same fair maiden as a "mealy-madonna-faced girl" (85).

The monster which Hugh is fated to slay is female. Neither Hugh nor Irene, who accompanies him on the quest, knows this at first, and only Irene knows it after the creature is slain and Hugh lies unconscious near its huge carcass. She sees the white monster's forelegs shaped like human arms: "woman's arms, and those were breasts, pointed like a sow's teats, between the arms and lower down the belly" (156). Even after Irene manages to extricate Hugh's body from underneath she does not tell him about the sex of the creature. But now that Hugh has slain this monstrous perversion of all that is female, he is free from the negative archetype. Gone from Hugh's troubled soul are both the cruelly nagging mother and the frail maiden needing protection. He is now able to achieve a normal relationship with a real woman. He finds in his companion—whom he once mistook for a boy—a woman he can love.

Like Hugh, Irene needs to escape, for like him, she has had only a negative experience with the opposite sex. She is sensitive about the loss of her father, feeling that she is "the daughter of a ghost" (74). The stepfather who has replaced him is a total perversion of the paternal. He abuses her mother when he is drunk, and tries to rape Irene when he is sober. Her teenage has been a nightmare of fear, knowing that his lustful presence lurked around every corner waiting to catch her alone. "Once he caught her behind the tractor shed, and she tried to joke with him and make fun of him, because she could not believe he was serious until he was all over her suddenly heavy as a mattress, smothering and brutal, and she got away with a moment of luck and a sprained wrist" (72–3). During this same period, her close friend is the victim of a rape. Irene becomes embittered about men and resolves never to fall in love.

Her younger brother had been her defender at home for a time, but in his adolescence he had come to reject her, along with females in general: "He spent his time with a male clique, adopting all their manner and rhetoric of contempt for the female, and sparing her none of it" (72). Her brother is lost to her, as her natural father is. She has no man to respect.

Forced to leave home, she has tried sharing an apartment with two friends, an unmarried couple, but this experiment has also failed. She has become a pawn in their continual altercations, finding that non-marital relationships are not any better than those formalized by marriage. She concludes cynically that "Love is just a fancy word for how to hurt somebody worse" (76).

Like Hugh, however, Irene also has an idealized image of the opposite sex. Just as Hugh wants only to serve the delicate blonde Allia, Irene wants only to follow the dark mysterious "Master" of the mountain village. He has been her secret love since she first encountered him. In appearance he is the opposite of hulking, straw-haired Hugh. The Master is "a spare, swarthy man with a hawk nose and dark eyes. . . . A harsh man, a dark man" (38). In manner he is laconic, authoritative, even threatening. But in her eyes he is heroic. "In his age, in his mastery, in his strangeness, in his hardness even" (90), he is the father she has never known, the brother who is gone, the lover who is yet to be.

Irene is thrilled when the Master asks her to accompany him on a mission northward to the city. What has promised to be a great adventure, however, ends in ignominy almost as soon as it begins. The Master is unable to walk more than a few yards toward the north when he is overcome with fear and weakness. He stumbles on the road, and runs back to the village, pushing her roughly aside. He fails her in the moment of danger as Allia had failed Hugh. Irene is sickened with disappointment and feels that she has no further reason to stay in her twilight world.

Irene's response to Lord Horn, Allia's father, is the reverse of her intuitive attraction to the dark Master. She finds him cold and develops an intense dislike for him. Lord Horn compliments her courage, however, and in a later moment of danger she recalls his words with warmth and gratitude. It is not until her final departure from the village that she begins to recognize him as an authentic father image.

He bids her farewell with a paternal warning: "Go without looking back, my daughter" (132).

On her return to the daylight world with her wounded companion, Irene encounters one more authentic masculine figure. The passing motorist whose aid she enlists—with considerable misgiving on her part—is a young man who is called simply Redbeard. Honest and humane, he is downright thrilled to be able to help out in the emergency. He enjoys the speeding trip to the hospital ("He was out of the car as he jammed on the brake at the emergency entrance" (180), and he delights in getting Irene coffee and a candy bar as she waits in the lobby. This kind of masculinity has been lacking in Irene's experience. "It is royalty that call each other sister, brother" (180).

Irene is now able to love the awkward young man whom she once threatened to expel from her "ain" country with a rock. She rents a small apartment for the two of them, where they will live when Hugh is released from the hospital. The book ends with their departure together in the car, she wearing the patched and battered cloak and he the stained leather jacket that they wore in their adventures across the river. Ten minutes from downtown in a garage apartment will be their "ain" country in the immediate future.

The journey into the twilight land across the river has been for both Hugh and Irene a journey into the depths of their own perturbed psyches. In that strange world they have encountered projections of their own anima and animus. They have also completed a quest by slaying the blind, fleshy monster and discovering thereby the treasure of their own sexual nature. They have moved from troubled adolescence to self-aware maturity.[9] Now they are able to call the chaotic world along the freeway their own country and accept its challenges, fortified by the reality of their own relationship.

Although the response of reviewers to this latest novel has been on the whole positive, it has been more enthusiastic than articulate. By no means an easy book to understand, it reads well enough on the surface to capture its audience, yet its deeper implications may well elude the casual reader. The double style, although suited to the subject of parallel worlds, may alienate readers who prefer their fantasy and realism straight. *The Beginning Place* in effect takes the central situation presented in *Very Far Away from Anywhere Else,* the alienation of two contemporary adolescents, and imposes on it the allegorical narrative of Book I of the *Faerie Queene.* A breezy concrete style depicts the realistic setting with humor and a careful eye for detail. Then, once the reader is settled in recognizable surroundings, he is whisked into a world where caves, monsters, and quests suddenly seem as mundane as supermarkets and freeways. All of this is allegorical, but not allegory. There is no one-to-one identification of one object or episode with a specific meaning. The obviously symbolic adventures are not explained in terms of easy equations. The twilight world of the psyche will seem a bit different to each reader, and each will go on wondering why the monster is white. Both rereading and further reflection are required for the reader to learn what river it is through which the Ganges flows.

Chapter Nine
The Language Of The Night and Other Essays in Criticism

Ursula Le Guin's interest in the craft of writing has produced several critical essays as well as works of fiction. Many of her best pieces of criticism are gathered in the collection *The Language of the Night* (1979), which derives its title from her defense of fantasy: *"We like to think we live in daylight, but half the world is always dark, and fantasy, like poetry, speaks the language of the night."*[1] Several of the essays are concerned with the nature and significance of both fantasy and science fiction, but the collection as a whole has a wider focus on the value of the imagination.

The book has five sections. The first section contains only one essay, "A Citizen of Mondath," which serves to introduce Le Guin the person and Le Guin the reader as well as the writer. The second section contains a group of nine essays on the specific subject of fantasy and science fiction. The third consists of a series of nine brief introductory statements to some of her own works. The final two sections contain extracts from miscellaneous items, including interviews and other talks as well as formerly published pieces.

"A Citizen of Mondath"

The title of the introductory essay, "A Citizen of Mondath," is drawn from Lord Dunsany, who was the first major literary influence on Le Guin. When she read his *A Dreamer's Tales* at age twelve, she was captivated by his "Inner Lands" (one of which is Mondath) and adopted them as her own country. For a time her early reading was concentrated on fantasy and science fiction although she found herself reading voraciously in all kinds of literature. This early reading experience, combined with her even earlier acquaintance with myth, legend, and fairy tale, however, shaped her future writing: "the great spaces of fantasy and science fiction are precisely what my imagination needs. Outer Space, and the Inner Lands, are still, and always will be, my country" (30).

But what exactly are SF and fantasy? Why do they appeal to the imagination of writers and readers? How are they different from each other? And are they truly literature or simply forms of escapism? These are some of the questions addressed in the essays in the second section. The key ideas emerging from her discussions are the central role of imagination—and therefore of imaginative literature—in the development of the human being, the value of both SF and fantasy as metaphors of the human condition, the distinctive nature of fantasy as a vehicle for exploring the collective unconscious (the Inner Lands), and the identity of ethics and aesthetics in literature.

For Le Guin imagination is the distinctively human faculty. She regards it as the essential faculty for developing the qualities of "humanness" as well as humaneness. If a child's imagination could be suppressed, he "would grow up to be an eggplant" (42). What is the imagination as she sees it? "The free play of the mind, both intellectual and sensory" (41): "play" in the literal sense of re-creation, and "free" in that the action is performed without any object of profit. She adds, however, that "free" does not in any way mean "undisciplined." She finds the disciplined imagination "the essential method or technique" of both art and science.[2]

Unfortunately in our culture although the imagination cannot be suppressed, it can be neglected and even worse, it can be warped. As a result many adults neglect genuine imaginative literature in favor of TV thrillers, hack romances, and pornography, all presumably "real." Catering to the starved imagination, "Fake realism is the escapist literature of our time" (42).

Le Guin defines the purpose of imaginative fiction "to deepen your understanding of your world, and your fellow men, and your own feelings, and your destiny" (43). To those who would accept this definition but apply it only to the great novelists like Dickens and Tolstoy, Le Guin would respond that both SF and fantasy can and should help us to understand human life much more than so-called "realism," which is perhaps "the least adequate means of understanding or portraying the incredible realities of our existence" (58). In our baffling, complex, even improbable world, both science fiction based on thought-experiment and fantasy based on myth and archetype offer viable metaphors of human life. "A scientist who creates a monster in his laboratory; a librarian in the library of Babel; a wizard unable to cast a spell; a spaceship having trouble in getting to Alpha Centauri; all these may be precise and profound metaphors of the human condition" (58).

Although both science fiction and fantasy—the scientist creating a monster and the wizard casting a spell—function as metaphors, they are, in Le Guin's view, essentially different from each other. Science fiction is concerned with the Outer Lands and is object-oriented in its presentation. As thought-experiments, the imaginary or secondary worlds of science fiction serve to clarify and glorify the primary world. Fantasy worlds, on the other hand, are not based on the objective world at all, but reflect instead the Inner Lands of the psyche. "The science fictioneer imitates the Creation; the fantasist emulates the Creator" (123).

As Le Guin explains in her introduction to *The Left Hand of Darkness*, science fiction is properly a thought-experiment, as the term has been used by Schrödinger and other physicists.[3] Its purpose, therefore, is not to predict the future but to describe the present world.[4] Its method of description is necessarily metaphorical. The speculations and the facts, the gadgets and the galaxies, are metaphorical not only of the objective world but of the subjective human beings whom they affect. "What good are all the objects in the universe, if there is no subject?" (116). At its best, science fiction as thought-experiment offers, "a promise of continued life for the imagination, a good tool, an enlargement of consciousness" (119).

But Le Guin finds that all too often American science fiction falls short of these goals. Unlike European science fiction with its strong intellectual tradition, American examples tend to be simplistic and solipsistic. Since almost every work in this genre is fundamentally concerned with the nature of the alien, it is disturbing to find that American SF writers still treat as alien women and socialists and anyone else who differs from the accepted ideal of militaristic male supremacy. Le Guin lashes out against this elitism which she sardonically characterizes as "a perfect baboon partriarchy, with the Alpha Male on top, being respectfully groomed, from time to time, by his inferiors" (99). Not surprisingly, her outspoken ideas about her fellow writers have engaged her in a few running debates in SF journals.

Fantasy

Turning from science fiction to fantasy is a shift from "the outside to the inside" (123) for fantasy is by nature an introverted genre. While the limitations and the strengths of science fiction are those of extraversion, fantasy gains its strength and suffers its limits from the depths of introspective selfhood. The fantasy world is not another planet in outer space but the inner world of the unconscious.

Le Guin defines fantasy as "a different approach to reality, an alternative technique for apprehending and coping with existence. It is not antirational, but pararational; not realistic, but surrealistic, superrealistic, a heightening of reality. In Freud's terminology, it employs primary, not secondary process thinking. It employs archetypes, which, as Jung warned us, are dangerous things. Dragons are more dangerous, and a good deal commoner, than bears. Fantasy is nearer to poetry, to mysticism, and to insanity than naturalistic fiction is. It is a real wilderness, and those who go there should not feel too safe. And their guides, the writers of fantasy, should take their responsibilities seriously" (84).

Taking her own responsibility as the author of the Earthsea trilogy seriously, Le Guin discusses these works in both "Dreams Must Explain Themselves" and "The Child and the Shadow." In the "Dreams" essay she speaks of the artist as magician, suggesting that the theme of wizardry is actually a metaphor of the creative experience. "Wizardry is artistry" (53). Like Tolkien she dislikes allegory, so that for her the metaphor should not be confined to an exact equation. Like dreams, fantasy novels must explain themselves.

"The Child and the Shadow" is concerned with the archetypal nature of fantasy. Like myths and fairy tales, as well as dreams, fantasies emanate from the unconscious: "they speak *from* the unconscious, *to* the unconscious, in the *language* of the unconscious—symbol and archetype" (62). Le Guin compares their effect to that of music, which cannot be described in the language of reason. The universal plot of literary fantasy is the quest journey, which is also an inward journey to the collective unconscious, where one encounters the archetypes that lead to self-knowledge.

The most significant archetype encountered on this journey is the Shadow, "the dark brother of the conscious mind" (63). Standing on the threshold between the unconscious and the conscious mind, the shadow represents "all we don't want to, can't, admit into our conscious self, all the qualities and tendencies within us which have been repressed, denied, or not used" (64). Le Guin offers a brief but perceptive analysis of characters from *The Lord of the Rings* as exemplary of the Shadow figure in fantasy. This archetypal approach, based on Jungian psychology, also illuminates her own use of a literal shadow in *A Wizard of Earthsea*.

In her essay "From Elfland to Poughkeepsie" Le Guin discusses the elusive subject of a style appropriate to fantasy fiction. Her premise maintains that there is a style uniquely suitable to fantasy, a style that would not work in a naturalistic novel for the same reasons that the style of the latter would fall flat when transferred to fantasy. The title of the essay encapsulates this important difference. Elfland is the domain of fantasy. Whether it is called Middle Earth, Narnia, or Prydain, it is still the magical secondary world of Elfland. Poughkeepsie, on the other hand, is not at all like Elfland. It is a specific town, with specific local and recognizable characteristics that have to do with the natural world of which it is a part. The inhabitants of Elfland and Poughkeepsie do not speak the same language. Dialogue from a book about the actual town cannot be substituted for dialogue in a book about the mythic realm. It would sound phony.

For her examples of successful Elfland style, Le Guin chooses works by E. R. Eddison, Kenneth Morris, and J. R. R. Tolkien. Quoting a brief passage of dialogue from each she demonstrates how and why these passages would seem out of place in realistic fiction simply because they have achieved the authentic resonance of heroic fantasy. Then, citing a passage from a recent work of fantasy, she demonstrates the reverse. Since this passage lacks the genuine ring of Elfland it can be completely transformed simply by substituting modern place names of the fantasy world. In short, a true fantasy has a distinctive style which will not permit Elfland to be called Poughkeepsie.

How to achieve this style is not so easily demonstrated. Le Guin points out the problems of writing with deliberate archaism, with mixed tone, with combined humor and heroism, and with several other pitfalls awaiting the novice fantasist. But ultimately, since the secondary world of fantasy represents the unique vision of its creator, the style is more than a mere ingredient in the book. The style is the book.

Le Guin's comments on fantasy—its nature, purpose, style—in *The Language of the Night* add up to a significant statement about a subject as yet little touched upon by literary critics. Although her remarks are scattered, with only the three essays just discussed exclusively devoted to this subject, they embody a consistent and intelligent aesthetic of literary fantasy.

Ethics and Aesthetics

For Le Guin the aesthetics of literature cannot be separated from the ethics of literature. She considers herself a moral writer, yet she

is obviously not the sort of writer who superimposes a "moral" on a
story. Her fictional world, however, incorporates a moral vision of
human life. She believes in science fiction and fantasy as serious literature capable of conveying such a moral vision. Her essays, like her
fiction, deal with the themes of integrity, alienation, cultural diversity, social stereotyping, education and politics. The moral value of
action in her novels is echoed in the moral perspective on writing in
her essays.

One of the social issues with which she deals in *The Language of the
Night* is feminism. In "The Stone Ax and the Muskoxen," a talk she
delivered at a world SF conference in Melbourne, Australia, she expresses her concern over the limited number of women in SF, in the
works, in the fans, and in the writers. She speculates as to the possible reasons for this paucity of women, suggesting perhaps their own
limited interest in the "wars or wiring diagrams" (229) school of SF
so popular in the American SF magazines, perhaps an acquired fear of
science and technology. She rejects the theory that SF publishing is
biased against women, for she has personally experienced almost none
in her career. Her only single experience with bias occurred in connection with the publication of a story in *Playboy,* for which the ed-
itors insisted on using her initials instead of her first name.

Perhaps, she further speculates, it is the fault of women who are
themselves afraid to let their imaginations loose, particularly since to
do so would involve them in competition with men. In response to
this hypothesis, she urges women writers to try their wings with SF.
"The practice of an art is, in its absolute discipline, the experience of
absolute freedom. And that, above all, is why I'd like to see more of
my sisters trying out their wings above the mountains. Because freedom is not always an easy thing for women to find" (230).

One brief but witty statement on the subject of feminism occurs
in her introduction to the works of James Tiptree, Jr. The name of
this particular author, James Tiptree, Jr., turns out to be a pseu-
donym for Alice Sheldon. Le Guin gleefully takes advantage of this
rare opportunity to mock those who like to comment on "masculine"
or "feminine" styles of writing. She quotes a prominent science fiction writer (whom she does not identify) who went on record as con-
sidering James Tiptree, Jr., an "ineluctably masculine" writer (182).
She then triumphantly concludes that the revelation of Tiptree's feminine identity must decisively "imperil all theories concerning the
woman as writer" (183).

Some of Le Guin's introductions to her own novels also touch upon the issue of feminism. In her introduction to *Planet of Exile* she admits that at the time of its writing she did not care whether her characters were men or women. She had not yet had her consciousness raised in respect to feminine issues. She feels, however, that she has effectively avoided stereotyping, not out of any conscious ideology but rather out of her habitual focus on the essential humanity of her characters. The "person" she tends to write about is neither a man nor a woman, but a complex human being. "On the superficial level, this means there is little sexual stereotyping—the men aren't lustful and the women aren't gorgeous—and the sex itself is seen as a *relationship rather than an act*" (143).

In a provocative essay called "Is Gender Necessary?," intended as an introduction to *The Left Hand of Darkness,* Le Guin explores the subject of feminism in broad, theoretical terms. She defines the "female principle" as anarchic. "It values order without constraint, rule by custom not by force" (165), in contrast to the male who enforces order and creates power structures. A further contrast is evident between the "driving linearity" of the male, which pushes forward to break the limits, and the "circularity" of the female, which values "patience, ripeness, practicality, livableness" (165–66). Le Guin, here as elsewhere, seeks balance and integration, the reconciliation of opposites wherein she feels that our society has failed because of its pervasive dualism.

If in the opinion of some feminists Le Guin does not go far enough in voicing their concerns in her fiction, it is because of that very integrity which equates ethics and aesthetics, refusing to sacrifice either to the other. She refuses, for example, to do violence to the English language by inventing a pronoun for he/she. Furthermore she does not accept the extreme position that sexual injustice is the root of most human problems. She does, however, reject the principle of patriarchy, which is the prevalent kind of domination in our world, agreeing that the will to dominate is the root of many, if not most, human problems.

Only once in Le Guin's fiction does the ethical aim threaten to overwhelm the aesthetic rather than coincide with it. In writing *The Word for World Is Forest,* she admits that she succumbed to the "lure of the pulpit" (151). She had been active in demonstrations against the war in Vietnam in the late sixties, and the novel became an impression of her outrage over the ethic of exploitation. Her protest

is aesthetically weakened by the character of Captain Davidson who
is a totally evil individual. Le Guin's admission is typical of her
frankness and honesty about her own work. The identity of art and
ethics holds true for her personal reactions to literature as well as for
her literary output.

Writers and Writing

Although Le Guin has published many reviews of single works
of science fiction, only two of the items included in this collection
are devoted to works of other writers. "The Staring Eye" concerns
J. R. R. Tolkien, and "The Modest One" is focused on Philip Dick.
Tolkien's *Lord of the Rings* is one of her favorite books, and she confesses readily to having read it several times to herself as well as three
times out loud to her children. She does not regard it as an influence
on her own writing, however, as she discovered it after she had found
her own voice in fiction. Her remarks on Tolkien's characters and on
the scope of his imaginative world are both sensitive and perceptive.

Philip Dick, on the other hand, has been influential on Le Guin's
fiction, although that influence is not her concern here. She finds
Dick's central themes to be "reality and madness, time and death, sin
and salvation" (176), but suggests that the reader may well miss
them because they are so entertainingly presented. His characters,
comparable to those of Dickens, she describes as masterpieces of the
ordinary: "what counts is the honesty, constancy, kindness, and patience of ordinary people" (176). Dick's vision, which some critics
have likened to the absurdist views of Kafka, represent for Le Guin
a triumph of moral clarity. She finds it neither absurdist nor despair-
ing but prophetically clear and whole, a consistent vision which per-
meates all of his works. Again like Dickens, he creates in his books
a single total universe.

There are scattered references throughout the book to several other
writers including major novelists like Tolstoy and Borges as well as
to science-fiction writers. These remarks are on the whole distinguished by their directness and by an acute perception of what good
writing is. They are also generous in spirit, for she never attacks a
fellow writer. Although she occasionally deplores certain tendencies
in bad writing, she cites them anonymously. The result is the valuable insight of a sharp critic tempered by the modesty of a practicing
writer.

For the would-be writers who come to this book seeking advice, the result may be disappointment. Le Guin does not offer any list of easy-to-follow-rules to become a great writer. On the other hand, there is much to be gleaned, both implicitly and explicitly, from her sensible commentary on her own writing experience. She asserts that she has always avoided the how-to-write texts, preferring to use only a dictionary and a manual of English usage. She also insists that the persons and places in her fiction are not invented by a deliberate, conscious process, but rather are found in her unconscious. This theory of creativity is at one with her philosophical Taoism, which also maintains that the laws of nature, aesthetic as well as scientific, are not imposed from without but reside within things, and are therefore to be discovered.

Perhaps Le Guin's subtlest advice to writers lies in her comments about the uses of myth. She is quick to warn the beginner that the "presence of mythic material in a story does not mean that the myth making faculty is being used" (75). A genuinely mythic dimension in a work of literature cannot be imposed that consciously. Much more is involved than mere imitation or even mere thievery, although "Theft is an integral function of a healthy literature" (75). True mythic awareness comes from within, arising "in the process of connecting the conscious and the unconscious realms" (79). Overt knowledge of actual myths is therefore not enough. "The artist who works from the center of his own being will find archetypal images and release them into consciousness" (80).

Whereas the practical side of Le Guin's advice to writers, then, consists of the admonition to get a dictionary and a handbook, the inspirational side involves contact with one's unconscious. Beyond that, she has one more suggestion: write. A writer learns to write by writing. Since the writer's creative experience is an inward matter, what he does in the material world is essentially irrelevant. She cites the Brontë sisters as an example. Writing is a solitary occupation, she warns, and writing courses and workshops can at best function only on the most superficial level. Because it is solitary, the art of writing also depends much upon the writer's self-knowledge. The writer's job is to tell the truth, but the truth of his own being is within, not out there in a textbook.

Although the last two sections of *The Language of the Night* are somewhat disappointing in that they consist of a miscellany of talks and brief extracts, the collection as a whole is excellent, and the essays in the first three sections are substantial and valuable. What also comes through this collection of essays on a broad range of topics is the personality of the writer, her likes and dislikes, her wit and wisdom, her devotion to her art and her own profound integrity about her own and others' writing. As one reviewer observed, "She comes through as a feisty, witty, extraordinarily sensible, tough, and honest writer and woman."[5] To read this volume is not merely to gain a new perspective on fantasy and science fiction but also to meet a writer, an engagingly human writer who is often funny, occasionally exasperating, but always likeable, and never dull.

Chapter Ten
Wild Angels and *Hard Words*

Le Guin has published two volumes of poetry, *Wild Angels* (1975), reprinted in the *Capra Chapbook Anthology* (1979), and *Hard Words* (1981).[1]

Wild Angels

Wild Angels is a slender volume consisting of thirty poems, many of them quite short. Although the individual poems are arranged in no particular order, they can be grouped by the reader into certain categories of subject matter. Some deal with the theme of nature, some with death, and a few are concerned with personal experiences. Beyond these three groups, which include most of the thirty poems, there remain a few single poems with a still different focus.

The longest personal poem in the collection is the autobiographical "Coming of Age." The first three sections of this seven-part poem refer to childhood: to Saint Ursula for whom the poet was named, to her brothers with whom she played, and to the imaginative world in which their creative young minds flourished. The fourth section is in memory of her father, Alfred Kroeber, to whom the collection is dedicated. The last three are largely concerned with her personal response to nature.

Among the group of personal poems are two dedicated to her children. "For Ted" is a vivid poem about the hawk to whom "all earth is prey" (316). "Für Elise" is about her daughter's study of the cello. Le Guin contrasts the range of beautiful sounds emanating from the room where Elizabeth is practicing her cello with the dull sounds coming from her own study: "a dry tak-tacking / and long silences" (315). Personal experiences are the focus of "Flying West from Denver," "Hier steh ich," and "The Offering." The latter is a witty, nine-line poem about a poem written while the poet is falling asleep. When she awakes, it is lost forever. She reflects poignantly that if it was good, she wishes to offer it to the "gods / of the great darkness / where sleep goes and farther / death goes" (301).

Another group of poems is concerned with the world of nature, ranging from specific rivers, trees, and mountains to a general vision of the idea of nature. Since Le Guin has called herself an arboreal writer, it is not surprising that two of the best nature poems are about trees. "Arboreal" echoes *The Farthest Shore* in its address to "O high ash tree, O rowan fair / red rowan on the hill" (302). Literally rooted in myth, "Arboreal" also draws on the Norse creation myth of the world tree. It begins with "The family tree has not got back / to trees yet," and ends with "child of Ygdrasil" (302). In "Rooftree" a house is metaphorically identified with a tree; a high house with a green roof, its green evolves from its deep roots. A volcanic mountain also takes on mythic stature in the "Mount St. Helens / Omphalos," where the mountain is seen as the center of the world, or world navel, with a mystical ring of seven stones on top.[2] Nature as idea is the subject of the "Tao Song," which equates nature with the Tao or the Way, ending on an optimistic note: "No one can lose it / for long" (319).

Another group of poems is concentrated on the subject of death: "The Darkness," "Dreampoem," and "Dreampoem II" are all highly personal visions. In "The Darkness" death inspires fear because it threatens the unknown. It appears in the faces of others and visits the houses of others, but the poet has not met death: "And so I fear the darkness like a child" (294). The two dream poems are allegorical. In the vision described in "Dreampoem" the poet walks with Death, who has three faces, one white, one brown, and one unseen. The white mouth tells her to wait a while, the brown mouth smiles, and the third mouth is still. The walk continues. "Dreampoem II" recounts another walk, "on no street / toward no end," in a city "where no one walks" (303). The mood of emptiness and futility is reminiscent of the dry dead land in *The Farthest Shore*. A much less personal and more intellectual death poem is "Archeology of the Renaissance." A wry comment on transience, this ironic poem concerns the unearthing of the tombs of Pico and Politian. Pico advised following the path of virtue while Politian urged to gather roses quickly. Both, however, are equally dead.

One poem in the collection combines the themes of death and art. In "Ars Lunga" Le Guin describes herself as "perpetually inventing new people / as if the population boom were not enough" (298). Since she does not want or expect life beyond the grave, however, she can enjoy living all those lives—"nine at once or ninety"—feeling vulnerable to death on all sides at all times, but therefore also feeling intensely alive.

Hard, compact, tense, the poems in *Wild Angels* achieve an economy rare in poetry, and quite different from Le Guin's fictional style. The vocabulary is straightforward, with a diction austerely avoiding the Latinate or the ornate. Many are told in the first person, but they are restrained and given to understatement. There is no confessional tone, nor is there much metaphor. The sparse surface is deepened by mythic roots rather than elaborated by figures of speech.

Hard Words

Le Guin's second collection, *Hard Words,* is both more substantial and more varied in style and subject. With its fifty-six poems arranged in five sections, the greater range of tone and content offer what the poet calls on the cover "a map of my mind."

The first section, containing eleven poems, is entitled *Wordhoard.* An Anglo-Saxon word, the title refers to the poet's private stock or treasure of words. It is analogous to the German word *Wortschatz,* meaning literally "word-treasure," but also meaning "dictionary." The particular poem which gives its title to the group is on the Anglo-Saxon subject of a dragon guarding its own hoard, or treasure. Speaking to the person who has come to beg a coin from the vast hoard, the dragon agrees to the theft of "the anger opal and the honor stone" but will not give away the pearl, "My own, my Egg" (4).[3]

Several of the other poems in this opening section, including the titular "Hard Words," are about the craft of writing. In "For Karl and Jean" she considers the actions of writing and carving as "grabbing at straws" and "bringing the world / to be by short hard repeated/blows" (3). "Invocation" expresses the desire to sing in such forceful language that even "the machines will gather round to listen" (7).

In many of these poems about writing, the creative act is likened to working with stone. Both "Hard Words" and "Translation" confess the appeal of "hard things," like granite and diamonds. More explicitly in "The Mind is Still" she describes her craft in terms of sculpting:

> Words are my matter. I have chipped one stone
> for thirty years and still it is not done,
> that image of the thing I cannot see.

> I cannot finish it and set it free,
>   transformed to energy.

(9)

She concludes wistfully that stone is "heavy in the hand" (9). Focused on the same metaphor, "The Marrow" likens the act of writing to seeking words hidden in stone:

> There was a word inside a stone.
> I tried to pry it clear,
> mallet and chisel, pick and gad,
> until the stone was dropping blood,
> but still I could not hear
> the word the stone had said.

(10)

Conscious effort to extricate words from recalcitrant stone does not necessarily work. It is only after the deliberate effort has ceased that the long-sought word suddenly appears as if on its own:

> I threw it down beside the road
> among a thousand stones
> and as I turned away it cried
> the word aloud within my ear,
> and the marrow of my bones
> heard, and replied.

(10)

With its precise dialectical structure, "The Marrow" is one of the best poems in this first group, which is interesting as a whole for its concentration on the art of writing as a hard struggle for hard words.

The second section of poems, "Dancing at Tillai," is quite different. These eleven exuberant, often strident poems contrast sharply with the understated style of the first section. The unifying element here is the dance. All of these poems are intensely rhythmical and lend themselves to a singing style of recitation. Many of them refer to drums, and there is an overall effect of a drumbeat. The poet dances, the god dances, the Dancing Master calls out the dance, the comets are called to dance, and the herdsman dances in the mountains. As the poem "drums" summarizes:

> Sun dance
> stone dance
> bone dance
> one dance
>
> sky dance
> bird dance
> word dance
> I dance.
>
> (28)

The most vigorous of these vibrant poems is the "Carmagnole of the Thirtieth of June" (20). The "carmagnole" was the carriage used to carry people to execution during the French Revolution. It later became the name of a popular revolutionary song and dance. The violent, jeering language of the poem, filled with exaggerated bravado, captures the mood of the revolutionary mob:

> I will grow fingernails
> ten feet long and walk on themlike stilts
> & breathe steam out of my nostrils
> & split boards with my eye.
>
> (20)

Some of its satirical jibes are quite current:

> I am WUMMUN, ta doody boo-bah.
>
> (21)

It ends in a crescendo with wild dancing on various parts of God's anatomy:

> when I dance on his eyes he wakes and all the stones
>   fall down ashes, ashes,
> all fall down.
>   Get up and dance, creation!
>
> (21)

Funny as well as shrill and hyperbolic, the "Carmagnole" is an effective tour de force.

The section concludes with the title poem, "The Dancing at Tillai." The subject is death, this time in a partly Hindu frame of reference. There are repeated allusions to Kali, the Hindu black goddess of death. The last stanza offers a description of the dancing deity Siva, whose picture is featured on the cover of *Hard Words*:

> his left hand points to the dancing foot . . .
> river and moon are in his hair
> his lifted foot is grace
> his lowered foot is sleep
> he dances in the center.

(30)

The illustration is from a fifteenth-century Indian bronze sculpture in the Portland Art Museum. Published originally as a separate series in the *Kenyon Review*, this group of "dancing poems" is a distinctive lyrical achievement.

The next section, comprising sixteen poems, is called "Line Drawings." The focus here is on geographical place. Included are personal impressions of several scenes in Oregon and elsewhere in the west and on the Pacific coast. There is also a long poem about Mount Everest and a short one about New York City. The brief New York lyric captures a past and present moment in New York, "Central Park South, March 9, 1979." The poet walks "between the weary horses and the trees" at age forty-nine, recalling her father who was but ten when he walked there in 1886, in "cap and bare knees; more likely / he ran, on the paths there, by the lake" (39). The few poems in this section not concerned with a personal experience of place are devoted to individuals, including "The Journey" for Joseph Needham whose book on Taoism much influenced Le Guin.[4] One is a sympathetic tribute to Richard III. "Did he forsee / the hump, the murders, and the theft / the withered hand, and all the Tudors made him?" (41).

The fourth section contains three long poems. Called "Walking in Cornwall," it describes the poet's deeply felt experience of seeing the landscape and learning the history of Cornwall. The vivid geographical descriptions evoke the profoundly ancient past. The "grass, forse and heather" of the present grow over the graves long ago unearthed.

The name of the town—Chun—is all that remains of a long forgotten language:

> Chun is a name
> in a tongue that no one speaks now
> but rocks and larks.
>
> (54)

Some of the names from the old tongue are exotic, like Men-an-Tol, and some are quaintly comic, like Woon Gumpus.

The unifying image in the Cornwall poems is stone. There are "walls / of spark-strown granite" (53), standing for "maybe eighty generations" (53); there are rings of stone and stones that mark the gateway; there are "rock-wall rings" (54); both stones that are cut and stones that are not yet cut ("We have left cut stone / a thousand years ahead of us" [57]). The stones that still remain after all of the other structures of civilization have gone suggest the great tranquility of the landscape:

> The roofs are off, the wooden walls are gone,
> the centerposts are gone, but not the hollowed stones.
>
> (60)

Le Guin's perspective in these poems involves a temporal view of landscape. What she sees now on her walking tour continually suggests to her what was there long, long ago. The imagery functions to intertwine past time with present space. This awareness is captured in the gnomic line: "Place is three fourths of Time" (60). "Walking in Cornwall" is thus primarily visual poetry whereas "The Dancing at Tillai" was primarily aural and rhythmic.

The fifth section of the collection, named "Simple Hill" from its introductory poem, is a miscellany of fifteen poems on a variety of subjects. Several are short personal lyrics, many based on a single figure of speech. The "I" frequently relating the poem is not always the poet, however; in "Cavaliers," for example, it is the voice of the meadow lamenting the destruction wrought upon its grasses by the cavaliers on horseback. ("I have gone to seed . . . O desolation!" [69]). This wide-ranging use of the first-person pronoun should be noted by the reader all too ready to assume that the "I" is always Le Guin.

Along with the lyrics in this section is a group of three dramatic monologues called "The Well of Baln," spoken in turn by Count Baln, his wife, and his daughter. The Count is "a nobleman of vast estate, / girthed like an oak tree" (71) and heir to a "house of seven hundred rooms" (71). His great wealth does not satisfy him, for he senses a hole at the center of his house and heart, into which fall "all the leaves and diamonds and hounds," all "the hours and eyes and words" (71). Baln's wife questions the strange fear that obsesses the Count and wonders about the empty cellar into which things seem to disappear. Baln's daughter has been down the well, down far enough to take a boat on the river to the country on the other side. These monologues are richly suggestive, leaving much unsaid. The homely diction is reminiscent of Robert Frost, but the mythic allusions are closer to William Butler Yeats.

Hard Words demonstrates a greater maturity and flexibility of style than evident in the earlier collection of poems. Although Le Guin is not as accomplished a poet as she is a fiction writer, she is a competent poet with an unusually versatile flair for verse forms and rhythm. Among her poems one finds a remarkable range: the dramatic monologue, the resonant mythic narrative, the raucous song, the delicate lyric, the fragile haiku. Both as a map of her mind and as an objective poetic achievement, this collection of Le Guin's poems is well worth reading.

Chapter Eleven

Miscellaneous Short Fiction

Thought-Experiments

Not all of Le Guin's short fiction has been collected in anthologies.[1] Several of her stories are available only in the periodicals in which they were originally published. Many of these stories are in the category of the thought-experiment which the author referred to in her introduction to *The Left Hand of Darkness*.

An almost classic example is "Schrödinger's Cat" (1974), a thought-experiment about a thought-experiment.[2] Based on physicist Edwin Schrödinger's experiments with quantum theory, it involves putting a cat into a box containing a loaded gun. When the box lid closes, it activates an emitter designed to emit one photon which has a fifty-fifty chance of striking a mirror, thereby activating the trigger. If the photon strikes the mirror, the gun will shoot the cat; if the photon is deflected, the gun will not shoot the cat. The observer must open the box to find out what happened. Before the emission of the photon, the system of the universe on the quantum level seems quite clear, but after the emission of the unpredictable photon, the system depends on an unknowable combination of two waves. Thus no one can predict the outcome. As one character in the story puts it, "God plays dice with the world!" (38). The only certainty possible in the universe is what the observer creates subjectively for himself.

With considerable humor and ingenuity, Le Guin combines the cat-in-the-box story with a number of other elements, including the theory of entropy. At the time of the story, the world is both heating up and speeding up. The narrator lists graphic details of the unbearable heat. Stove burners are turned on in a vain attempt to cool them off, and touch is virtually impossible: "a kiss was like a branding iron" (35). Speed is evidenced in the movement of the worms like subway trains through "the writhing roots of roses" (36). The narra-

tor wants to report these events although nothing can possibly matter
any more. He mocks his own "Ethica laboris puritanica, or Adam's
disease," which is incurable except by "total decephalization" (34).

Much of the humor derives from the style. Metaphorical language
is literalized. While most things are burning to the touch, the cat's
fur remains cool: "a real cool cat" (36). The expostulation of the
young mailman who suddenly appears in the narrative—"Yah!.,"
"Wow"—leads the narrator to nickname him Rover and ever after refer to him in canine terms. A young woman characterized as "pretty
well gone to pieces" supports her head in the crook of her right knee
and hops on the toes of her right foot, leaving her left leg, arms, and
trunk lying in a heap.

The theme of entropic process is deftly interwoven with the box
experiment. At the end, the narrator and the mailman breathlessly
open the box only to find that there is no cat in it at all. Just as they
lift the lid of the box, the roof of the house lifts off. An end-of-the-
world story with a difference, "Schrödinger's Cat" is a delightful
tour-de-force.

A different kind of thought-experiment is recounted in the story
with the unusual title, "The Author of the Acacia Seeds and Other
Extracts from the *Journal of the Association of Therolinguistics*" (1974).[3]
The authors of the three journal extracts assume the existence of both
art and language among the animal and plant species. The first extract introduces a tentative translation and interpretation of a manuscript found in an ant hill. The message is written in "touchgland
exudation" on acacia seeds artfully laid in rows at the end of a tunnel
leading off a deep level colony. The second extract announces an expedition to investigate the language of the Emperor Penguin. A research specialist, already an expert on Dolphin, has received a Unesco
grant for the purpose. The third and final extract, written by the
president of the Therolinguistic Association, considers the nature of
art and language. Challenging the theory that art, like language,
must communicate, this writer postulates that plants, too, have art.
He wishes to rally support for further study of "non-communicative,
vegetative art" and in a visionary glimpse of the future foresees the
geolinguist not only understanding the delicate lyrics of the lichen
but even discovering the "atemporal, cold, volcanic poetry of the
rocks" (163).

The three journal extracts are written in precise language, with no
hint of parody or exaggeration. The sympathetic descriptive adjec-
tives applied to the language of insects and birds reveal real sensitiv-

ity, and the mystical speculation that plant poetry may use "the meter of eternity" suggests a oneness with nature that the empath Osden would admire.

"Selection" (1964) might be a more conventional "hardcore" SF story, were it not for its sly, wry ending.[4] The narrative takes place in a future galactic bubble colony, where all marriages are arranged by a highly sophisticated sociometric computer. Operated by a trained specialist in sociometrics, the computer takes into account everything from DNA patterns to enzymes in order to assure both optimum-offspring and maximum contentment. The details are carefully supplied by the author, who concentrates on one recalcitrant couple opposed to the efficient system. Joan vehemently objects to marrying Harry, whom she loathes. In the given situation, however, she has no choice but compliance, and the marriage takes place in spite of her protestations. One day when the newlyweds are out skiing, Harry is seriously injured in an accident, and the emergency awakens a new sentiment in Joan. The marriage becomes a success after all, and a year later Joan proudly shows her infant son to the sociometrist who arranged the match. In the last paragraph of the story, the confident sociometrist returns to his computer cards, and the reader learns the final stage of his scientific spouse selection process. By-passing the complex computer, he drops the namecards of fifty young men into his hat and draws.

The tight narrative is well-sustained, and the final twist comes as a complete surprise. A balance between the ultraefficient, computerized system and the vagaries of human nature adds a dimension of meaning, making the story much more than a merely gimmicky SF yarn.

"The Diary of the Rose"

"The Diary of the Rose" (1976) has a biographical as well as literary interest for the Le Guin reader.[5] After the story had been nominated for the annual Nebula award, Le Guin publicly withdrew it from further consideration in protest against an action taken by the Science Fiction Writers of America. That organization, of which she had been a member for several years, had revoked an honorary membership it had bestowed on the Polish writer Stanislas Lem because of some unfavorable remarks he had published about American science fiction. Le Guin resented this dishonoring of a fellow writer.

The story offers a compelling, somewhat chilling SF narrative with a psychological twist. It is a first person account in the form of a diary written by a woman doctor, Rosa Sobel, who deals with mental patients. She specializes in the psychoscope, a highly sophisticated machine that projects thoughts on to a screen in pictures. The psychoscopic projection of images helps her to understand what is going on in the disturbed minds of her patients. The educational and therapeutic purpose of the diary is to record all of her spontaneous thoughts while dealing with her patients, both for the benefit of her own development and for the future training of others. As a result the style is clinical, straight-forward, impersonal, with an attentive care to literal details and a meticulous avoidance of emotional response. The enterprise is by definition ironic, in that the writer is so highly trained professionally as to be almost incapable of the sort of spontaneity called for in a diary.

The immediate subjects of Dr. Sobel's diary are her two new patients, a depressed, middle-aged woman and a young engineer referred to the hospital after an outbreak of violent behavior. The woman proves easy to treat with conventional hormone therapy. Essentially a dull person, she even has dull dreams. The man, however, is quite different. It is not clear at first why he has been hospitalized because he denies having committed any violent acts. He claims instead that one night he was awakened, interrogated, beaten and drugged, after which he was arrested. He is cooperative with Dr. Sobel, whom he respects, but although he is willing to work with her and the psychoscope he confesses his horror of being subjected to the so-called ECT, an electric shock treatment. She assures him of her preference for psychoscopy as an "integrative rather than a destructive instrument" (19). But he learns through her that a once renowned intellectual, Dr. Arca, has been subjected to the ECT and as a result has lost all memory and indeed all identity. It is not until she reports these confidential details to him that she herself becomes fully aware of the outrage that has actually occurred.

The relationship between doctor and patient is sensitively portrayed. As she ostensibly learns about him by watching his mental images on the screen of the psychoscope, she also learns about herself. Her training has made her too impersonal, even mechanical, in handling psychological problems, but the full humanity of this young engineer comes through to her as a profoundly new experience. At one point when she is watching the images he is producing, she sees on the screen a strikingly beautiful rose. "The shadows of one petal on another, the velvety damp texture of the petals, the pink color full of sunlight, the yellow central crown" are more like a living, growing flower than a "mentifact" (10). She is moved by its vivid quality but does not yet connect it with her own name. Shortly after, when she sees some of the mental images of his childhood, she again feels deeply touched and realizes that she is not being as coldly analytical as she is supposed to be. "I can't say what it is, I feel honored to have shared in the childhood he remembered for me" (16).

The developing relationship also signals a growing irony, for it is clear that her study of him through his mental images projected on the psychoscope produces more of an effect on her than on him. By opening up his inner thoughts and memories and sharing them with her, he is in effect contributing to her own personal growth. Whereas her diary was initiated as a clinical account to be used for professional training, it becomes more and more personal until she realizes that she will not be able to show it to her superior. At the point when she realizes that her patient has what she calls a "political psychosis," that is, he is a liberal in an authoritarian state that will not allow liberals, she realizes that she has no one to turn to for advice. She continues the diary but hides the loose pages which she feels are now potentially dangerous.

At this point she is, of course, a different person from the blindly obedient, well-trained psychoscope operator who started her new diary with a touch of pride in her new patients. She has worked inside a sane, integrated mind for several hours a day for six weeks, whereas in the past she had worked only with the mentally disturbed. She has discovered that the alienation of the political liberal is not the product of his mind but of the repressive society. With growing horror she knows that he will indeed be given the ECT treatment and follow the unfortunate Dr. Arca into oblivion. But there is nothing she can do.

At the end of the story, she greets the young man on the morning after the ECT. He does not recognize her. He has lost his memory and his identity, but he has conferred identity on her. "I am Rosa. I am the rose. The rose, I am the rose. The rose with no flower, the rose all thorns, the mind he made, the hand he touched, the winter rose" (24).

"The Diary of the Rose" is typical of Le Guin's psychologically oriented science fiction. The futuristic prospect, the technological materials, and the laboratory setting are stock features of science fiction, but what makes the story a success is the characterization. Told from Rosa's point of view, the narrative leads the reader from her state of innocence to her growing awareness of the horrors taking place in her world. In her sessions with her patient, the reader becomes familiar with both the inner workings of his rich, well-integrated personality and of her as yet undeveloped potential for sympathy, understanding, and love. The ending is shocking, not only for the actual event but also for the reversal of human identity that has taken place. The mind that has been destroyed has created a new one in its place.

Although it is idle to speculate as to whether this story would have won the Nebula, it clearly has the power and originality that established it as a worthy candidate. Perhaps because it did not win, however, it has not been as frequently collected as some of Le Guin's other stories, but it is well worth the reading.

"The Eye Altering"

Le Guin's story "The Eye Altering," published in the anthology *The Altered Eye* (1976), is a product of a science-fiction writing workshop.[6] The workshop itself was her own idea. With her experience as writer-in-residence at similar American events, she suggested this transglobal workshop to the 33rd annual World Science Fiction Convention held in Melbourne, Australia, in 1975. All of the twenty selected participants wrote their own stories and criticized the others, with the result that the initial draft in each case benefited—or suffered—from nineteen detailed critiques.

Le Guin's own contribution to this workshop, "The Eye Altering," was written in two differing versions. The original story is printed along with the several separate commentaries of fellow workshoppers. Le Guin's response to their critiques is also included, and the somewhat revised story appears at the end of the volume. Le Guin acted on some of the suggested revisions but rejected others, and the second version is tighter in language and structure than the first.

"The Eye Altering" takes place on the planet New Zion, settled by Jewish refugees from Earth. Life is difficult for the settlers both psychologically because of the drab, gray sky and physically because of the allergic reactions that make adaptation dependent on continual dosages of metabolizing pills. Several settlers are sickly, including the central figure, Genya, who was born on the planet twenty-four years ago. The older settlers maintain one Living Room as a nostalgic retreat. In this room artificial lighting simulates Earth sunlight in piquant contrast to the depressing native atmosphere. On the walls are pictures of Earth, many of them enlarged photographs. The delicate youth Genya, who is talented artistically, paints a picture of Earth which is startling in its authenticity. Never having seen Earth, he has achieved the Earthlike scene while looking at the dismal prospect of New Zion. What the painting reveals is that Genya is actually better adapted to the new planet than are the older settlers. Taking "meta" pills all of his life has been, in fact, a serious mistake, for his eye is native to the natural beauty of the planet. For him it is not ugly and alien, and his supposedly intense allergic reactions are, in fact, produced by the pills. His is the "altered eye."

The two slightly dissimilar versions of the story offer a useful insight into the writing process. As Le Guin explains in her introductory comments, her published stories usually have undergone two thorough revisions. In this case the story has profited from the advice of several outside readers. Noting minor changes in wording is a valuable lesson in the art of literary revision. One reader objected to "warty" modifying "orange," but Le Guin retained the image as a valid simile. On the other hand, she removed the word "non-adaptive" used twice on the last page in favor of the less pseudo-technical phrase "fitting a pattern."

Either version of the story is entertaining reading, but would-be writers will want to read both.

Children's Stories

Le Guin has written two works for young children, *Leese Webster* (1979) and "Solomon Leviathan's Nine Hundred and Thirty-First Trip Around the World" in *Puffin's Pleasure* (1976). (The latter, however, has been published only in the English anthology and is virtually unavailable to American readers.)

Leese Webster is about an artistic spider who lives in a deserted palace. As a young spider, Leese weaves the kind of web that her family, the Websters, had always woven. Enjoying her privacy in the bedroom that long ago belonged to a princess, she wants to experiment with different kinds of web. She begins to imitate the designs she sees in the carpet and on the paintings which adorn the walls. With patient practice, she learns how to weave her ideas so that her new webs achieve designs with leaves and flowers, huntsmen and hounds.

Her fellow spiders scorn her artistic webs because they can catch no more flies than the ordinary kind, but Leese does not mind going hungry. She does mind, however, what she regards as a flaw in her new webs. Unlike the jewels in the throne room of the palace where she was born, her webs do not have any colored light in them. They are only gray.

One day Leese's quiet room is disrupted by the entry of two women who are helping to clean up the palace and convert it into a museum. Their brooms terrify the spider, but the women are awed by the beautiful web and rush to tell the proper authorities about it. The tapestry experts examine the web with care and decide to place it under glass in what they will now call the Room of the Silver Weavings. Although the web is preserved for future generations of tourists, Leese finds herself without a home. A kindly cleaning woman shakes her off the broom out of an open window so that Leese is able to start life anew in the outdoors. At first the spider thinks she is dead, but gradually she perceives new beauty in the reflections of the stars. As she weaves her new web overnight, dew begins to form on the strands. At first she is distressed, but as dawn comes the light of sunrise makes the drops on the web shine like jewels. Leese has now made the most beautiful web ever.

While tourists admire the tapestry web in the Room of the Silver Weavings, Leese happily spins outdoors what seem to her even lovelier webs that shine with the jewels of the sun.

With its sensitive illustrations by James Brunsman, *Leese Webster* is an appealing book. The central action of the story is carefully structured and fully resolved. The artistic ambitions of the talented young spider are first fulfilled in the fine tapestry that becomes a museum piece, but her own dissatisfaction with her work lingers. It is not until her web catches the sparkle of sunlight on dew drops that she is able to match the beauty of the jewels she admired so much. The resolution of the action is not only aesthetically satisfying, but meaningful. Leese's triumph comes about as a result of what seems to her a catastrophe. When she is first thrown out of the window, she thinks she is dead. Later, when the drops of water cling to her web at night she thinks they will spoil it. Only the light of dawn reveals to her the bejeweled beauty that she has at last achieved.

The spider here is the figure of the artist. Le Guin has used the spider as an image of the master-patterner in the Earthsea trilogy. Leese is portrayed as a dedicated artist, quite willing to go hungry for her art and not at all dependent on the praise of others for her satisfaction. As she happily spins in the deserted room, her sole aim is to create beauty. She is also a highly original artist, not content to re-create the old art forms. Her dissatisfaction spurs her on to ever greater achievement.

The story is told consistently from Leese's point of view. When she finds herself outside, she thinks she has landed in an extremely large room. When the maids refer to a broom, the word terrifies her. There is also humor in her response. Thinking herself dead, she opens at first only one eye, then after a tentative look around, opens the other seven.

The language is never prosaic or condescending. There are a few words which children might not recognize, like "festooning" and "crevices," but both the clarity and the lyrical sound of the prose are satisfying to young readers. Enhanced by its resonance of the Arachne myth, it is enjoyable reading for adults as well, confirming C. S. Lewis's conviction that good children's literature is good literature.

Chapter Twelve
Critical Summary

Since Ursula K. Le Guin at fifty-five is still at the peak of her writing career, a critical overview of her literary achievement is not yet possible. As her most recent publications, *The Beginning Place* and *Hard Words,* clearly demonstrate, she is also still experimenting with new forms, so that another new book is likely to be not simply an addition but also an innovation. Whether she will, as some have speculated, turn to mainstream fiction or whether she will, as others have predicted, create yet new and richer forms of fantasy, remains to be seen. What is possible at this time is to survey the critical response to her published work so far, noting the directions in its development, culminating in her current reputation as an outstanding writer.

Survey of Criticism

Le Guin's first books did not attract any serious critical attention. The Hainish trilogy received only brief notices in SF magazines and quickly went out of print. Her first works to merit acclaim were *A Wizard of Earthsea* (1968) and *The Left Hand of Darkness* (1969), followed shortly by *The Tombs of Atuan* (1971), and *The Farthest Shore* (1972). All of these novels were award winners: *A Wizard of Earthsea,* the *Boston Globe*-Horn Book Award; *the Tombs of Atuan,* The Newberry Honor Book; *The Farthest Shore,* the National Book Award; and, most dramatically, *The Left Hand of Darkness,* both the Hugo and Nebula awards for the best science-fiction novel of the year. In 1974 the double honor was conferred on *The Dispossessed,* making Le Guin the only writer to win both of these prestigious awards twice. In addition to the novels, three short works were award winners during this period: *The Word for World Is Forest* (1972) and "The Ones Who Walk Away from Omelas" (1973), both Hugos, and "The Day Before the Revolution" (1974), a Nebula.

Along with these stunning awards—all, however, in fantasy and science fiction, a disadvantage from the viewpoint of the critical establishment—came a delayed critical recognition. In general the Earthsea trilogy received more attention in England, where fantasy is a highly respected genre, and the SF novels more in this country, where science fiction has a vast following but still remains a marginal genre in the academic world. When the *New York Times* somewhat belatedly reviewed the Earthsea trilogy, it called upon the English poet Robert Nye to do the job. In contrast the *Times Literary Supplement* published full reviews of each volume by Naomi Lewis, who praised the whole for its "total realization of place, time, customs, laws of behavior, of magic."[1] Serious discussion of Le Guin's science fiction, however, followed quickly upon success of *The Left Hand of Darkness*. The widespread acclaim afforded this novel in effect conferred retroactive value on the earlier Hainish trilogy, which was subsequently reprinted in hardback and reviewed adequately for the first time over a decade after its initial appearance.

Although Le Guin's reputation as a science-fiction writer was definitely established after the publication of *The Left Hand of Darkness,* discussion of that novel involved considerable controversy. A major challenge to its international acclaim was voiced by fellow science-fiction writer Stanislaw Lem, who objected that the theme of androgyny is not sufficiently integrated into the plot of the novel. A further, somewhat related, objection was expressed by feminist critics, including Joanna Russ, who complained that the androgyny theme fails because the inhabitants of Gethen all seem to the reader to be exclusively male, rather than bisexual.[2] In this controversy a major champion of the novel was Canadian critic Darko Suvin, who described it as a "truly civilized fable on human love and trust independent of (though deeply concerned with) maleness or femininity."[3]

Le Guin's next double winner, *The Dispossessed,* also provoked a lively controversy among reviewers, which helped to enhance her already firm reputation. The *Times Literary Supplement,* which had praised the Earthsea trilogy, found *The Dispossessed* a disappointment.[4] American critics have debated the work's merits and shortcomings, their opinions ranging from Suvin's appraisal of "masterpiece" on the dust jacket to Russ's complaint that the novel displays too much telling and not enough showing.[5] The mere fact of this controversy is important, for it reveals that Le Guin has to that extent escaped the science-fiction ghetto and entered the realm of serious academic consideration. In 1975 she received recognition in both camps, with both a special issue of *Science-Fiction Studies* devoted to her work and a seminar of the Modern Language Association concerned solely with her fiction.

In spite of this recognition in 1975, Le Guin's fiction is still not adequately reviewed. The short stories in particular have been neglected. Even the two collections, *The Wind's Twelve Quarters* and *Orsinian Tales*, have received little attention. Thomas J. Remington's article relates three of the stories—"Nine Lives," *The Word for World Is Forest*, and "Vaster Than Empires"—to themes in the novels, and James Bittner's essay offers the only substantial exploration so far of theme and form in the Orsinian collection.[6] Only one major review article appeared in connection with *The Language of the Night*. S. J. Edelheit's review in the *Boston Review* is an extended and sensitive statement about that work in its relationship to the fiction.[7] As for *The Beginning Place*, token reviews in *Time* and *Newsweek* were content with mere plot summary followed by routine praise.[8] Apparently the main problem inhibiting reviewer response to this latest novel is the question of genre, which has been a stumbling block for Le Guin throughout her career so far.

The Problem of Genre

Le Guin's earliest difficulties in achieving publication were caused by the genre problem. Her first stories were set in the imaginary country of Orsinia, but were neither fantasy, nor science fiction, nor realism. As a result they were repeatedly rejected. She learned that in order to be published in this country, one has to write pieces which are easily categorized.[9] When she aimed deliberately to write a clearly definable science-fiction story, she found a ready market for it.

Although the publications continued steadily once they had started, the genre problem returned to plague Le Guin in a different way at the height of her success. The problem afflicted even her greatest triumphs, that is, the Earthsea trilogy, *The Left Hand of Darkness,* and *The Dispossessed.* The Earthsea trilogy was labeled not only fantasy, which in this country was not regarded seriously in the late sixties, but also children's literature. As a result it did not receive proper critical attention. The special issue of *Science-Fiction Studies,* for example, neglects the trilogy altogether. The case of *The Left Hand of Darkness* and *The Dispossessed* was not a matter of neglect because of genre but of misinterpretation based on genre. While their recognition as science-fiction novels gained her both awards and an international reputation, it also narrowly categorized her as an SF writer.

Much of the negative commentary that met both of these novels was based on generic assumptions. Rather than extending the definition of science fiction to include her richly innovative techniques, several commentators attacked the novels for not adhering to an accepted narrow definition of science fiction. What is especially significant about both of these novels is that they have in fact extended the limits of science fiction. Fortunately a few excellent interpretive essays have opened the way to future reading of Le Guin's fiction as "literature," not merely as science fiction.

A few critics deserve special attention for their perceptive treatment of individual works in ways that transcend generic boundaries. The first serious recognition of the Earthsea trilogy as more than children's literature was Eleanor Cameron's article on the work as "high fantasy," which recognizes Le Guin's sophisticated use of anthropology and psychology in developing the major themes of names and shadows.[10] Peter Nicholl's review of *The Farthest Shore* in the British journal *Foundation* also argues that the trilogy transcends the category of juvenile fiction and compares Le Guin's work favorably with that of Tolkien and Lewis.[11] He finds her morality subtler than Tolkien's and her metaphysic more convincing than Lewis's. With praise for style as well as content, he considers the trilogy her finest achievement to date.

After much debate about the relative merits and shortcomings of *The Left Hand of Darkness,* Martin Bickman's essay on form and content in the novel marks a significant break-through.[12] He points out that several of the earlier readings of the novel fail to take into account Le Guin's use of point of view. According to Bickman, Genly Ai functions as the structuring consciousness of the narrative, channeling the reader's response accordingly. He also indicates that although this kind of unity in form and content is expected in the traditional novel, it has been overlooked in this case because of the science-fiction label.

Similarly *The Dispossessed* is redeemed from its generic labels by George Turner's interpretive essay on pattern and meaning.[13] Turner compares the novel's structure with that of a literary classic, George Eliot's *Daniel Deronda,* thus avoiding the SF category altogether. Concentrating on the relationship between the structural pattern and the thematic content, he then shows how Le Guin's and Eliot's novels are alike in their parallel presentation of contrasting societies. Like Bickman's, this essay demonstrates the critical validity of approaching the Le Guin novel as novel.

Recent Trends in Criticism

During the flurry of critical activity that followed Le Guin's novels winning prestigious awards, for the first time a few attempts were made to see her fiction as a whole. Along with the pioneering articles which considered her novels as works of literature rather than as examples of formulaic fantasy or science fiction, a few critics chose to deal with themes and techniques in all of her published fiction to date. To do so was in itself to regard her as a novelist rather than a science-fiction writer, to approach her work as one might approach Dickens or Forster rather than Asimov or Dick. Some of these essays dealing with her work comprehensively were written in languages other than English, a testimony to the international standing she had achieved by about 1975.

Douglas Barbour's essay in *Science-Fiction Studies* (1974) was the first to consider Le Guin's fiction as a whole, apart from the Earthsea books, noting themes and images that appear throughout.[14] As his title "Wholeness and Balance in the Hainish Novels of Ursula K. Le Guin" indicates, Barbour is concerned with the overall influence of Taoism, but he is also concerned with the quest theme, the imagery of light and darkness, and ability to create whole cultures convincingly. His study ranges over the six Hainish novels, but he deals with the Earthsea group of novels independently.

Also in 1974 Robert Scholes undertook a careful scrutiny of Le Guin's fiction in his article "The Good Witch of the West." Although beginning with a comparative study of the Earthsea trilogy with Lewis's Narnia books, Scholes moves on to consider *The Left Hand of Darkness*. Unlike some of the critics of this novel, he sees it as a unified achievement focused on the relationship between the main characters. He also finds the Earthsea books as much of a classic as the Narnia chronicles. His praise of Le Guin is in terms of the traditional novel as well as science fiction. Not only is she "the best writer of speculative fabulation" in the country today, but she also "deserves a place among our major contemporary writers of fiction."[15]

In 1975 two articles dealt with an overview of Le Guin's fiction to date. Rafael Nudelman, a Russian theoretical physicist, offers a subtle analysis called "An Approach to the Structure of Le Guin's Science Fiction." Using the methods of semiotics and structuralism, he studies the relationships between part and whole and between time and space in her fiction. He focuses on the structural principle he calls

Iconicity: "the 'lower' level of the narrative form is a similarity, an image, the isomorphic sign of a more general or 'higher' formal level." According to this principle the narrative structure, usually in the form of a journey, is isomorphic with the textual structure, in which the "scattered elements strive toward oneness."[16] The overall structural pattern in Le Guin's fiction is thus a dynamic movement away from fragmentation and toward unity. Structure and content are an organic whole.

Somewhat similar in its optimistic conclusions about Le Guin's open universe although it is not based on structuralism, Darko Suvin's essay "Parables of De-Alienation: Le Guin's Widdershins Dance" is focused on *The Dispossessed* and "The New Atlantis" but clearly has implications for all of her works.[17] Suvin explores two kinds of alienation, external and internal. External alienation is imposed by oppressive government and society, but internal alienation is brought about within the individual psyche. In *The Dispossessed* he finds Shevek's theories of time a correlative to the political revolution. Shevek's alienation is both external and internal, and his temporal theory together with the revolution attempts to overcome both forms. In "The New Atlantis" the alienation of the individual and the society in a contemporary setting is juxtaposed to the emergence of a new collectivist and harmonious society. Alienation is in itself a contrary movement (a "widdershins dance") but it leads in turn to a new harmony, a pattern that applies to the early trilogy as well as to the later novel and short story.

In 1976 George Slusser's pamphlet, *The Farthest Shores of Ursula K. Le Guin,* included the Earthsea trilogy in its survey of the novels to date. Because of his emphasis on moral themes, such as the nature of evil, his focus is quite different from other assessments. He regards Taoism as a major influence although he neglects *The Lathe of Heaven.* In tracing Le Guin's development through the nine novels from 1966 to 1974, he finds certain definite directions. He notes a movement away from heroes to complex protagonists, away from straightforward narration to experiments with points of view, and away from external to internal evil. Slusser disagrees with critics such as Suvin in that he finds the tenor of Le Guin's fiction growing more pessimistic. The experiment on Urras betrays "unregenerate human nature" and in both "The Day Before the Revolution" and "The New Atlantis" he finds that "the individual life ends in death, the collective existence in annihilation."[18]

In 1977 *Science-Fiction Studies* carried a two-part essay translated from the French, written by Gerard Klein, an economist and science-fiction writer-editor.[19] In the first part Klein assesses the pervasive pessimism in American science fiction, and in the second explains how Le Guin manages to avoid it. Assuming the Marxist position as formulated by Lucien Goldmann, that is, that the real subject of a work of literature is the current situation of the social group the author belongs to, Klein delves into the attitudes of the social group of American SF writers. He finds that they are the middle class, technologically oriented group who feel threatened by recent changes in the world economic and social structures. Because of their concern about these threats to their own values, their fiction is dominated by a tone of pessimism. Le Guin, on the other hand, as Klein goes on to explain in the second part, does not belong to that group. Her own background is intellectual and academic, focused on anthropology and history. As a result her values are rooted in cultural diversity and relativity rather than in technological progress. She also avoids the trap of identifying the future of the world with the future of her own social group, as so many SF writers seem to do. An underlying optimism therefore pervades Le Guin's ethnological science fiction. Her created worlds illustrate Levi-Strauss's theory in *Race et Histoire,* that is, that cultural diversity is a natural phenomenon and civilization is a process not a linear progress. Klein also attributes Le Guin's worlds of cultural diversity to the fact that she is a woman, freed from the obsessive male urge toward aggression. This view is in keeping with the ideas about war as rape expressed by Le Guin in *The Left Hand of Darkness* and "The Eye of the Heron."

Opposed to Slusser's sense of pessimism in the fiction and closer to Klein's recognition of her optimism is Susan Wood's vision of Le Guin's celebration of life in her 1978 essay, "Discovering Worlds: The Fiction of Ursula K. Le Guin." Wood stresses the creative imagination and applies Le Guin's journey motif to the evolving form of her novels. These works are a series of voyages of exploration, journeys into the creative unconscious where new worlds are discovered and given shape through language. Since discovery is the focus, the novels celebrate the diversity of life and accept the possibility of ever new worlds. For Wood there is a definite decline in the later works, such as *The Word for World* and *The Dispossessed* because there moral ethical patterns are imposed rather than discovered, a process contrary to Le Guin's own convictions expressed in *Dreams Must Explain Themselves.* Wood also views the Le Guin protagonist, whether scientist, or wizard, or traveler, as a figure of the creative artist, also in accord with Le Guin's own assertions about wizardry as artistry as they occur in the Earthsea books. On the whole Wood's essay is balanced and perceptive, wisely based on the author's own ideas about her fiction.

The essays of Barbour, Scholes, Nudelman, Suvin, Slusser, Klein, and Wood are valuable both for drawing attention to pervasive facets of Le Guin's work and for suggesting possibilities for future study. Although they deal with her fiction as a body rather than with individual works, however, they are still limited in scope, partly because of the growing body of work available for study. Now that several additional novels, short stories, essays, and poems have been added, there is rich and complex material awaiting further critical attention.

Present and Future

Although a critical overview is still premature, a progress report is very much in order. At mid-career Le Guin has already made major contributions not merely to contemporary fantasy and science fiction but also to contemporary American literature. The Earthsea trilogy ranks with the acknowledged fantasy masterpieces of Tolkien and Lewis; *The Left Hand of Darkness* stirred critical acclaim and controversy in Europe as well as the United States, establishing Le Guin as an SF writer of international rank; and *The Dispossessed* which she labeled "an ambiguous Utopia" has engaged the concern of utopian critics who conclude that its brilliance will obviate the need for further utopian writing over the next several years. In addition to these three achievements in three separate areas of fiction, she has written award-winning short stories in still different genres, such as "The Ones Who Walk Away from Omelas," a philosophical parable, and "The Day Before the Revolution," which, although about the founder of an imaginary world, is in itself a mainstream story about old age and death. A poet and essayist as well, Le Guin has also written an historical novel and a variety of entertaining short pieces covering the gamut of realism, fantasy, science fiction, and combinations thereof. Ursula K. Le Guin is a literary presence, a major voice in American literature, who cannot be circumscribed in any generic literary ghetto.

What are the distinctive traits of this versatile and gifted writer? First and foremost is her myth-making ability. As reflected in the title of one of her early interviews—"Meet Ursula: She Can Shape You A Universe"—she has the ability to create a completely coherent and convincing secondary world, with authenticating details of language, history, myth, climate, geography, calendar, flora, and fauna. The authenticity is confirmed by much more than superficial details of landscape. Drawing on her anthropological background, Le Guin is able to create cultural concepts for her imaginary societies. Concepts such as "kemmer" and "shifgrethor" on Gethen, the stone-pounding ritual on Werel, the worship of the Nameless Ones on Atuan, and "mindspeech" as it occurs throughout the Hainish works, give depth and inner configuration to her invented worlds.

Le Guin's mythopoeic imagination is gracefully fulfilled and embodied in her elegantly precise style. In her hands language is a flexible instrument, and she is equally adept at humor, vivid description, straightforward suspenseful narrative, stream-of-consciousness, and nuances of dialogue. Her flair for the apt metaphor spices her expository as well as imaginative prose, as when she predicts that the child whose imagination is neglected will "grow up to be an eggplant." In total contrast, the epic description of the flight across the Gobrin Ice has sustained power and magnitude, modulated with delicacy in handling the sensitive human relationship involved. An added feature of her stylistic prowess is her ability in naming. Characters, places, and alien concepts all seem to have exactly the right original name, affirming the author's contention that she "discovers" rather than "invents" names.

Characterization is also unusually strong in Le Guin's fiction. Her gallery of fictitious portraits is filled with memorable characters: Wold and Odo as portrayals of old age, Shevek as a sensitive, troubled intellectual, naïve Genly Ai as one struggling for understanding, the proud youth Ged and reluctant priestess Tenar, the alienated adolescents Owen and Natalie, Hugh and Irene, and—not to omit the nonhuman world—the superbly ancient dragon Kalessin, with a glint of humor in his cold, yellow eye. Neither flat nor static, Le Guin's characters experience both internal conflict and moral growth. To do justice to either Ged or Shevek, to cite just two examples, one would have to recite their development in full, for they mature through experience. As a result many of her characters are convincingly contradictory: courageous and fearful, humble and proud, lonely and gregarious. In short, they are real.

Narrative structure is also a distinctive feature in Le Guin's fiction. Almost none of her novels falls into a pattern of simple linear plot. Even in her early fiction, she experiments with the circular journey as structure as well as theme. She later tries basing structure on point of view (e.g., *The Left Hand of Darkness*), and she creates parallel and double structures (*The Dispossessed* and "The New Atlantis"). All of these structural experiments involve to some extent manipulating point of view, and all are at the same time exact manifestations of theme. Never simplistic, Le Guin's fiction aims at an organic interweaving of plot, theme, character, and structure. The use of musical motifs in several of her works, especially in "The New Atlantis," *The Beginning Place,* and "An Die Musik," hints strongly at a structural analogue in musical form. The parallel and mutually affective worlds in *The Beginning Place* and "The New Atlantis" are instances of contrapuntal structure.

Still another striking feature in her fiction is Le Guin's use of imagery, both verbal and nonverbal. The verbal imagery is, of course, a molecular unit of her writing style. The nonverbal images, however, tend to resonate in the reader's memory long after finishing the novel. Like C. S. Lewis, who began his Narnia stories when he envisioned a fawn carrying an umbrella, Le Guin often begins her novels with a concrete image. The genesis of *The Left Hand of Darkness,* for example, was her vision of two people dragging a sled across the ice. Other evocative images are the heron at the pool ("The Eye of the Heron"), the rowan tree at the center of the grove *(The Farthest Shore),* the daisy growing in the cracks *(The Lathe of Heaven),* the patterning frame *(The City of Illusions),* the stone of power *(A Wizard of Earthsea).* Certain images are precisely associated with character, for example, the hawk with Ged; some function as thematic setting, for example, the tombs of Atuan. Most radiate meaning from their own center, transcending any of the separate components of the work in which they appear.

Mythopoeic imagination, character, style, imagery, and structure are all qualitative features of Le Guin's fiction. Yet they do not add up to the sense of the whole. There is in her fiction a vision that transcends even these distinctive elements. Le Guin's fiction offers a thrilling personal vision of a universe, a whirling, expanding infinitely peopled universe, with harmony in its vast movement and unity in its complex diversity. Her personal voice, like that of all great writers, resonates from its roots in tree and stone to its ultimate reach beyond the stars. She has already created a galaxy with profoundly human relevance, and her reading public can only wait with soaring expectancy for what will follow next.

Notes and References

Chapter One

1. Joe de Bolt, "A Le Guin Biography," *Ursula K. Le Guin: Voyager* (Port Washington, N.Y., 1979), p. 13. I am much indebted to this excellent brief biography.
2. Ibid., p. 14.
3. Theodora Kroeber, *Alfred Kroeber: A Personal Configuration* (Berkeley: University of California Press, 1970), p. 141. This biography gives a lively picture of family life in the Kroeber household.
4. De Bolt, *Le Guin: Voyager*, p. 15.
5. Ibid., p. 17.
6. Claude Levi-Strauss, *Tristes Tropiques* (New York: Atheneum, 1968), p. 58.
7. For a detailed discussion of this subject, see Karen Sinclair, "Solitary Being: The Hero as Anthropologist," de Bolt, *Le Guin: Voyager*, pp. 50–65.
8. See especially "Dreams Must Explain Themselves," "The Child and the Shadow," and "Myth and Archetype in Science Fiction," all reprinted in *The Language of the Night* (New York, 1979), pp. 47–56, 59–72, 73–82. See also chapter 9 below.
9. "The Child and the Shadow," *The Language of the Night*, pp. 63–64.
10. Le Guin's major sources of information about Taoism, apart from her own reading of the *Tao Te Ching*, are Holmes Welch, *The Parting of the Way* (Boston; Beacon Press, 1966) and Joseph Needham, *Science and Civilization in China* (Cambridge: Cambridge University Press, 1962). Quotations from Lao Tse and Chuang Tse serve as chapter headings in *The Lathe of Heaven*.
11. "Dreams Must Explain Themselves," *The Language of the Night*, p. 55.
12. For an interesting comparison, see C. S. Lewis's "Illustrations of the Tao" in the appendix to *The Abolition of Man* (New York: Macmillan, 1947). Although Lewis is a Christian, he finds that the Tao as natural law is reflected universally in all civilizations, and he quotes from sources widely different in time and place (Babylonian, Hindu, ancient Roman, Norse, Biblical, Chinese, and Renaissance English).
13. Lin Yutang, trans., *The Wisdom of Laotse* (New York: Random House, 1948), p. 216, p. 79.

Chapter Two

1. *Rocannon's World* was reviewed briefly in *Magazine of Fantasy and Science Fiction* 31 (December 1966): 32. All three novels were reviewed when they were reprinted in paperback in the 1970s.

2. *The Language of the Night,* p. 136.

3. *Rocannon's World* (New York, 1966). Subsequent page references are to this edition. *The Language of the Night,* p. 134.

4. Le Guin's adaptation of the story is based on Padraic Colum, *The Children of Odin* (New York: Macmillan, 1920).

5. Again Colum's *The Children of Odin* is the main source. Part 2 of Colum's book is entitled "Odin the Wanderer."

6. *Planet of Exile* (New York, 1966). Page references in text.

7. *The Language of the Night,* p. 141.

8. *City of Illusions* (New York, 1967). Page references in text.

9. Le Guin notes that *City of Illusions* gave her the chance to use "my own 'translation' (collation-ripoff) of the *Tao Te Ching.*" *The Language of the Night,* p. 147. For other studies, see chapter 1, n. 10.

10. Welch, *The Parting of the Way,* p. 21.

11. Ibid., p. 24.

12. *The Language of the Night,* p. 146.

13. Ibid., p. 147.

Chapter Three

1. On 6 April 1973 a *Times Literary Supplement* reviewer wrote, "After Earthsea lore, with its weight and substance, most other modern fantasies must ring thin." Susan Wood remarks that "Le Guin's best work, the Earthsea trilogy, derives its great strength from the direct translation of ideas into shared experience." "Discovering Worlds: The Fiction of Ursula Le Guin," *Voices for the Future,* ed. Thomas D. Clareson (Bowling Green, Ohio: Bowling Green University Popular Press, 1978), p. 175. For similar views see Eleanor Cameron, "High Fantasy: A Wizard of Earthsea," *Horn Book,* April 1971, pp. 129–38; George Edgar Slusser, *The Farthest Shores of Ursula K. Le Guin* (San Bernardino, Calif., Borgo Press, 1976).

2. "The Child and the Shadow," *The Language of the Night,* p. 65.

3. Le Guin complained about "adult chauvinist piggery" among American publishers and reviewers. She noted that "English readers are grownup enough not to be defensive about being grownup," and applauded the fact that juvenile fantasy is reviewed with respect in English newspapers. See "Dreams Must Explain Themselves," *The Language of the Night,* p. 55.

4. Le Guin explains that she did not invent but rather discovered Earthsea. "I did not deliberately invent Earthsea. I did not think 'Hey wow—islands are archetypes and archipelagoes are superarchetypes and let's build us an archipelago!' I am not an engineer, but an explorer. I discovered Earthsea." *The Language of the Night,* pp. 49–50. The names which appear on the map of Earthsea were discovered in her unconscious. This aesthetic of discovery is also implicit in Taoism, according to which true laws exist in things and are, therefore, to be found, not imposed. The Taoist world view is one of immanence, not transcendance.

5. Among primitive peoples personal names are carefully kept from general knowledge. In many cases each individual has a secret name which is never mentioned except in solemn ritual. See James Frazer, *The Golden Bough* (New York: Mentor, 1959), 1 vol. abr. ed., especially "Tabooed Words," pp. 235–46.

6. "The Child and the Shadow," *The Language of the Night*, p. 64.

7. *A Wizard of Earthsea* (New York, 1968). Page references in text.

8. The bird is symbolic of the soul in folklore over the world. See Frazer, *Bough*, pp. 199, 266. In medieval drama death was represented by the release of a bird from a cage.

9. In ancient times bactyllic stones, or meteorites, were held to be sacred. Upright stones were also associated with the world center, the source of life. For discussion of some of these traditional beliefs, see Francis Hitchin, *Earth Magic* (New York: Pocket Books, 1976).

10. See John Pfeiffer, "But Dragons Have Keen Ears: On Hearing 'Earthsea' with Recollections of Beowulf," de Bolt, *Le Guin: Voyager*, pp. 115–27.

11. "Dreams Must Explain Themselves," *The Language of the Night*, p. 55.

12. *The Tombs of Atuan* (New York, 1971). Page references in text.

13. For further discussion of early feminine religious practices, see Esther Harding, *Women's Mysteries* (New York: Bantam, 1971).

14. Erich Neumann, *The Great Mother*, trans. Ralph Manheim (Princeton: Princeton University Press, 1955).

15. Ibid.

16. For discussion of the complex history of the labyrinth, see John Layard, *The Lady of the Hare* (London: Faber & Faber, 1944).

17. Rollin A. Lasseter, "Four Letters About Le Guin," de Bolt, *Le Guin: Voyager*, p. 100.

18. "Dreams Must Explain Themselves," *The Language of the Night*, p. 55.

19. For further discussion of the cosmic tree and the world axis see Mircea Eliade, *Patterns of Comparative Religion* (New York: Sheed & Ward, 1958).

20. *The Farthest Shore* (New York, 1972). Page references in text.

21. James Bittner has pointed out the apparent influence of Rilke's tenth elegy on Le Guin's landscape of death, particularly the Mountain of Pain. Rilke refers specifically to the Stars of the Land of Pain and to the mountains of Primal Pain. See Rainer Maria Rilke, *Duino Elegies*, ed. J. B. Leishman and Stephen Spender (London: Hogarth Press, 1939).

22. The analogy to Shakespeare's Prospero is worth noting. Prospero, however, discards his wand deliberately.

23. The *Odyssey* also offers alternative endings, but one is in the form of a prophecy. The poem ends with Odysseus in his palace, having cleared it

of the suitors. In the prophecy offered in his journey to the land of the dead, however, he is told that he will leave home again and go on to a land where the people have never known the sea and never use salt with their food.

Chapter Four

1. I am relying here on the ingenious but convincing chronology worked out by Ian Watson, "Le Guin's *Lathe of Heaven* and the Role of Dick: The False Reality as Mediator," *Science-Fiction Studies* 2 (March 1975):67–75. See chart, p. 68.

2. *The Left Hand of Darkness* (New York, 1969). Page references in text.

3. For discussion of the novel's unity see Martin Bickman, "Le Guin's *Left Hand of Darkness:* Form and Content," *Science-Fiction Studies* 4 (March 1977):42–47.

4. "Winter's King" was originally published in *Orbit V* (1969). It is reprinted in *The Wind's Twelve Quarters* (New York, 1975), pp. 85–108.

5. David Ketterer, "*The Left Hand of Darkness:* Ursula Le Guin's Archetypal 'Winter Journey,' " *New Worlds for Old* (Garden City, N.Y.: Doubleday, 1974), pp. 76–90.

6. Northrop Frye, *Anatomy of Criticism* (Princeton: Princeton University Press, 1957), pp. 131–242.

7. For fuller discussion of this myth see N. B. Hayles, "Androgyny, Ambivalence, and Assimilation in *The Left Hand of Darkness," Ursula K. Le Guin,* ed. Joseph D. Olander and Martin Henry Greenberg (New York, 1979), pp. 97–115.

8. "Ketterer on *The Left Hand of Darkness"* *Science-Fiction Studies* 1 (July 1975):139.

9. The phrase is from Peter Brigg, "The Archetype of the Journey in Ursula K. Le Guin's Fiction," Olander and Greenberg, *Le Guin,* p. 49.

10. For discussion of the symbolism of sacred space and the sacred Center of the World, see Mircea Eliade, *The Sacred and the Profane,* trans. Willard R. Trask (New York: Harcourt Brace, 1959), pp. 20–67. Eliade develops the idea that "the true world is always in the middle, at the Center, for it is here that there is a break in plane and hence communication among the three cosmic zones" (p. 42).

11. Jeanne Murray Walker, "Myth, Exchange and History in *The Left Hand of Darkness," Science-Fiction Studies* 6 (1979):180–89.

12. Stanislaw Lem, "Lost Opportunities," *SF Commentary* 24 (November 1971):22–24. Reprinted in *Women of Wonder,* ed. Pamela Sargent (New York: Vintage, 1975).

13. *SF Commentary* 26 (April 1972):90–92. Reprinted in *Women of Wonder.*

14. "Is Gender Necessary?" *The Language of the Night,* p. 168. This essay first appeared in *Aurora: Beyond Equality* (Greenwich, Conn.: New Directions, 1976).

15. Introduction to *The Altered I: An Encounter with Science Fiction,* ed. Lee Harding (Carlton, Victoria, Australia: Nostrilia Press, 1976). See also the poem "Amazed" in *Hard Words* (New York: Harper & Row, 1981), p. 75. The last two lines of the poem read: "I am not I/but eye."

Chapter Five

1. *The Lathe of Heaven* was first published in 1971 in *Amazing Stories Magazine* when "Vaster Than Empires and More Slow" first appeared in *New Dimensions 1.* *The Word for World Is Forest* first appeared in editor Harlan Ellison's anthology *Again, Dangerous Visions* (1972). Page references are from the following editions: *The Lathe of Heaven* (New York, 1971); "Vaster Than Empires and More Slow," the reprint in *The Wind's Twelve Quarters; The Word for World Is Forest* (New York, 1976).

2. Douglas Barbour discusses Taoist ideas in *The Lathe of Heaven* in "*The Lathe of Heaven:* Taoist Dream," *Algol* 21 (November 1973):22–24. Ian Watson attributes some of the distinctive features of this book to the influence of Philip Dick. See his "Le Guin's *The Lathe of Heaven* and the Role of Dick: The False Reality as Mediator," *Science-Fiction Studies* 2 (March 1975), 67–75.

3. According to one popular tradition, the year 1998 will be the fateful one because Christ died in the 1998th week of his life. See *The People's Almanac,* ed. David Wallechinsky and Irving Wallace (New York: William Morrow & Co., 1978), p. 639.

4. Quotations are from *The Wisdom of Laotse,* ed. and trans. Lin Yutang (New York: Random House, 1948).

5. The cyclical journey is a continually recurring motif in the fiction of Le Guin, both stated and enacted in narrative structure. Ged returns home to the isle of Gont at the end of the Earthsea journey. Shevek and Falk-Ramarren return to their home planets. The Odonian revolutionary maxim in *The Dispossessed,* "True journey is return," echoes the alien's "to go is to return."

6. Theodore Sturgeon, *National Review,* 4 February 1972, p. 106.

7. Ibid.

8. Le Guin's short commentary on the television production appears in *TV Guide* (5 January 1980).

9. A chart providing dates for each of the Hainish works appears in Watson, "Le Guin's *Lathe,*" p. 68.

10. Although Le Guin did not know it at the time of writing, the Athshean attitude toward dreaming closely resembles that of the Senoi people of Malaya. The Senoit culture is largely based on training in and use of the dream. Not only are their dreams seen as meaningful and as the basis for solving personal and social problems, but also their dream state and waking state are regarded as equal. It is particularly interesting to note that the

Senoi have not had a murder or a war for centuries. See "Synchronicity Can Happen at Almost Any Time," *The Language of the Night*, pp. 152–54.

11. For further discussion see Sneja Gunew, "Mythic Reversals: The Evolution of the Shadow Motif," Olander and Greenberg, pp. 178–99.

12. Le Guin admits an obsession with trees. In her introduction to "The Word of Unbinding" in *The Wind's Twelve Quarters*, she remarks, "I think I am definitely the most arboreal science fiction writer" (p. 65). Reflecting this preoccupation, her short story "Direction of the Road" is told from the viewpoint of the tree. *The Wind's Twelve Quarters*, pp. 244–50.

13. The stanza of "The Garden" relevant to Osden's remark is as follows:

> Meanwhile the Mind, from pleasures less,
> Withdraws into its happiness:
> The Mind, that Ocean where each kind
> Does straight its own resemblance find;
> Yet it creates, transcending these,
> Far other Worlds, and other Seas;
> Annihilating all that's made
> To a green Thought in a green Shade.

Chapter Six

1. *The Language of the Night*, p. 111.

2. See Le Guin's introduction to "The Day Before the Revolution," *The Wind's Twelve Quarters*, p. 260.

3. Ibid.

4. All page references are from *The Dispossessed* (New York: Avon Books, 1975).

5. See "Taoist Configurations: *The Dispossessed*," de Bolt, *Le Guin: Voyager*, pp. 153–79.

6. Shevek originated in Le Guin's childhood memory of Robert Oppenheimer as a young man. She recalled "a thin face, large clear eyes, and large ears," and a personality that was attractive: "attractive, I mean, as a flame to a moth." *The Language of the Night*, p. 111.

7. Robert C. Elliott, "A New Utopian Novel," *Yale Review* 65 (December 1975): 257.

8. Peter Brigg, "The Archetype of the Journey in Ursula K. Le Guin's Fiction," Olander and Greenberg, p. 55.

9. Lasseter, "Four Letters," de Bolt, *Le Guin: Voyager*, p. 109.

10. *Time*, 5 August 1974, p. 84. Although brief, this anonymous review has high praise for the style of the novel, "remarkable for its sinewy grace."

11. See Le Guin's introduction to the story in *The Wind's Twelve Quarters*, p. 251.

12. All page references are from "The Ones Who Walk Away from Omelas," *The Wind's Twelve Quarters,* pp. 251–59.

13. All page references are from "The Day Before the Revolution," *The Wind's Twelve Quarters,* pp. 261–77.

14. All page references are from *The Norton Anthology of Short Fiction,* ed. R. V. Cassill (New York: W. W. Norton, 1978), pp. 397–416. The original publication in 1975 (see bibliography) was not available to me at the time of writing.

15. The number seven, comprising the ternary and the quaternity, is symbolically associated with completeness and perfection. J. C. Cooper, *Encyclopedia of Traditional Symbols* (London: Thomas & Hudson, 1978), summarizes the number seven as follows: "The number of the universe, the macrocosm. Completeness; a totality. With the three of the heavens and the soul and the four of the earth and the body, it is the first number which contains both the spiritual and temporal" (p. 117).

16. Lasseter, "Four Letters," de Bolt, *Le Guin: Voyager,* p. 109.

17. Slusser, *The Farthest Shores of Le Guin,* p. 9.

18. Darko Suvin, "Parables of De-Alienation: Le Guin's Widdershins Dance," *Science-Fiction Studies* 2 (November 1975): 257.

19. For further discussion of this idea see Timothy R. O'Neill, *The Individuated Hobbit* (Boston: Houghton Mifflin, 1979). The loss of Atlantis (or, in Tolkien's case, Numenor) signifies the "real beginning of Man's movement to one-sidedness, and the powerful affect-image associated with renewal" (p. 163).

Chapter Seven

1. All references to the three Le Guin works are from the following editions: *The Wind's Twelve Quarters* (1975); *Orsinian Tales* (New York: Harper & Row, 1976); and *Very Far Away from Anywhere Else* (New York: Atheneum, 1976).

2. "Semley's Necklace," for example, is a prologue to *Rocannon's World;* "The Rule of Names" and "The Word of Unbinding" are the germinal stories for *A Wizard of Earthsea* and *The Farthest Shore;* "Winter's King" introduces *The Left Hand of Darkness.*

3. Le Guin quotes Carl Gustav Jung in *The Wind's Twelve Quarters,* p. 201.

4. Henry Vaughn, an early seventeenth-century mystical poet, is best known for his visionary poem, "The World." Besides the opening lines, two lines from the last stanza, although not quoted, are paraphrased by Hughes, "O fools (said I), thus to prefer dark night / Before true light."

5. *Atlantic Monthly* (December 1975), p. 118.

6. *New Republic* (7 February 1976), pp. 28–29.

7. Bittner's excellent article is "Persuading Us to Rejoice and Teaching Us How to Praise: Le Guin's *Orsinian Tales*," *Science-Fiction Studies* 5 (1978):215–42.

8. The remark appeared originally in "The Crab Nebula, The Parmacium, and Tolstoy," *Riverside Quarterly* 5 (1972):89–96. This article is the source of Bittner's title.

9. Bittner, "Persuading Us," p. 235.

10. Marcia Hoffman, *Library Journal* 51 (1 October 1975):2086.

11. *New Statesman* 93 (10 June 1977):787.

12. *Educational Journal* 62 (May 1978):90.

13. *Horn Book* 53 (February 1977):57.

Chapter Eight

1. All quotations are from the following edition: *Millennial Women*, ed. Virginia Kidd (New York: Dell, 1978), pp. 124–302.

2. For discussion of the place of the household in the symbolism of the center, see Mircea Eliade, *The Sacred and the Profane*, trans. Willard Trask (New York: Harcourt Brace, 1959), pp. 20–65. According to Eliade, in traditional societies the household is sanctified by cosmological symbolism. Each dwelling is symbolically situated at the Center of the World. Le Guin's interest in the symbolism of the center is also reflected in her poem, "Amazed":

> The center is not where the center is
> but where I will be when I follow
> the lines of stones that wind about a center
> that is not there
> > but there.

> (*Hard Words*, 75)

3. *Ms.*, July 1978, p. 35.

4. *Bulletin: Center for Children's Books* 32 (November 1978):46.

5. All page references are to *Malafrena* (New York: Berkley-Putnam, 1979).

6. *Times Literary Supplement*, 11 April 1980, p. 416.

7. Allan J. Mayer, *Newsweek* (1 September 1980), p. 74.

8. All references are to *The Beginning Place* (New York, 1980).

9. The theme, but not its treatment, recalls both the Earthsea trilogy and *Very Far Away from Anywhere Else*. Owen and Natalie, the young protagonists in *Very Far Away from Anywhere Else*, are similar to Hugh and Irene in their isolation and alienation as well as in their need to escape parental oppression.

Chapter Nine

1. *The Language of the Night*. The title is taken from this Le Guin statement quoted on the dust jacket. Page references in text.

2. It is interesting to compare Le Guin's remark about the disciplined imagination in both art and science with Albert Einstein's remark that "the gift of fantasy has meant more to me than my talent for absorbing positive knowledge."

3. Le Guin published a short story called "Schrödinger's Cat," which is a thought-experiment about a thought-experiment. See chapter 11.

4. Not all science-fiction writers agree. Isaac Asimov, for example, accepts predicting the future as a legitimate, even inevitable function of the science-fiction writer.

5. S. J. Edelheit, *Boston Review,* September–October 1979, pp. 5–6, 13.

Chapter Ten

1. *Wild Angels* (Santa Barbara, Calif., 1979), pp. 275–319; *Hard Words* (New York, 1981).

2. Cf. the ring of nine stones in *The Tombs of Atuan*.

3. *Hard Words*. Page references in text.

4. Joseph Needham, *Science and Civilization in China,* 5 vols. (Cambridge: Cambridge University Press, 1954–70).

Chapter Eleven

1. Since this book went to press, a new anthology of Le Guin's stories has been published which includes some of those discussed in this chapter. *The Compass Rose* (New York: Harper & Row, 1982) includes "The Author of the Acacia Seeds," "The New Atlantis," "Schrödinger's Cat," "The Diary of the Rose," and "The Eye Altering" as well as several other stories.

2. *Universe 5,* ed. Terry Carr (New York: Random House, 1974), pp. 33–41. Cat lovers will be pleased to know that the idea of using a cat in an experiment is Schrödinger's, not Le Guin's.

3. "The Author of the Acacia Seeds," *Fellowship of the Stars,* ed. Terry Carr (New York: Simon & Schuster, 1974), pp. 155–63.

4. "Selection," *Amazing* 38 (August 1964):36–45.

5. "The Diary of the Rose," *Future Power,* ed. Jack Dann and Gardner R. Dozois (New York: Random House, 1976), pp. 1–23.

6. *The Altered Eye,* ed. Lee Harding (Melbourne, Australia: Nostrilia Press, 1976), pp. 108–17. Variants used in the story "The Eye Altering" are included.

Chapter Twelve

1. "The Making of a Mage," *Times Literary Supplement*, 2 April 1971, p. 383; "Earthsea Revisited," *Times Literary Supplement*, 28 April 1972, p. 484; "A Hole in the World," *Times Literary Supplement*, 6 April 1973, p. 379; *Observer*, 4 May 1971, p. 36; 30 July 1972, p. 32; and 15 May 1973, p. 39.

2. "The Images of Women in Science Fiction," *Red Clay Reader* 7 (Charlotte, N.C.: Southern Review, 1970), pp. 35–40.

3. Darko Suvin, "The SF Novel in 1969," *Nebula Award Stories 5*, ed. James Blish (Garden City, N.Y.: Doubleday, 1970), pp. 193–205.

4. *Times Literary Supplement*, 20 June 1975, p. 704.

5. Joanna Russ, "Books," *Magazine of Fantasy and Science Fiction* 48 (March 1975):41–44.

6. James W. Bittner, "Persuading Us to Rejoice and Teaching Us How to Praise: Le Guin's *Orsinian Tales*," *Science-Fiction Studies* 5 (1978):215–42.

7. *Boston Review* (September–October 1979), pp. 5–6, 13.

8. See *Time* (11 February 1980), p. 86 and *Newsweek* 96 (1 September 1980), p. 74.

9. "You must either fit a category, or 'have a name,' to publish a book in America." "A Citizen of Mondath," *The Language of the Night*, p. 28.

10. Eleanor Cameron, "High Fantasy: A Wizard of Earthsea," *Horn Book* 47 (April 1971):129–38.

11. Peter Nicholl, "showing children the value of death," *Foundation 5* (January 1974):71–80.

12. Martin Bickman, "Le Guin's *The Left Hand of Darkness:* Form and Content," *Science-Fiction Studies* 4 (March 1977):42–47.

13. George Turner, "Paradigm and Pattern: Form and Meaning in *The Dispossessed*," *SF Commentary* 41–42 (February 1975):65–74.

14. Douglas Barbour, "Wholeness and Balance in the Hainish Novels of Ursula K. Le Guin," *Science-Fiction Studies* 1 (Spring 1974):164–73; see also "Wholeness and Balance: An Addendum," *Science-Fiction Studies* 2 (November 1975):248–49.

15. Robert Scholes, *Structural Fabulation: An Essay on Fiction of the Future* (Notre Dame, Ind.: University of Notre Dame, 1975), pp. 77–99.

16. Rafael Nudelman, "An Approach to the Structure of Le Guin's Science Fiction," *Science-Fiction Studies* 2 (November 1975):213–14.

17. Darko Suvin, "Parables of De-Alienation," *Science-Fiction Studies* 2 (November 1975):265–74.

18. Slusser, *Farthest Shores of Le Guin*, p. 58.

19. Gerard Klein, "Discontent in American Science Fiction," *Science-Fiction Studies* 4 (March 1977):3–13; "Ursula Le Guin's Aberrant Opus: Escaping the Trap of Discontent," *Science-Fiction Studies* 4 (November 1977):287–94.

Selected Bibliography

PRIMARY SOURCES

A. Books

The Beginning Place. New York: Harper & Row, 1980.

City of Illusions. New York: Ace Books, 1967, 1974.

The Dispossessed. New York: Harper & Row, 1974; Avon Books, 1975.

The Farthest Shore. New York: Atheneum, 1972; Bantam, 1975.

Hard Words. New York: Harper & Row, 1981.

The Language of the Night. New York: Putnam's, 1979.

The Lathe of Heaven. New York: Charles Scribner's Sons, 1971; Avon Books, 1973.

The Left Hand of Darkness. New York: Ace Books, 1969.

Malafrena. New York: Berkley-Putnam, 1979.

Orsinian Tales. New York: Harper & Row, 1976; Bantam, 1977 (short stories).

Planet of Exile. New York: Ace Books, 1966, 1974.

Rocannon's World. New York: Ace Books, 1966, 1974.

The Tombs of Atuan. New York: Atheneum, 1971; Bantam, 1975.

Very Far Away from Anywhere Else. New York: Atheneum, 1976; Bantam, 1978.

Wild Angels. Santa Barbara, Cal.: Capra Press, 1975.

The Wind's Twelve Quarters. New York: Harper & Row, 1975; Bantam, 1976 (short stories).

A Wizard of Earthsea. Berkeley, Cal.: Parnassus Press, 1968; New York: Ace Books, 1968; Bantam, 1975.

The Word for World Is Forest. New York: Putnam's, 1976; Berkley, 1976.

B. Selected Short Fiction

"The Author of the Acacia Seeds and Other Extracts from the *Journal of the Association of Therolinguistics.*" In *Fellowship of the Stars.* Edited by Terry Carr. New York: Simon & Schuster, 1974.

"The Diary of the Rose." In *Future Power.* Edited by Jack Dann and Gardner Dozois. New York: Random House, 1976.

"The Eye Altering." In *The Altered Eye: An Encounter with Science Fiction by Ursula K. Le Guin and Others,* edited by Lee Harding. Carlton, Victoria, Australia: Nostrilia Press, 1976.

"The Eye of the Heron." In *Millennial Women,* edited by Virginia Kidd. New York: Delacorte, 1978.

Leese Webster. New York: Atheneum, 1979.
"The New Atlantis." In *The New Atlantis and Other Novellas of Science Fiction,*
    edited by Robert Silverberg. New York: Hawthorne Books, 1975.
"Schrödinger's Cat." In *Universe 5,* edited by Terry Carr. New York: Ran-
    dom House, 1974.
"Selection." In *Amazing Fact and Science Fiction Stories* (August 1964).
"Solomon Leviathan's Nine Hundred and Thirty-First Trip Around the
    World." In *Puffin's Pleasure,* edited by Kaye Webb and Treld Bicknell.
    Harmondsworth: Puffin Books, 1976.

SECONDARY SOURCES

1. Books
De Bolt, Joe, ed. *Ursula K. Le Guin: Voyager to Inner Lands and Outer Space.*
    Port Washington, N.Y.: Kennikat Press, 1979. An anthology of essays
    about Le Guin's life and work. See entries below under Cogell, De
    Bolt, Lasseter, Molson, Pfeiffer, Sinclair.
Olander, Joseph D., and Greenberg, Martin Henry, eds. *Ursula K. Le
    Guin.* New York: Taplinger, 1979. A collection of critical essays. See
    entries below under Alterman, Brennan and Downs, Brigg, Crow, Es-
    monde, Gunew, Hayles, Remington, and Smith.
Slusser, George Edgar. *The Farthest Shores of Ursula K. Le Guin.* San Ber-
    nadino, Calif.: Borgo Press, 1976. A pamphlet surveying the novels
    with a particular concentration on the nature of evil.

2. Articles
Alterman, Peter S. "Ursula K. Le Guin: Damsel With a Dulcimer." In *Le
    Guin,* edited by Olander and Greenberg (see principal entry above), pp.
    38–63. A study of the Romantic influence on Le Guin's vision of na-
    ture, focused on *The Word for World Is Forest* and "Vaster Than Empires
    and More Slow."
Barbour, Douglas. "Wholeness and Balance in the Hainish Novels of Ur-
    sula K. Le Guin." *Science-Fiction Studies* 1 (March 1974):164–73;
    "Wholeness and Balance: An Addendum." *Science-Fiction Studies* 2 (No-
    vember 1975):248–49. An analysis of the holistic vision of Le Guin's
    five Hainish novels.
Bickman, Martin. "Le Guin's *The Left Hand of Darkness:* Form and Con-
    tent." *Science-Fiction Studies* 4 (March 1977):42–47. An examination of
    the structure of the novel, establishing Genly Ai as the structuring
    consciousness of the narrative.
Bittner, James W. "Persuading Us to Rejoice and Teaching Us How to
    Praise: Le Guin's Orsinian Tales." *Science-Fiction Studies* 5 (November
    1978):215–42. An interpretation of the *Orsinian Tales,* stressing their

nature as "tales" rather than "stories" and examining their double perspective, aesthetic and historical.

Brennan, John P. and Downs, Michael C. "Anarchism and Utopian Tradition in *The Dispossessed.*" In *Le Guin,* edited by Olander and Greenberg (see principal entry above), pp. 116–52.

Brigg, Peter. "The Archetype of the Journey in Ursula K. Le Guin's Fiction." In *Le Guin,* edited by Olander and Greenberg (see principal entry above), pp. 36–63. A study of the archetypal journey, with attention to travelers, destinations, and landscapes, and with emphasis on Rocannon, Genly Ai, and Shevek.

Cameron, Eleanor. "High Fantasy: A Wizard of Earthsea." *Horn Book* 47 (April 1971):129–38. An early appreciation of the world of Earthsea and a discussion of the value of high fantasy.

Cogell, Elizabeth Cummins. "Taoist Configurations: *The Dispossessed.*" *Le Guin: Voyager.* Edited by de Bolt (see principal entry above), pp. 153–79, 207–9. The major principles of Taoism—following the model of nature, the theory of letting alone, and the eternality of change—as they apply to *The Dispossessed.*

Crow, John H. and Erlich, Richard D. "Words of Binding: Patterns of Integration in the Earthsea Trilogy." In *Le Guin,* edited by Olander and Greenberg (see principal entry above), pp. 200–40. Traces the patterns of individuation, the pattern of balance, and the patterns of movement from social disorder to order.

De Bolt, Joe. "A Le Guin Biography." In *Le Guin: Voyager,* edited by de Bolt (see principal entry above), pp. 13–28. Brief but highly informative biography based largely on interviews and family records.

Esmonde, Margaret P. "The Master Pattern: The Psychological Journey in the Earthsea Trilogy." In *Le Guin,* edited by Olander and Greenberg (see principal entry above), pp. 15–35. An interpretation of the Earthsea trilogy as a psychological journey toward wholeness, involving integration of the shadow and acceptance of personal mortality.

Gunew, Sneja. "Mythic Reversals: The Evolution of the Shadow Motif." In *Le Guin,* edited by Olander and Greenberg (see principal entry above), pp. 178–99. Traces the image of the shadow through the novels, elucidating the spectrum of meanings it achieves.

Hayles, N. B. "Androgyny, Ambivalence, and Assimilation in *The Left Hand of Darkness.*" In *Le Guin,* edited by Olander and Greenberg (see principal entry above), pp. 97–115. An exploration of the dualities in the novel in terms of the traditional myth of androgyny and the interplay of mythic and everyday modes.

Jameson, Fredric. "World-Reduction in Le Guin: The Emergence of Utopian Narrative." *Science-Fiction Studies* 2 (November 1975):221–30. A study of multiple narratives and five major themes in *The Left Hand of Darkness.*

Ketterer, David. "The Left Hand of Darkness: Ursula Le Guin's Archetypal Winter Journey." In *New Worlds for Old: The Apocalyptic Imagination, Science Fiction, and American Literature.* Garden City, N.Y.: Doubleday Anchor, and Bloomington: Indiana University Press, 1974, pp.
   76–90. Approaches the novel through archetypal myth criticism, finding it an example of an epistomological apocalypse.
Lasseter, Rollin A. "Four Letters About Le Guin." In *Le Guin: Voyager,*
   edited by de Bolt (see principal entry above), pp. 89–114. In the form
   of open letters to a "friend and challenger," a close study of each volume in the Earthsea trilogy, with an emphasis on the symbols of the
   inner journey.
Molson, Francis J. "The Earthsea Trilogy: Ethical Fantasy for Children."
   In *Ursula K. Le Guin: Voyager to Inner Lands and Outer Space,* edited by
   de Bolt (see principal entry above), pp. 128–52. Proposes the term
   "ethical fantasy" for the trilogy, which is intended to teach as well as
   please, concerning its youthful characters in serious ethical choices.
Nudelman, Rafael. "An Approach to the Structure of Le Guin's Science
   Fiction," translated by Alan G. Myers. In *Science-Fiction Studies* 2 (November 1975):210–20. A structural reading of the Hainish novels,
   with plot assessed as movement toward oneness, a spatio-temporal journey toward unity.
Pfeiffer, John R. "But Dragons Have Keen Ears: On Hearing 'Earthsea'
   with Recollections of Beowulf." In *Le Guin: Voyager,* edited by de Bolt
   (see principal entry above), pp. 115–27. Demonstrates that knowledge
   of *Beowulf* can enrich appreciation of the Earthsea trilogy, which, like
   the early epic, uses alliteration, the kenning, and gnomic sayings.
Remington, Thomas J. "The Other Side of Suffering: Touch as Theme and
   Metaphor in Le Guin's Science Fiction Novels." In *Le Guin,* edited by
   Olander and Greenberg (see principal entry above), pp. 153–77. Fo-
   cuses on the themes of loneliness and need for human relationships in
   three short works, "Nine Lives," "Vaster Than Empires and More
   Slow," and *The Word for World Is Forest.*
Scholes, Robert. "The Good Witch of the West." In *Structural Fabulation.*
   Notre Dame, Ind.: University of Notre Dame Press, 1975, pp. 77–99.
   Both a study of *The Left Hand of Darkness* and a comparison of the
   Earthsea trilogy with the Narnia chronicles of C. S. Lewis.
Shippey, T. A. "The Magic Art and the Evolution of Works: Ursula Le
   Guin's Earthsea trilogy." *Mosaic* 10 (Winter 1977):147–63. An explo-
   ration of religious and philosophical implications of the trilogy, sug-
   gesting myth-breaking as well as myth-making features.
Sinclair, Karen. "Solitary Being: The Hero as Anthropologist." *Le Guin:
   Voyager,* edited by de Bolt (see principal entry above), pp. 50–65. An
   analysis of Le Guin's heroes as participant-observers, outsiders with understanding of inside problems.

Smith, Philip E., II. "Unbuilding Walls: Human Nature and the Nature of Evolutionary and Political Theory in *The Dispossessed.*" In *Le Guin,* edited by Olander and Greenberg (see principal entry above), pp. 77–96. A consideration of Le Guin's anarchism as influenced by the theories of Kropotkin.

Suvin, Darko. "Parables of De-Alienation: Le Guin's Widdershins Dance." *Science-Fiction Studies* 2 (November 1975):265–74. A view of the overall movement in Le Guin's fiction toward a nonalienating, collectivist society opposed to the dominant ideas and values of our own civilization.

Turner, George. "Paradigm and Pattern: Form and Meaning in *The Dispossessed.*" *SF Commentary* 41/42 (February 1975):65–74. An interpretation of *The Dispossessed* focused on form and involving an extended comparison with the structure of George Eliot's *Daniel Deronda.*

Walker, Jeanne Murray. "Myth, Exchange, and History in *The Left Hand of Darkness.*" *Science-Fiction Studies* 6 (July 1979):180–89. A study of the function of myth and kinship exchange in the novel, based on the structural theories of Claude Levi-Strauss.

Watson, Ian. "The Forest as Metaphor for Mind: 'The Word for World Is Forest' and 'Vaster Than Empires and More Slow.' " *Science-Fiction Studies* 2 (November 1975):231–37. A reading of the two works from the perspective of the forest as metaphor for mind.

Wood, Susan. "Discovering Worlds: The Fiction of Ursula K. Le Guin." In *Voices for the Future,* Vol. 2, pp. 154–79, edited by Thomas D. Clareson. Bowling Green, Ohio: Bowling Green University Popular Press, 1978. A comprehensive study of Le Guin's novels based on the author's own theory of creativity as discovery.

Index

Acculturation, problem of, 9
Agnen, 41
Aldebaranians, 63
Alienation, 9, 130
All-Alonio, 20–21
Allegory, 117, 124, 128
Allia, 120–22
Alliteration, 31
"Altered Eye, The," 148
Alterra, 16–18
Ambisexuality, 46, 51, 57
"An Die Musik," 3, 103
Anarchy, 7, 74, 78–79, 81, 131
Anarres, 75–85
Androgyny, 48–50, 53, 58–59, 153
Anglo-Saxon, 31
Angyar, the, 13, 15
Anima, 6, 48, 120, 123
Animus, 6, 48, 123
Ansible, 46
Anthropologist-heroes, 5, 7
Anthropologists, 2, 4–5, 70
Anthropology, cultural, 4–7, 19, 46, 158, 160
"April in Paris," 3
Archetypes, 4–7, 9, 25, 48, 128, 133
Archipelago, 29
Archmage, 27, 29
Arha, 33–34, 36; see also Tenar
Arren, 38–42; see also Lebannen
Asgard, 101
Athsheans, 68–70, 72, 113
Atlantic, 3, 91
Atlantis, 88–89, 91
Atuan, 32, 159, 161
Augmentor, the, 62, 66
"Author of the Acacia Seeds, The," 144

Balance, Taoist ethic of, 25–57
"Barrow, The," 102
Beatles, the, 66
Beginning Place, The, 6, 109, 116–17, 123, 152, 154, 161
Belle, 87–91
Beowulf, 31
Bickman, Martin, 58
Bildungsroman, 45, 76, 115
Bittner, James, 100–101, 105, 154
Borges, Jorge, Luis, 118, 132
Breisingamen necklace, 10
"Brothers and Sisters," 102

Cameron, Eleanor, 155
Celtic mythology, 118
"Child and the Shadow, The," 27, 128
Children's literature, 27, 44, 149, 155
Chinese philosophy, 6
Christianity, 6–7, 23, 102
Chuang-Tse, 6, 60, 74
"Citizen of Mondath, A," 125
City of Illusions, 14, 19, 22–24, 44, 52, 161
Cloning, 96
Cob, 40, 43
Cogell, Elizabeth Cummins, 78
Collective unconscious, 5–6, 126
Coming of age, 6, 38
"Conversations at Night," 103
Creechies, 68, 113

"Darkness Box, The," 94–95
Davidson, Captain, 68, 70–72, 132
"Day Before the Revolution, The," 74, 85, 152, 157, 159
Death, 33, 38, 42
"Diary of the Rose, The," 145, 147
Dick, Philip, 132
Dickens, Charles, 3, 126, 132